Matthew Bennett is a 22-year old British author and student from British Columbia, Canada. He takes pride in controversial and bold ideas and enjoys unseating readers from their comfort zone. Matthew served just under 18 months in the CAF, and at just 22 years old he has committed himself to success in the form of literature. As a new author, he relies heavily on using experience from military service and his travels across the world for inspiration to develop mind-bending concepts into absolute page-turners. *The One Being* is his first novel.

This book is dedicated to the Bennett family.

Matthew Bennett

THE ONE BEING

AUSTIN MACAULEY PUBLISHERS™

LONDON • CAMBRIDGE • NEW YORK • SHARJAH

Ordering Information
Quantity sales: special discounts are available on quantity purchases by corporations, associations, and others. For details, contact the publisher at the address below.

Publisher's Cataloging-in-Publication data
Bennett, Matthew
The One Being

ISBN 9781643787688 (Paperback)
ISBN 9781645369097 (Hardback)
ISBN 9781641822145 (ePub e-book)

Library of Congress Control Number: 2020916015

www.austinmacauley.com/us

First Published (2020)
Austin Macauley Publishers LLC
40 Wall Street, 28th Floor
New York, NY 10005
USA

mail-usa@austinmacauley.com
+1 (646) 5125767

To Austin Macauley Publishers, for believing in my book and granting me the opportunity to publish it.

I

"Our world has been desecrated, burned, and utterly ruined. The people who took this land for granted before us wanted to thrive with comfort and luxury and all the nice things in the world so badly that they would rather kill anyone who opposed this idea than live with the fact that they would have to forfeit just a little bit of their perfect, protected life. Nine world wars ravaged the Earth, eating up every easily available resource. Forget oil. Water and even clean air were the most valuable resources of the time. Nobody seemed to care about human life anymore, so long as they thought they could one day live in a world that they so desperately craved once the violence had ended. Truth be told, we haven't had a single generation of people that hasn't seen or been affected by war in nearly five hundred years. That brings us to today, in the Valley. After the most recent ninth world war ten years ago, the globe was divided into two parties, or factions if you will, the Valley, which is us, and the inland. You need not worry about the inland because we won't hear from or speak to them for a while, decades, some predict. Now we live in peace, with the resources we need to survive, but not much else. That's why we only shower once a week, and we eat twice a day. There was a time in which people could shower daily and eat three or four meals a day, but politics got a hold of the world and weapons followed in a similar fashion. I am proud, though, to live in a world of peace despite the ruin. We have the chance to appreciate the simple things in life. Anyway, enough with the boring stuff. I can see three of you are asleep by now anyway! Who wants to talk about the mysteries and secrets in our world?" Mr. Hoxel speaks out in British twang with pride to the drowsy rows of pupils' chairs in front of him.

With suspicion, interest, and a faint hope in heart, Adam stands there, calmly rocking back and forth in patience as Mr. Hoxel continues to lecture in his history class, a class that he'd reckon nowadays to be the most important of all. He speaks with dignity and a sense of true valor, which Adam thinks he rightly should, as an ex-military man himself. There aren't many of them left. The lights of the classroom dim to a dusky brown amongst a yellowish amber-colored hologram that appears from thin air. Several objects begin circling the center of the room, lighting up Mr. Hoxel's poorly groomed beard as his firm accent elaborates.

"The dimension relics. This is a set of artifacts that supposedly existed many years ago, left to legend now. It's what our parents would tuck us into bed to at night, the tale of the Corinthians and the Chalice or the Nordic wars over the Scythe, and every story ended in the same way. Some hero falls head over heels for a damsel in distress, losing sight of what their main goal was – to secure the artifact they sought out in the first place. However, as usual, love takes precedence. I digress. Nobody knows how many of these strange objects drift across the universe. It has been rumored that if all of these artifacts were to be brought together in the same place, their power would be unstoppable." Mr. Hoxel snaps his ruler sharply across his desk to split the cadence, much to some sleeping students' dismay. "So many years went by as our population believed that these objects were nothing but a myth, nearly thousands! Until twenty-four years ago, on May 23rd, 2313, when one of these mystical treasures was allegedly discovered." He explains quietly, breaking shortly after the word 'allegedly' as if disappointed. Several students perk up while others remain unchanged.

"But what was it, sir?" one student asks impatiently.

"I still wonder myself; you know. It was rumored to be the divinity sphere, an orb said to be able to eternalize one's soul. This artifact should present the power to exile or create whatever one desires to and from the universe. They say it takes you another plane of existence more commonly known in folklore as 'the aether' where they could live safely forever. Of course, science has never proven that anything even close to such an astonishing feat could possibly exist. These stories have fallen helplessly into myth over the ages, and the Upper level has deemed them to be officially untrue." Mr. Hoxel tilts half of his mouth downward after speaking, opening his eyes briefly as if to recognize a lost friend. Melancholy gently riddles his face. He claps and the lighting returns to normal. The hologram disappears in an instant. An eager student shoots up his hand and starts speaking only after Mr. Hoxel nods in his direction.

"So what, sir? Nobody ever proved these artifacts existed. So what's the point? It seems odd. Why are we learning about this, sir?" he asks politely. Mr. Hoxel explains himself in response quite hastily.

"That's exactly it, Jackson. This is all just stories and, as part of your history education, not only do you get to learn what is history, but you also must understand what isn't. It's odd that I even have to teach this to you but, yes, there are people out there who still believe that these things exist! And the Upper level doesn't want anyone wasting their life searching for something that isn't real," Mr. Hoxel explains himself quite hastily. "Aaand it looks like time is up for today. I'd just like to quickly remind you that you have a test tomorrow on world wars three through six, and the study package will be uploaded to your grafts as soon as I'm done in a few minutes with Adam. Does anyone have any final questions?" None of the students raise a finger. "Good, see you tomorrow." The students rapidly pack their bags silently and almost synchronously, leaving the classroom without a word. Adam opens his mouth readily once the wooden door closes.

"Very impressive, Mr. Hoxel. Say, how long have you been working here now? My graft tells me fifteen years, isn't it?" he asks, looking down at the back of his hand. An external mechanical replication of the hand's bone structure is attached to the back of his hand. Projecting up from the tiny one-inch screen on it is a sharp, blue hologram. It lights up with an array of information detailing the professor.

"Yes, sixteen next month, sir," he replies with confidence.

"Excellent, and how do you think you're doing here at America University?" Adam asks him.

"I must say I believe I'm doing my job well. I enjoy it and approach it with enthusiasm. Really, though, I'm just thankful for a stable job. Suppose you have any feedback for my performance review, sir?" Mr. Hoxel responds with an eagerness that Adam has not seen in years. Outstanding!

"Your class was," Adam takes a breath, knowing that discussing the topic of artifacts is strictly prohibited outside of the classroom, "perfect. I'd like to congratulate you on a score of ninety-six. For this work, I'll be happy to recommend a promotion for you on one condition," Adam states, sneering.

"I'm listening, sir. What can I do to improve your American experience?" Mr. Hoxel chuckles lightly with joy.

"Tell me, what else do you know of these artifacts? More specifically, the one they call the divinity sphere?" Adam inquires, lowering his voice to a soft whisper upon mentioning the subject.

"Well, sir, I know the rules around here, but I am a fanatic for lore if you want to put it that way," Mr. Hoxel explains in polite British manner, clapping once to dim the lights as he spins his grafted hand. He transforms the room into a dazzling show, pulling up a detailed projection hologram of the relic in question. "The divinity sphere, as I mentioned earlier, is said to contain the power to save the user in another dimension, a mythical place we cannot prove exists, to live forever, unharmed. The power that comes with living in this dimension is supposed to be unthinkable! There are many scriptures written in books about this relic, and it often comes to light that even that may not be the full extent of its powers. This orb here is the one that was supposedly discovered in 2313. I would do anything to know that these relics exist. Dear me, how incredible!" Mr. Hoxel speaks softly, entranced by the illusion rotating slowly in front of him.

"So, how exactly would one ever wield such immense power? It seems like quite the responsibility, don't you think?" Adam inquires further. A pair of carved eyebrows pop up suddenly.

"Yes, yes. You see, that's where you're wrong, sir. No disrespect at all, but in order to open or use any of the unspoken relics," Mr. Hoxel reduces his volume to a mere whisper, "one would need an unimaginable source of energy, comparable to that of a paradox, black hole, or even a wormhole." His eyes go berserk as he explains the prophetic theory. "Even now with the technology of grafts and the beginnings of intergalactic travel, it would take another few hundred years or more to produce such power. The effects are perfect, but achieving them, phew! Good luck." Mr. Hoxel fiddles anxiously with his chunky thumbs as he elaborates further on the divinity sphere. Adam claps once to kick the lights back into gear again, breaking the stillness.

"Wow, you are evidently quite knowledgeable of the subject, and you have impressed me. I'll gladly inform the Upper level of your work, Mr. Hoxel. We'll keep that last conversation between us, eh? That'll be all from me." Adam winks sharply. He flicks his hand up and waves a quick goodbye as he exits the classroom. He hears a faint 'good day, sir' from down the hall as he turns the next corner of the school's hallway. Adam wonders as he strolls down the hall how, if at all possible, a treasure that already has such power could still have more undiscovered abilities. He rushes to his vessel of safety outside. His feet pitter-patter against the damaged, dusty ground as he approaches the mostly hollow, levitating glass sphere. The side closest to him opens upwards, granting an elegant entrance. He crouches to get inside to sitting on a glowing snowy leather chair stitched carefully with red patterning all the way around. In a moment of settling, he allows the sphere to enclose upon him. Holographic lights flicker precariously on a small control panel in front of his relaxed body.

"Welcome back, Adam," a fluid voice announces, as if from nowhere. The combination of unreal controls begins to move autonomously as Adam sits to observe the wild outdoors.

"Thanks, Silver. Take me to the Dawne. While you're at it, send my employee evaluation to Simon," Adam responds.

"Of course, initiating Upper level access," the operating system calls to him. The sphere levitates upwards above the horde of scrambling box cars below, shooting him toward a prodigious towering structure. It stands two hundred stories tall, an immense construction cascading over everything as far as the eye can see. The reflective black crystal, coronium, discovered on Mars, sparkles boldly in the roaring sun. Its harmonious edge catches the flutters of sunlight in an incomparable manner. The wildly impressive feat stands alone with its oval windows, each encrusted with glistening diamonds on their smooth edges. Many of these fabulous openings find themselves prettily patterned with travel pods. Adam looks to its jagged but smoothed out titanium-tipped peaks and thinks about how incredibly lucky he is to have the opportunity to be where he is today. The controls in front of him start moving around as a holographic file slides out of the side of the pod, bouncing back a green 'sent' message. The sphere continues to rise above the chaos below, streaking forward. Adam can't help but feel a touch of desperation for all the people left down there, the poor and the tired. He peers down at the glass with a tiny sentiment of self-disgrace. Watching harmlessly as hundreds of people fight to get in line to send mail to the other side, he sits comfortably.

"Upper level one hundred and forty-five. Travel time was thirty-eight seconds, six seconds slower than yesterday," Silver says smoothly as the sphere slides gracefully up to one of the higher levels of the enormous black crystal tower. One of the diamond-patterned windows on the far-right side opens to allow the spherical pod to fit perfectly into the hole presented. A quick hiss from the side of the sphere touching the Dawne and the pressure difference resolves, connecting the sphere to the building. The elimination of toxins allows a much higher quality of air into Adam's lungs as he takes a deep, slow breath of purified air.

"Thank you, Silver, I needed that. Hey, would you mind fetching me that old ball from the living room, the one on the mantelpiece?" Adam says out loud as he climbs out of the pod. He steps out into the stainless white apartment, where each and everything is in place, clean, and without dust.

"You're very welcome, sir. Give me one moment," Silver calls back to him, now from inside the apartment. Adam leaves a darkened briefcase in the pod before walking over to the dinner table, stopping for a second to catch a glimpse of himself in the mirror. His musky, gray eyes appear older to him each day under a charcoal-black head of neatly groomed hair. He perches himself at the dining table alone in front of an absolute feast. One steaming-hot half chicken, three pepper-seared potatoes, a head of broccoli, and four garlic-roasted brussel sprouts lie out in a delicately organized manner. They come together to form an art piece on the gold-rimmed plate resting in front of him beside silver cutlery. He takes his time ingesting a rich meal as a mechanical arm, running across the ceiling of the apartment, enters the lobby room and moves toward the dining table with a quiet robotic hum. It slows to a steady halt in front of Adam where he removes the object from the robot's grasp and holds it in his hands. Soft fingers rotate it around ever so carefully, slowly examining. It rests in his hands almost perfectly, being about the size of a microwavable bag of popcorn. The object in front of him is truly spherical in shape, marked all over with inscriptions that even he cannot understand. His mind drifts into dark and long-lost corners.

"Silver, send this to John. Have him analyze this, but make sure it stays on the down low. I don't want anyone knowing what's going on," Adam vocalizes into the vacant room.

"Sir, I must remind you that covert activities are forbidden without express permission of at least sixty percent of the Upper level. Would you like to proceed, sir?" Silver's smooth robotic voice calls back. Her arm begins to move over to the spherical object in his hand, keeping claws open for both the plate and the object.

"Override it! I made you. I know you can find the loophole," Adam says with a charming touch.

A flashback becomes vivid in his mind, blinding him from even the silky, hot taste trapped inside of his mouth. Sparks of a memory whiz through his mind as everything else darkens.

A deep orange sun is settling into the horizon, befriending a few clouds to tickle the sky, working together to materialize streaks of pink and light red. In front of him, miles away, the poverty-ridden streets erupt into chaos once again.

"Adam, I..." a woman with long, soft blond hair cries as she attempts to speak, perched upon a luscious green hilltop beside Adam, who strokes her hair gently. The naturally beautiful peak overlooks a nearly completed construction of the Dawne. Off to the right lies a type of bare chaos they are too familiar with. On the left of the Dawne, nothing but a few broken and beaten houses few and far between, which are rid of inhabitants, rest in the shadow of the Dawne. They sit to rot in an expanding mass of sand.

"Yes, sweetheart?" Adam responds after a few seconds of silence.

"To celebrate all of our countless years together, and what is probably gonna be our last, I have something to give to you," she tells him with tears running down her face.

"Honey, you know that if I could get you into the Upper level, then I would do it. But we both know I'd be killed and so would you," Adam says, agitated, without hesitation. "Anyway, I'm sorry, baby. Let's just enjoy the moment. What do you mean you have something for me? That's just not necessary. You should be keeping the money for yourself," Adam tells her.

"Yes, sweetie, I know, but you always get me something for our anniversary and it's okay. This one didn't cost anything." She wipes away the tears and puts a smile on, knowing that moments like these would end soon.

She reaches into the damaged burlap sack behind her and rummages around for a second, spreading around the dirt inside of it. She pulls out what looks like a towel wrapped in on itself into a ball. Adam seems confused, and one of his eyebrows bounces up momentarily.

"This is for you. You know, because you're always crying at emotional movies. I thought you might want to hold on to something so you don't get those fancy clothes of yours all soggy with your tears. Pretty good, huh? Gotcha!" She lights up with excitement, laughing and enjoying herself in the warmth of the day's fading sun. Her tears, however, fail to hide away beneath the blazing rays.

"Uhm, thank you, babe, but I mean," he tries to ask but can't finish because the woman beside him interjects.

"Oh, hun, relax. Haha! It's not actually a towel. Look." She pulls on the cloth mess and it falls off swiftly like an orange peel. "Now this is an ancient artifact, oooooh." She raises her left hand, playing the piano with her fingers and opening her eyes wide, leaning slightly toward him. "Now, babe, we all know the fairytales of those things that don't actually exist, but my grandfather believed that this really was one of them. And I mean, I know it can't be true and that it's all myth and legend, but it's a family heirloom that we've had for generations., So here it is, the Stevenson family heirloom. I want you to have –" Her voice is cut off instantly, but not by words. Adam throws his arms around her with a hefty force, almost sending the two of them down the hill.

"Oh my goodness! This is incredible. Seriously, this must mean so much to you… I couldn't ever thank you enough. It's beautiful," Adam says in response to her little ramble. They both sit in a brief silence, broken only by the calm whistle of the wind, a wind which brushes the leaves of a nearby tree and suppresses the distant roar of rampant chaos. "The only thing better in this world than you would be for the both of us to escape from the Newgrounds." He sighs desperately. "It just gets worse every day; the lack of food and freshwater is ruining what's left of our society." Another slow breath exhales from his mouth. "I'll find a way to get you into the Upper level," he gently kisses the top of her head, "away from this shit." A few minutes trickle by as they sit together, with her head wholeheartedly resting on his shoulder.

"Hey, babe," he says, and then he gives a failed attempt at a wink that makes him look like he is just blinking strongly. "Look," he repeats a couple of times.

"You are adorable," she says, planting a kiss on his forehead and holding his neck, "but you'll never be able to wink with one eye, honey," she finishes, winking at him charmingly. Eventually, the woman stands up slowly and picks up her bag. She starts stuffing the dirty brown rug-like blanket that lies flat beneath them back into it. Adam looks at her and cracks a baby smile for just a second before having to channel his energy into holding back a tear gone rogue. She smiles at him with a comforting and loving grin. One of her tears balances on the verge of being freed from the still gaze her eyes hold with his.

With raised suspicions and a touch of blurry vision, Adam swallows the last bite of a once-delicious home-cooked meal. He clamors the cutlery together onto his place for the metal arm to hastily swerve back and collect.

II

A restless six hours of sleep haunts Adam as he dreams fearfully of the past and the future. His only reliable asset is himself. He wakens suddenly, startled from the blackness in his brain. After spending twenty or so minutes in a delicate rain-shower, he steps out onto the heated floor to dry himself with an alarmingly white silk-cotton-blended towel. He picks up a small object the size of a raisin from the flat surface beside his sink and pops into his mouth, opening his mouth just moments later to reveal a sheen clean smile into the mirror above the faucet. As he walks out of the bathroom, one of Silver's mechanical pieces opens up, moving with him to blow comfortably warm air at a gusting pace. This flops Adam's fringe up and down like a ping pong ball, drying his entire head of dreamy hair in six seconds flat. He promptly dresses in a divine leather, brown-colored camel hair, and chiffon suit and heads toward the transportation pod. He seats himself inside and relaxes, knowing the flight will be taken care of for him.

"Good morning, sir. Current outside temperature: thirty-eight degrees Celsius. A slightly overcast day is expected. Humidity is at thirty-seven percent. Today's important tasks: firstly, meet with John to rendezvous about your inquiry. Secondly, you have the national conference of global preservation. That's all for now. Remember to smile, sir. The Upper level is always here to help," Silver exclaims quietly.

Adam looks to his left to see the date written out on a screen not entirely opaque. 'November 23rd, 2237.' The pod remains stuck to the side of the building like a spheroidal stick insect. It zips away from his room, zooming upward a few levels to its destination.

"Arriving at Level One Hundred and Ninety, sir," Silver tells him. The pod matches seamlessly once again with the perfectly formed opening in the side of the building and the front swings open to the inner side of the edifice. He climbs out with ease. The encasing walls of the floor are crafted magnificently out of a flawless glass. The deep purple of coronium complements the walnut wood, and there is an astonishing array of technology that New grounders could only ever dream of. Easily, the room stretched from end to end of the

Dawne. It must have been one of the biggest rooms of the entire construct, if not the biggest. If not for the colossal computer hub in the center of the room, it would be nearly empty. An enormous island of greens, blues, and yellows on screens spot the middle of the room. They tower over Adam and his colleagues by about two feet, maybe more. Beneath the complex construction of computers and diagrams is the most objectively confusing set of controls – buttons here, levers there, and even keys on vertical platforms. Adam strolls over to a man slightly taller than him, and even a touch wider in the shoulders.

"John, it's good to see you. I'm assuming you got my late-afternoon delivery last night. Have you made any headway?" Adam lowers his voice to communicate softly.

"Morning, buddy, thanks for that by that way. I sent it here to get analyzed last night under a password-protected program. I came in a few minutes early today and I don't know much, but whatever that thing is, it has a coronium center. I mean, it's got to be worth an absurd amount of money. Tell me, Adam. Where in the *heck* did you get this?" John asks almost nervously.

"Well, that doesn't matter, but I appreciate you taking the time to look at it. Do you think you need some more time to see if you can find anything else?" Adam shoots back a bit quickly.

"I already ran all the tests I can. I'll send it back down to you when you head upstairs for the conference," John explains confidently, lifting an eyebrow. His eyes veer off to an opaque jet-black circular cubicle that is just about the right size to contain Adam's orb.

"Thank you. I really ought to get up there now, actually," Adam responds.

"Well, as representative of the modern science division, we wish you good luck as our team leader. Go make a difference, man," John speaks as he walks back to the control center in the middle of the open floor concept. Adam steps back over to the pod rather hastily and clambers aboard.

"Silver, you know where to go," Adam speaks out loud.

"Taking you to Floor Two Hundred, sir. You will be slightly early. The conference begins at 09:30. Current time: 09:18. Shall I engage invisibility to avoid awkward social contact?" the voice synthesis asks politely. Adam lets out a mild whimper to insinuate a positive response. "Here we are, sir," Silver responds to his quietness. The orb-shaped pod slides vertically in a harmonious manner up the side of the Dawne. Upon reaching the brow of the magnificent rooftop, the machine shimmers and becomes entirely transparent. The invisibility prevents his presence from being detected, noticeable only from the outside. Adam can still see everything inside his pod without an issue. From the outside, however, the entirety of the pod is permeable to all light. Arriving at the top, the pod slows to a careful halt. The craven sun rays glimmering off the crest of the Dawne and onto Adam's skin create a peaceful and calming image, an image that, comparing to the screaming streets of Newgrounds, can be considered perfect. Adam bides his time, absorbing the perplexing spectacle of the world. It doesn't take long to appreciate what has been salvaged of the human race. In a moment of false paradise, he smiles to himself. The clock strikes and he removes himself from the comfort of the chair, navigating under the swinging door to stand upon the glass-encased rooftop. Several other people swarm the same level, each dressed in an exquisite manner, one that cannot be frowned upon by even the richest of the rich, a manner which defines the reality of a broken economy. An economy reminisce of what once was. Adam's spine trembles in the fear that they are making all the same mistakes again. He paces around a grand, smooth oak table to find his card on the oval masterpiece. 'Modern medicine: Helena. Resource mining: Rory. Modern science developmental technology: Adam. Ah! Perfect.' He finds his card and cools his heels behind the maroon-carpeted grandfather chair.

"Two minutes until we roll," an unenthusiastic voice taunts. Everybody else on the sparkling roof level quickly takes their respective positions behind the evenly spaced seats. Adam looks left to see Rory, and on his right is James. His card reads: *'Experimental Time Technologies: James.'*

"Hey there, Adam, how's things these days?" James asks tenderly amongst the rolling whispers in the room.

"Ah, you know how it is. I'm just hoping that the news we have will go down well, but we'll see what happens," Adam attempts to subtly change the subject.

"Ha! You and I both," James says back to him. Adam continues his visual venture as his eyes investigate. To his right, he can see the Newgrounds over the edge of the Dawne. Thousands, maybe millions, of people are lined up in the streets. Some people seem to be pushing around to get a good view, but they have all stopped now. The mass of people looks up with hope at several immense screens that are currently dark, but Adam and everyone else knows what happens next. Not a word echoes in the valley for a stinging moment, until the voice called out once more: "Thirty seconds." Everything stops. Silence rings through the air like icy knives through skin. Nothing is the sound, like emptiness, wind, crows, and sand blasting silently across a naked desert. The human ear captures nothing more through the tense air.

"Five, four, three, two," the voice calls out once again. Immense holographic numbers display on the table in correspondence with the counting, although the visual countdown includes the number one. The host of people at the table sits down in eerie synchronicity. One man, however, remains standing at the end of the table and begins blurting boldly in the heat of the blazing star above them.

"Good morning, ladies and gentlemen of the valley! Who's having a good morning? AHA! I know I sure am! It's your favorite host David here," he speaks while looking up at a hovering orb invented by Adam himself, transmitting flawless image and sound across the nation.

"We are all gathered here today to enjoy the spectacle of debate and problem-solving by everyone's beloved Upper level!" He very clearly overemphasized the words 'Upper level.' A horrific wave of 'boos and nos' erupted volcanically from the Newgrounds below so powerfully that it can be heard faintly from the tip of the Dawne. David continues to speak, despite hearing the chaos that is so fiercely being formed.

"Let's get right into it now. Last year, we discussed the possibility of reuniting the two sides of the world once again. We have longed for peace between the valley and the inland for some time now. With a good memory, you can recall last year's conference." David takes a seat as a short video clip plays with the most beautiful audio quality imaginable. It begins with David speaking ever so proudly while wearing a suit vastly different than his current attire.

"To mark the ten-year anniversary of not only a successful reign of the Upper level but the finalization of construction of the Dawne, we are happy to announce that a peace treaty is finally within our reach. We hope that in the next twelve to twenty-four months, we can *finally* reunite the sides of our war-torn world. That's right, ladies and gentlemen. You may all be able to see your sisters, brothers, and grandfathers, or even that long-lost dog you haven't seen in eleven years." A roar of cheering and screaming is shown from the people among damaged bungalows and dusty streets. People are pushing one another around, jumping up and down, and going absolutely berserk in reaction to the news. The video clip ends abruptly as the on-screen cheering attains a destructive level. The camera cuts back to David who stands up once more to take his place on screen.

"We are beyond ecstatic to announce to you fine people that a peace treaty with the inland has been CONFIRMED! That's right…" His enthusiastic speech goes on. However, the attention of most people is drawn to the sudden silence from the valley. The inhabitants listen intently to the riveting news and soon explode into a disruptive excitement. This continues for several minutes while David discusses details of the yearly conferences. Without being heard by a majority of people, he states that the yearly conference allows each department to present themselves. Everyone gets their say on what they've done to improve human life despite the many years that people have had to endure in ruin due to global war.

Nearly half of an hour goes by as David walks around and even on top of the table in his excitement, approaching each head of the assorted departments. More often than not, they reveal something that was generally uninteresting to the public and doesn't get much of a reaction. A large variety of leaders are giving the typical 'we-are-making-great-progress-and-we-are-excited-to-reveal-news-next-year' but they often fail to deliver on their promises. There are a few, though, that impress the crowd, such as the miner's new railway that is designed to get many of the common folks' working family member in and out of work twice as fast as before. Every now and then, the crowd would explode into a shockwave of a roar, tearing apart the fragile air. About forty-five minutes from the beginning of the conference, David makes his way over to Adam while he skips excitedly across the pristine table to begin interviewing him.

"Here he goes. Take it away, ADAM! From modern science developmental technologies, tell us what news you have for us." David halts his sprint over the table to Adam, pushing a button on his hand graft. Adam's graft sparks up and a series of lights emerge from around his chair, giving him the floor. The orb camera turns midair to focus on his perfectly smooth face as he takes a stand, holding hands with James, encouraging him to stand up with him.

"Well, it is my honor to announce a breakthrough in our science department. I've been working with James here from Time Tech and we have actually, for the first time in human history, successfully discovered a way to communicate between time periods. Yes, and actually we have a theory that we wish to present to our half of the world, to you people of the valley and our fellow Upper level members. If you'll hear us out." Adam talks to the orb with little anxiety, whereas James looks like he can barely keep a smile down. His hands jitter as fast as his teeth despite a few encouraging nudges from Adam. David takes over for a quick second to speak to the audience.

"Well, I'll be. Ladies and gentlefolk, *this* is why we have the very best up here. So we can do what needs to be done. So maybe one day, we can resurrect the ancient prosperity of our world," he pauses for a short moment for a breath and what one could easily say is an overdramatic break. "Adam. That sounds just marvelous! Why don't you elaborate for the beautiful people of the valley here today?" His voice curls up. His flawless hand directs the orb back to Adam.

"Our idea consists of communicating with people from the past." A slight break emanates, slow and steady. "It may be possible to avoid all of these world conflicts. If we take a look at our world, we have had nine world wars, each more dreadful than the last. With this technology, it just might be possible to avoid any of this. If we harness this tech, we could communicate with the people who lived hundreds, even thousands, of years ago and warn them of what is to come, preventing these wars. We could theoretically transform the world as we know it to be rid of these wastelands, and perhaps everyone could live in a building such as the Dawne." A sliver of sweat slides down his sensitive spine. "We may be, just maybe, able to prevent all of this mayhem. We aim to create a true paradise for not just one percent of our population, but for all. We can reshape the world, and we are so close to reinventing life as we know it." Adam stops talking, taking a breath of relief. The energy inspirits a powerful vibe.

"Wow! Just WOW! That right there, that is some revolutionary news. Well, my fellow valley-goers, it seems we have our options wide open!" David exclaims himself in a truly explosive manner. Adam has never seen a man with such invigorating energy. The screens actively display images of the overwhelming crowds below, stuck in the decaying streets. They are yelling, hollering, and fighting. An absolute burst of outrage overcomes the people of Newgrounds as they begin pushing one another around while many others are cheering in relief-filled happiness. A camera zooms right in on a couple of burly men, one of whom maintains a lengthy, bright orange beard of epic proportions. His current physical competitor has dark brown locks covering half of his face, though he must have been skinnier than the other guy underneath the natural mask by the look of the width of his face. The two are locked in a two-limbed arm wrestling with gritted grins. A live video focuses in and the camera starts to pick up audio. The gingery one speaks first, likely far too indulged in their altercation to notice his live stream to the general public.

"You think this's good, huh? You're probably thinkin' that ain't no way that can go wrong, uh? Well, I got news for you, sonny boy! I got family on the other side. I lost my freakin' wife to the ninth war! If I don't see 'er again because of people like you, you're nev'r gonna hear the end of it, and that's a Bilbo guarantee!" He's screaming at the smaller brown-haired man and gives him a forceful push with a grunt behind his last word. The other man contests back an inaudible mumble to the ginger, who claims to be Bilbo, striking his legs and flattening him. The ginger beard flops up as the great back hits the ground, smashing sand aside. They both lie on the ground now, one on top of the other. While in control, the smaller man rages out at him.

"What are you saying!? Do you want to fix this forsaken world we live in? It's shit! Nothing about this place makes me, you, or any of us happy. If there's a way to resurrect a better world, then for shit's sake, do it!" He leans in much closer, spitting on the raging red beard. "I can't stand people like you." He gets up and walks away after pushing Bilbo's hands into the ground as a sign of finality. Barely a moment passes before the camera shuts off. Its absence pushes a silent broadcast, a brief blackness. Everyone halts in shuddering anticipation. A few fists keep flying through the partitioning valley and the sounds of those fights are carried hollowly through the arid, threatening air. Adam can just feel that the people of Newgrounds are staring slightly vacantly at the dead screens, waiting for more. There is nothing. Adam can see David talking to somebody through his graft and wonders what might be going on. His suspicions are answered not a second later as David snaps his finger to reboot the autonomous-looking camera. He starts speaking once again, though this time not nearly as energetically. The poor man looks as though life has literally been sucked out with a vacuum from his wild heart.

"Hello, members of the valley. At this time, we would like you to calmly return to your homes. You may have the rest of the day off from work. The Upper level will get back to you with more news before the end of the day. Stay tuned in to your grafts. That's all for now," David begrudgingly informs the people of Newgrounds below. Those at the table atop the Dawne know, however, that not only that half of the commoners' grafts no longer work, but they are highly unlikely to actually return home without a fuss. Like the professionals they claim to be, the department directors walk over to the side of the building, gazing down. Protected by a stunted wall of glass no higher than Adam's shoulders, they watch what happens below – fights, screaming, and bloodshed. Adam hears something from several meters away from an anonymous voice.

"If only we had the numbers for a police force," one-woman sighs.

"I mean really, just look at the poor things. This is why we need a military," another woman says. A man nearby, Rory, calls back much more loudly than the soft-spoken words of the women.

"No. This is exactly why we don't," he spits.

"Listen, guys, bickering about that isn't going to solve anything. I've already spoken to the Top Four. They told me they're going to call us shortly. Just relax. They mentioned something about a democratic decision for once in their lives, so let's just see where this goes," David explains to Adam and the others. It's common knowledge that as head of Newgrounds' public relations, he is often the first one to know all of the relevant details. He needs time to make it sound the way that it should. The rooftop crowd is fully aware that if the Top Four are required, then things have taken a turn for either the worse or, in any case, the dead serious. The holographic screen above the perfectly carved table lights up again. It appears to show four slender figures seated comfortably on a pristine paper-white couch.

"Good day, children! Alex, Trevor, Samantha, and I are here to discuss things with you. Obviously, we saw what just happened and, we will be frank, there are some people who aren't happy. By some, we mean probably forty to fifty percent of Newgrounds' population," she speaks with a soft and slow voice, calming to all within earshot despite what appears to others as a very serious matter. The male to her right continues for her.

"Yes, as Alessia was saying, many of them are concerned, and it's not that this newly developed technology is bad. But it may not have been the solution the people wanted to hear just minutes after being told they could have had the chance of reuniting with their families," he explains to them the cause for concern. "So just imagine yourselves in their shoes. Ten years ago, one of the greatest wars among the nine annihilated the planet. Just months prior to that, we were finally starting to pick ourselves back up from World War Eight. In the frustration of wartime, for the ninth time, an evacuation from major cities was called once again. I'm sure you all remember how urgent the capitalists were to move bodies. People were thrown left, right, and center, dragged out of houses and workstations and shoved into whatever van they could find, leaving hundreds of thousands of families separated," he pauses for a second, taking a breath to try to comprehend the severity of the issue. "With a global population of less than five million, that's a considerable dent in the morale of today's world. So, have some compassion when you think about what these people have to deal with," he stops and gazes downward as though disappointed.

"Exactly. Thank you, Trevor," Alessia addresses him and then her audience once again. "So, we have decided that in order to prevent a revolution or, mother forbid, even worse, that there will be a vote." With the startling comment, everyone looks around at one another, taken aback. Without a dash of hesitation, Rory speaks up.

"Ma'am, I hate to object but we haven't given the right to vote in ten years and everything has run pretty smoothly."

"Well, Rory, if that's how you see things, then maybe that's the reason we do need to change history. We need to give something a chance and restore humanity before we end up just another part of history. The justification behind this rationale is because there are two options. The first is that we don't go through with it and the future generations will hopefully thrive anyway with the upcoming peace treaty. Although if we go through with this, we will literally be rewriting history. Everything we know could change in an instant. Our world could not exist. We could be gone, some of us maimed, killed, or not even born. It is likely that we won't be in power, but at least everyone would be able to have somewhat of a happy life, together as a species. Better that than some sociopathic complex. The four of us see this as an outrageously ripe opportunity for not just us but for them, too. We may be facing the biggest political dilemma we have probably ever seen. We don't have an option to please everyone. There will be fights. There will likely be deaths, but it is *finally* for the greater good," Alessia elaborates. "Additionally, with the way things are going with our power supply, we might not be able to last as long as we think. We've had a preposterous number of graft failures recently and we can't keep up with demand, people. If there is a time that we need to act, it's now," she dictates. Adam speaks up instantly.

"So, that's it then. We put it to a vote, and what will we, or more specifically, you, do with the people who don't get their way?" he questions.

"You leave that to us. It might not be perfect, but it will have to work. There's a reason we're here because we've had to make decisions before," the other male, presumably Alex, retorts.

"We'll send out a graft message to the public and let them know that a vote will occur at some point in the near future. You all deserve some time to think this over and send any suggestions our way. We still have some details to work out, but they'll all be included in the message you get later. That's all. For now, we need to get on with things," Alessia hints further, but a stinging quietness permeates the air. Each person in the vicinity with Adam has an expression of admittance on their face, sulking ever so slightly in acceptance. Alessia looks around cautiously for three or four seconds before the holographic screen shuts off. For a brief second, they all stare behind where it is and into the glass wall.

"Well, I think the best thing we can do is go back to work and think things over with our teams, see if we can come up with something to please the crowd. Until then, looks like we're out of luck. I'll see y'all when I see you," David announces. He trudges over to one of the several identical pods and climbs in before he gets sucked down the outer surface of the Dawne. A multitude of 'byes and goodbyes' scurry around the room as the powerful gathering of people does the same, moving back to their pod to take a speedy route back to work. Adam follows the trend as he makes a choppy exchange with Silver. His eyes become rapidly enthralled during the five seconds it takes him to get back to work – the sunset, the women, and a beautiful life that's painless and invincible, like youth but so far from it. He arcs his hand to his forehead, making way for a big push from the fingertips and a well-rehearsed uncanny eyebrow movement. He arrives at work again, only halfway through the brutal sun's loop around the Earth.

"Silver, announce a meeting at 12:15 for my staff, please, and if you could arrange the left side of the room during lunch break so that we have a place to sit, it would be appreciated," Adam requests.

"No problem, sir. Message sent. I will begin organizing in thirteen minutes, at 12:10," Silver transmits. Adam's feet meet the work floor once again as they whisk him toward John. The two of them discuss the issue as Adam explains the details of what was idealized during the rooftop conference video chat. In agreement, John respectfully takes a spot at the table beside Adam where they continue to wag their chins until quarter past. In the meantime, their grafts ping as a release of information from the Top Four illuminates their hands. They gather the floor staff, about six or seven people, and give them a detailed rundown. Surprisingly enough, John kicks off, leading the discussion.

"Alright, guys. The Top Four have said that they intend to release a message to the public of a rather... experimental nature. They've indicated to us that a vote will take place sometime soon. The basics of the voting situation are that everyone will have two options. On one hand, we will go ahead with contacting the past in an attempt to prevent the global conflicts that have gotten us into the state we are in today, which we know as the original plan. The second option is," he sighs and holds a longing gaze to his left, "the technology will be preserved, or at least unused to allow the option of people reuniting with their families again due to the closing deal on the peace treaty with the inland," John disclosed. "Our main goal here is to ask you, as a team or as individuals, if there is anything you think that could improve the possibility of us going ahead with the original plan. If we can sell it better to the people out there, it would make a world of a difference," he continues. Several ideas bounce back and forth between members. After some heated discussion and grilling questioning, the group arrives at a unanimous conclusion.

"Is there any way we could convince voters that there is an effective, maybe even foolproof, method of changing the past in the case that we establish communications?" one-man inquiries from across the sturdy table.

In immediate response, the gears begin to grind in Adam's mind. What if they could come up with something new? Something to revolutionize the idea of peace. He keeps thinking. His mind wanders amongst the conversation around him.

A belief system, myth, and images of the object in his room flood his complex mind's eye. The days of his relationship with a lover have passed, but what if he could see her again? His mind transforms into a train launching into full steam-operated power. It hurls through a dissociated puzzle of ideas and continues to rummage, grasping at the corners of a greater idea: peace. What if everyone worshipped one person? One man. A world with some cultural background. A history. Adam's mind continues to scamper up and down, left and right, picking up ideas and attaching them to this one great idea: a collective. He hears little and sees next to nothing as his expanding mind swamps all perception. This one thing or this one being could be the reason for behaving well. You could impress it, and perhaps *believing* that behaving well could grant you entrance to a place after death so that you could see your loved ones again. Better yet, those who do misbehave will go to a place less desirable. Not everyone would have to believe it for it to work. Sure, humans are incredibly intelligent but, if made convincing enough, they will believe it, especially in the early ages! It needs a name and some fine tuning. OH! It can be written into a book like a set of laws, but in order to make it more interesting, perhaps it can be presented as a novel. Yes. It will be filled with all the glorious and horrifying examples of behavior a human can undertake. What happens to those who act in such a manner will be demonstrated, too. The rug-rat dashing around within Adam has almost every piece needed to finish the construction of this colossal idea. It places logical reasoning here, an entertainment piece there. Tap-tap from the hammer and the final nail sinks in. That's it. The answer to the world wars, the fighting, all of it. The reigning concept above all else in this alternate reality. A reason to fight for a better world, for everyone else, and for your own hidden selfish reasons. Religion.

III

"YES!" Adam yells, out of character.

"See! I'm glad someone agrees that Martha's not pregnant, she's just fat." John exclaims as he nods happily.

"Oh no, pardon. Uh, I found a way out of this. I think I've figured it out," Adam voices.

"We're all ears," John fires back, shuffling his hands into a more professional manner to reduce the stature of his profane comedy.

"In agreement with what Robert said about convincing the people, and maybe even the Top Four, of a way to maintain peace in the past." Adam answers readily.

"Uhm. That was nearly ten minutes ago, but sure, what's your idea?" a man across the table, Robert, responds. Adam takes time to explain what he came up with – the whole idea, the one being above all, the realms of afterlife, including a good one and a bad one, all of it.

"So, in summary, the big picture is that there are beings, or maybe one being that is all-powerful and all-seeing. This idea should give people a reason to behave, a reason to maintain peace and order. I know it's quite farfetched, but I've got to believe it will work," Adam details as he scratches his head. "We need to try something outside the box. I think we can make people believe, from the beginning of civilizations, that there is something or someone watching our moves, who we ought to impress. Theoretically, it should generally improve not just personal behavior but interpersonal and even international relationships. There will have to be rules and laws, but that's the basis," Adam publicizes. The group remains cautious for a short while, looking unsure what to make of such an abstract concept. Every few seconds, a hand would shoot up for a brief instant before its owner would silently retract it, accompanied by center-of-the-face-oriented eyebrows and a perpendicular glance. "If anyone has anything to add to it, I would be happy to modify the idea," Adam announces. There is no movement in response. "Right, then let's get to it. John, come with me. The rest of you, continue perfecting the technology so that we can run without faults. We don't have enough power these days for wasted attempts," Adam encourages. The group disperses from the table as mechanical parts in the floor begin automatically disassembling the space, putting chairs and tables in their original spots. Adam spares a few minutes to explain the grandeur and details of the menacing task he holds ready for John: creation of the scripture.

"Just to be clear, Adam, you want this book to feature you, me, and my brother, James? And the plan is to act through a series of emotionally charged events that highlight why people ought to act a certain way. In the same light, I should highlight what is not okay and preach the idea that certain behaviors are incorrect. Is that right?" John inquiries.

"Yes, and be creative, but not crazy. It needs to be believable. If you want, I can hook you up with David so you can get started?" Adam politely appeals.

"Oh yes, definitely, that would make things much easier. Thanks, Adam." John says back. The members of the teams separate to endure a taxing workday, delving diligently into their individual tasks. Adam gets in touch with David for John and asks James if he would be okay with being represented in the book as himself, John's brother. Meanwhile, John clenches his fists in the corner of the room. His long nose and short hair complement his lips that dance in focused frustration. *'The revolution,'* he writes down. *'The spirit,'* he tries again. He scribbles down several ideas before crumpling them up and tossing them into the trash where they are instantly incinerated to dust. The team works tirelessly until early sundown, at which point they return to their respective pods and, in succession, their apartments. Adam arrives once more to the dinner table with a plate of mouthwatering steak and potatoes steaming in front of him. He notices that the orb that he sent up for analyzing has arrived back on his table. Silver must have placed it there. Then, her voice echoes around the room as he sinks his teeth through the buttery potatoes topped with perfectly seasoned gravy.

"You have a message, sir. Permission to open it?" Silver's mollifying robotic voice chimes in. Adam examines the lights that twinkle bleakly on his hand where he becomes informed of development from the Top Four. He motions smoothly with two fingers and the picture on the graft grows into a projection before his rot-gray eyes. A series of words in a large block of texts hovers above the table surrounded by other smaller pieces of information such as the current time, the topic of the message 'announcement,' and the sender 'the upper level.' It shimmers bravely in a blue lighter than the oceanic color that nestles the rest of the softly emboldened text.

The following information is available to all valley persons.

"Good evening, members of the valley. It is our pleasure from us at the Upper level to announce to you fine people of Newgrounds that there will be a democratic vote occurring next week on Monday at 14:15 sharp. This vote will determine the very future of the human race on Planet Earth. One option available to voters will be to rewrite time in an attempt to create a better world. On the contrary, you may vote in favor of keeping things the way they are, in the hopes that the peace treaty will commence. Of course, this will one day allow you to see long-lost loved ones. There will only be two options. Avoiding voting will result in a week's power loss in your block. For those of you without functioning grafts, a general voting station will be set up in the courtyard in front of the Dawne. Transportation to and from will be provided for those who live over thirty minutes away by foot.

"For those in Sector Four, the train will stop for pickup at 09:00. For those in Sector Three, the train will stop for pickup at 10:30. For those in Sector Two, the train will stop for pickup at 12:00. For those in Sector One, the train will stop for pickup at 13:15. Several trains will leave the courtyard at 16:30 on a return journey," Silver speaks out. "A diagram of the sectors illuminates the dining room, zooming in for each sector. Sector Four in green looks to be over half of a thousand kilometers away, where Sector One in red appears to be not much further than ten kilometers from the Dawne." She continues fluently, "We urge you to make the choice you feel will be the best for everyone, and yourself, of course. Voting is mandatory. It must also be noted that power supplies diminish every day and that it is time to learn from the mistakes of our ancestors. Please take these factors into account. We will hear from you on Monday – the upper level." Silver's beautiful voice flows naturally.

The following information is available to members of the upper level ONLY.

"Dear fellow upper levelers, in correspondence with the first message, you should be advised that there are significant risks in either choice. We know your families are no longer with us or down in Newgrounds in a majority of cases. We hope you'll make the right choice. Finally, if you would like to add to the suggestions given in regard to the plan, any help is appreciated. Since the reveal of information to the public, Newgrounds' relations department is receiving an overwhelming number of questions to which we don't yet have the clearest of answers. Topics of hot discussion are as follows: 1. How exactly can we be sure peace will be maintained and that the people of the past won't ignore us? 2. Who will contact the past on our behalf? 3. How long will the process take? Good luck and get back to us as soon as possible – the Top Four," Silver concludes. Her words finish explaining the end of the paragraph as Adam stares with one raised eyebrow at the object on the table.

"If everyone kept your secret for so long, what are you? What could you possibly be? Surely you can't," he whispers to himself, chewing a tender beef loin as the hologram closes. His head sinks slightly below his linked fingers as the juices melt in his mouth. His gaze brushes up just over the tips of his index fingers, deep into the sphere. He speaks up after swallowing a large mouthful, noticing the disappearance of the hologram. "Oh no, Silver! Bring that back up, please. I need to tell the Top Four something." He opens his palm, shooting the hologram back to the center of the table. The utensils scoop up the remainders of the alluring meal and deliver them to a moistened mouth. A mechanical arm bends from the ceiling to remove the clean plate.

"Voice recording for message typing active, sir," Silver reports.

"Alessia, Alex, Trevor, and Samantha. I'm sending this transmission in response to your voter's information package. I can't help you with who exactly should communicate to the past because I don't know everyone in the business. It's not really my area of expertise. I will disclose that I am interested, but maybe not perfect for the job," Adam specifies. "What I do know, however, is that the entire process will be complete in less than a day. Because of the nature of time travel, the operator here, in our day, will be able to talk to whoever it is from the past and guide them through their lifelong quest in a matter of hours. For example, if the said person needed three days to complete a task, it would only be a second or so for us, just the twist of a knob and we would be speaking with the same person just three days later. Every change that they instill will happen instantly if it is to affect our world. The entire planet could transform entirely between lunch and dinner," he asserts, pausing for a breath before explaining his grand idea. "Also, in regard to your first question, I think I may have an answer. It's a bit farfetched but I have a good feeling you'll like it." He explains the entire plan to them quite intricately, withholding not a smidge of information. Adam divulges into details of the story John will be writing. The physical scripture, on paper, will allow people the ability to follow along without any confusion from ambiguity. He proceeds, explaining that the behavior instilled by this belief will spread peace globally. He finishes, claiming that even if the idea of this omniscient being is changed between nations. It wouldn't matter because it will always be about peace. The propulsion of information from his mouth slows down to a halt.

"Would you like me to send the message, sir?" Silver asks him, displaying a vast textbox in a dazzling show of blue.

"Send it," Adam replies.

One minute goes by, and another, and another. He waits cautiously. Are they reading it yet? Should he have reworded things? Will they like it? Who knows? In the presence of a rising moon, he slips into an astonishingly soft gray nightgown. He pretends as though he isn't waiting as he prepares thoroughly for a perfect night's sleep. *Ping!* There it is! *Ping!* He looks at his hand to see the luscious green glow from his skin bloom into the darkness. With the knowledge that green indicates the presence of a new message, he hops on into bed and flips his palm face-up.

"Silver, read this out to me," he calls out with anticipation.

"No text received, sir. There is only a video file. Permission to open it, sir?" she responds. Adam simply nods and an image bounces up in front of the bed. A powerful jazzy string of notes starts booming out.

"Never gonna give you up!" A classic joke filled with musical energy echoes through the entire apartment. Adam's jaw drops. His eyes screw inward from wide open to an aggressive glare. He ogles oddly at the other side of the bed for a few moments, contemplating what's next.

"Silver! That's not funny. I can see that it's from the Top Four. Show me what's really on the message," Adam cranks out.

"Yes, sir, my apologies, just a bit of Evelyn's handiwork at play there," Silver tells him. Adam swallows, peering straight down for a split second. "Opening text," she continues. The deep azure-tinted words sprawl out amongst the air molecules in the room as Silver initiates reading aloud.

"Adam, you have honestly impressed us with much more than we could have hoped for. This, well, this is excellent. We've done a touch of editing, but we can assure you that a message for all valley members will be distributed regarding your idea tomorrow. We will also need a copy of John's book before the plan is initiated if we go ahead with it. In response to your interest in taking part as our representative, we would be happy to have you, should no one else step forward. We'll get back to you with more tomorrow on that. Thank you for this idea, Adam. You have been an enormous help in changing our world. Rest well for tonight – the Top Four."

A cheesy grin smacks into his face as his eyes skim through the words. He reads them once more to be sure as the smile extends, stretching his lips to his ears. A sense of accomplishment rushes through his veins, tingling the nerves. At last, his hard work is paying off. With the acknowledgment that there is still much work to do, he closes the marvelous display with a flick of his fingers and does the same to dim the lights.

Dreams are complicated. They aren't always easy to understand. Adam wonders far too often whether his dreams mean anything.

She stood there on that hill all alone this time. Her brown rags get caught adrift in the wind behind her. The sun decorates her entire body with a shimmering shower of golden glitter. She is merely a cocoon concealing an object against her abdomen using her right hand. A smile emerges from the left corner of a soft mouth and stretches far across to the right. A sparkling row of teeth burst into reality. Baby-blue eyes and a nose smoother than the most weathered valley adorn her perfect face. Adam wishes to know what it means.

He awakes with a startle as the image cuts to black. Flipping over on to the other side, still warm and exceedingly comfortable, he checks his graft for new messages. There's nothing. He goes through the morning routine seamlessly, preparing himself for what could be an interesting day at work. There isn't an experience he can think of that beats a bowl of orange yogurt and crunchy cereal in front of a glowing sunrise. A few minutes later, his feet greet the magnificent floor of his workplace to begin the tireless laboring grind.

"Morning, Adam!" John calls out from across the room. With a face that oozes ecstasy, he rushes over to Adam's side. "Okay, so, I have a basis for the book. I did some groundwork, but I haven't finished details or fully fleshed it out yet, but you can take a look," John finishes. "It's my first time *really* writing anything of importance..." The words ring with an odd familiarity. Adam walks over to the opposite side of the room with John, intrigued. The very first line strikes him with pride.

"In the beginning, there was God."

"God? Is that the name of our make-believe being?" Adam queries.

"Yes, do you like it? I asked Harper and he liked it, so." John returns with a touch of hope.

"Don't doubt yourself. That's an interesting name. I like it. Nice work, man," Adam tells him patiently. He lowers his voice, "Look, I got a message last night from the Top Four and they love the idea. Religion, the text, everything. They said they'd make some minor adjustments, but it's a go. They'll need a copy of the finished book by Sunday. You have a name for it yet?" Adam asks, rifling through pages with sheer content.

"I've got a few but the one I think I can get behind the most is 'The Bible,' and to support it, I created an adjective to describe things that come from it as 'biblical,'" John says back to him delightedly. Adam nods slowly in approval with pouted sideways lips. The pair of them continues working on their respective responsibilities. Tearing through simulation after simulation, they perfect one performance issue after another.

John begins to script the Bible.

Two o'clock rolls around to be met with a slew of alerts from each person's graft. Their hands expulse a harmonious green. The workplace skids to a sudden halt. Each person in the room directs their attention to the main assembly in the middle of the room as a male voice calls out from the ceiling and walls.

"The following message is for all valley members." There is a slight pause, and a screen of text covers all screens on the center console as one big box. "Dear citizens of the Newgrounds, we are happy to announce that we are adequately prepared to carry out this alternative option. You have no need to worry about logistical issues. While we still have four days to find the perfect representative of who we are as a whole, we are pleased to confirm that once we unlock the technology's abilities and move forward, the process will take less than a full day. For further explanation, read the attached textbox in your own time. Secondly, the method with which we will maintain peace in the past will be through something revolutionary called religion. This concept was developed recently from the Dawne and is presented to you in the following basic idea. We will convince people from years ago that there is a being that exists above all, watching our every move. The premise we designed is that people must behave in a certain way in order to achieve a sense of self-satisfaction for appeasing and following the laws of this being. In return for adequate actions, we have crafted the idea that they will be granted access to a blissful realm in their afterlife. The rules outlining these behaviors will be specified in scripture that is currently under production from our science departments. In addition, it will be mandatory for all members of the valley to attend or watch two seminars in regards to details of this topic in order to fully understand it so that you can make a fully informed decision when it comes to your vote on Monday. All working departments and businesses will have mandatory seminar times today and tomorrow from 15:30 to 16:30. That's all for now – the Upper level," the voice concludes. The men and women in the room cheer halfheartedly initially. Shortly after, however, their work chamber explodes in applause for one another.

They spend hours under the trance of a mind-bending focus on troubleshooting one issue after another until each person's graft begins blinking amber slowly. The time reads 15:30 on each of their palms as they finish up their tasks for the day and gather around the center console once more. The outer lights dim, keeping the center console well-lit behind a black projected screen. The very first thing shown is a simple textbox recapping what was mentioned earlier in the announcement. The repeated text rolls steadily with automated speech for a few minutes and then draws to a black close. A flash spurts from the screen in a blank white burst before a dreadful series of images begins revealing itself. The premiere of the show reveals images of houses on fire, cutting between bombs being dropped and cities being wiped flat, a wasteland after a prosperous potential. The camera slides underground. Dust falls from a steel roof as the observer pans downward to expose an endless sea of human life forms. Millions of people are packed tightly against one another in an emotional frenzy. An unbelievably behemothic and untasteful room with walls of beds and ladders on either side surrounds the carnage of screaming bodies within.

"This world is no more," a deep voice thunders. "We have a way to change the past to create a better tomorrow through religion," the crackling man echoes. "So, you want to know what religion is? Let's start with the basics. Here's you." The flickering sound of a camera shutter plays in rapid succession, clicking multiple times a second. The screen produces a live picture of a stick-figure man smiling and waving to the camera against a paper canvas background. "Here's God." A much larger man with a curly beard adorned with a white gown and scruffy hair stands beside the smaller man who is, in comparison, the size of the greater man's toe. A stunning symphony on the piano decorates the sound in a playful tune.

Focusing in on the smaller stickman, the camera zooms right into the smaller one's face. He is clearly puzzled, as a question mark appears above his head. "God created all life and is the reason you exist." The little man squeaks an 'oh' with a wide facial expression. Tiny little marks expulse from his limbs in stop-motion as he bounces with his cheeky comment. He follows it joyfully with a smooth and simple smile. The video zooms back out, and back in again, to god's face. "He has the power to create and destroy anything. He created the universe. He has lived long before you and will live long after you die because his life is eternal. He will let you live happily, but only if you follow his rules." With a zoom outward, another question mark pops above the little guy's head. The much larger and more detailed man snaps his fingers. In a flash, a book appears in front of him. He grabs it, and as he passes it to the little one, the book shrinks down to an appropriate size for him, though it seems very thick. "You must obey these rules for as long as you live, and he will allow you and your family to exist happily." The little man grabs the book from the larger figure's finger and hugs it tightly. "If you do not obey the rules, however, you will be punished after death with eternal torment." The observing angle swings down to underneath the floor on which the two men stand, showing a layer of fire on the bottom of the screen. It becomes enraged, singeing the feet of the innocent man before it dies down again.

"That's a bit much. Don't you think?" John inquires.

"Yeah, sshh," Adam comes back with a response.

"This only happens to the ones they call 'sinners,' but you, my good friend, will be safe in eternal delight because you followed the simple rules," the voice continues. The view pans upwards to reveal yellow circles above other people's heads who have clearly flown with birdlike wings and risen to the better place.

"This is just one view of the one we call God. Though he may be all seeing and all powerful, many nations may view him differently in some form or other." The larger man and the smaller man are cloned several times over the screen as it pans outward and to the right. The copies are each slightly different, some with different skin colors or different clothing. The clone variants are spread across the globe and allocated to different areas of the planet as the voice continues to explain. "The only constant is that God exists to establish peace among a growing world. However, he *only* exists because people believe in him. It's likely that you're wondering how people are ever going to believe such a tale. Many of you will have questions about what sort of person this God will be. For the answers to all of your queries and concerns, big or small, you must read a copy of the book of rules to be released in two days," the voice concludes.

"Two days!? I can't have it done in two days. Oh shit, alright guys, sorry. I'll watch this another time. I've got some work to do!" John exclaims with a rapidly oscillating voice. "Silver, get me in touch with James. I'll need his help." Adam watches as John walks over to the darkened area behind them and begins to work.

Intrigued by what the Top Four has done with his idea, he is quite impressed. Motion pictures are shown in a sort of stop-motion of people coming together as one to worship the larger man. They join hands and close eyes, humming and singing as one blind entity. As the camera reverses outward, it reveals a spinning orb among a vast concoction of stars, a promiscuous blue and green Earth, rather than a dry beige and orange one. The shuttering sound draws to a halt as the screen darkens.

From the blackness, a few slides of information slip by, including fewer engaging messages. Adam sits with the group to finish watching the presentation. The lights restore their original brightness after the seminar ends, allowing people to clean up their things and begin packing. Adam scurries over to John in anticipation, who assures Adam that things will be taken care of now that his own brother, James, is on board. Adam begins to flip page after page of the book, and minutes passed by without hesitation. He gets to the thirtieth and, so far, final page. The muscles on his face relax, and he smiles.

"John, I've got a great feeling about this. That's some compelling work. Keep it up," he reassures John with a hint of enthusiasm. In the air-conditioned paradise, hours creep past without much of a fuss. Adam attempts to relax as the sun falls behind the curvature of the Earth with a live stream of John's rule book as it's written. The video feed levitates in the quality air while he occasionally mixes in some intermittent old TV programs.

The following day starts up in routine as Adam wakes to a harmless apartment. Some oat-filled breakfast sends him on his way upstairs to work where he commands the crew through rigorous examinations. Nimble fingers operate on each part of the machinery as mindboggling physics is used to complete and modify their calculations – testing, testing, and trying over and over again. Sweat-layered time presses closer and closer to their spines as they work tirelessly to remove every possibility of failure. With the racing hour hand of the clock, the cauterizing sun travels through the sky to hover several degrees above a ruinous horizon. Half past three rolls around yet again and the group wastes no time plopping themselves before the enormous screen. Similar to the day prior, an old-style cartoon rolls and begins describing to the dangers of what can possibly occur from doing this – the scientific complications that can occur. The seminar continues for just under an hour, leaving a general message that there is a chance that things may not go toward the best of interests. In essence, they are informed that both paths for their future present potential issues whether it be contacting the past or establishing the peace treaty, although the message assures that the Upper level will do everything in their power to produce the best outcome for their desperate world.

This Friday night ends with Adam, John, and James sitting together in a semicircle of sorts to load in the last few words in the book they have officially denounced as 'the bible.' Their wise eyes rest little through a burning sunset and the freezing wisps of an early night. After some time, they arrive at a checkpoint in their daunting task. They edit the piece to fix any errors and send it off to the Top Four, as requested. With a bested but a conquering state of mind they decide to return to their individual floors for a well-deserved slumber.

With a tired mess of redhead hair, Adam sits up in his bed. Without a word, the synthetic curtains draw open to reveal a marvelous image. Like clockwork, the sun breaks through the solemnity settled in the far edges of the land to burn away a curdling icy chill. Adam tears himself from the comfort of warm sheets to prepare for the day ahead. With the bible complete, he knows that a Saturday to remember is brewing. As he sits down for a readymade breakfast, his graft glows a gorgeous green. His fingers twist to display a projection of the new message. Silver's settling voice reads out the display.

The following information is available to all valley persons.

"Good morning, valley-goers. Here at the Upper level, we have carefully constructed the very rules for our religious pretense. Attached is the book named 'the bible.' You will find it maybe slightly different than expected – in the form of a story rather than a list. We discerned that this would be best to maintain the attention of our predecessors. Please open the attachment and read as much of it as possible before the voting ceremony on Monday. In addition to the digital file, you will all receive a physical copy of this book throughout the day. Regards, the Upper level," Silver enunciates.

The entire valley receives a copy through the remaining operational grafts with the message. Meanwhile, thousands of drones spew from the bottom of the Dawne, carrying enormous crates. The massive collection of machines soars through the wilted air with packages for millions of people to stumble upon amongst their morning scrounge for food. Adam finishes the last bites of his perfectly poached eggs.

Over the next few hours, news updates culminate quickly. The observing cameras of the Upper level catch the fascinating responses from the Newgrounds' folk. A surge of riots erupts after people have had the chance to read the rules that are implied through the characters' actions in the book. Throughout the day, fires ignite with rage nationwide. People's houses are torched while others literally brawl to the death in the streets. Utter calamity riddles the disorganized community with violence and outrage. The entire fiasco could be interpreted as a powerfully exaggerated version of what occurs normally in the slums of the Newgrounds.

While relaxing in his living room, Adam takes a few steps over to the window to observe in person what he has heard about. Astonishing! Though difficult to make out details from over a hundred and fifty stories up, it seems as though there are hundreds, if not thousands, of books strewn carelessly about the walkways. Papers fly above huts and houses like dust in the wind. They trounce around unmoderated, often making the place dirty. It's been worse, but the fights just never seem to stop. The news updates continue to roll in as the death toll rises one by one. A failed infrastructure comes alive. Arguments lead to arson over the simplest of things. Hopefully, Adam ponders that the vote will revolutionize the catastrophic world around him and change things for the better permanently.

IV

The night before the great Monday event, though, incurred some interesting midnight stimulation.

There is blackness as thick as fog. It is no better than the haze that once covered the Earth. The silence was fitting. It isn't today or yesterday. It's more like a while ago. Turning over and over in an attempt to clear some of the fog of mystery, he stands alone, yes. He is standing. He looks down at his feet and then back up as his arms become visible. There is something between his fingers and his thumb, though details are difficult to recount. The heavy and dark fog swirls around him, preventing the penetrating glow of whatever is beyond from disrupting him. His arm is outstretched. He is speaking, or at least he thinks he is. His mouth moves with the intent of passing some sort of message, something that he believes to be important. He feels alone, but almost not. A whisper of words manage to break the foggy barrier and seep into his eardrum, but it isn't exactly distinguishable. It can be more accurately described as a collective shout, supportive in nature. With deeper focus, he trains his sleeping mind on cracking the details. The smoky aura displaces itself from his rugged, worn feet. Nothing but leathery sandals hold them in place. He stands upon a rock or construct of some kind. The noises grow somewhat familiar. The more he speaks, the more he can see the trail of white smoke peel from his lips as it disappears into whatever he holds in his hand. Round in shape and foreign in origin it must be. His words transform into sound waves which he feels are not only bolstered by this strange device but are more… believable maybe? The device is outputting a similar substance into the air, shooting out from the back with more than enough force to make its way through the horrific black vapor. A ray of light pokes through the other side to reveal, vaguely, hundreds of disfigured bodies pounding up in the air with an exterior member. Up and down they all go as the cheering accelerated. In the very moment, he realizes what is happening. The fog thickens up and closes him off completely from everything. The device… he knows exactly what it is. 'This ability,' he thinks, 'can prove useful.' He can't put his finger on it, but it feels more like memory than just another dream.

It seems confusing. Something very familiar about it resonates with him, however. Then, in a moment, he understands. The impossible becomes reality, and a spark burns within him.

Dreams never really are his favorite, but this one he likes.

At the very least, he thinks he likes it, until it changes.

Reclamation Day, April 2nd, 2319, he remembers in flashes. Such a significant time in the history of the modern world!

His dream begins the day before. On April 1st, everyone has to take a test through their graft to test intelligence. Results are sent to a collapsing government to determine a reform in society. It is the decision to see who would populate the Upper level and Newgrounds. The test is over now. It is the day following, on the second of April, when the results are announced… or rather enforced. He remembers the pain. The fuzziness surrounding the dream evaporates as the torture ensues. The front door comes collapsing down as a squad of armed men scream behind several men in suits. Their words are mildly unintelligible, not because of false memory but a rugged voice. The burly man who leads the gunmen shouts out.

"Newgrounds' member, Evelyn. Upper level member, Adam." Without a moment to think in between, an electric surge of adrenaline releases within his body. Dread and fear corrupt every vein and vessel.

"No. It's not possible," he replies quickly, trying to talk calmly to them. Their words echo hauntingly in his mind.

"Sir, we're going to need you to come with us." One man extended a hand, reaching for Adam, but he pulled away.

"No. Not without her," he tells them firmly. His heart beats from his chest out into the open world. He can feel it pounding against his skin. It would burst open any second.

"Sir, there is no time and no other option. Come with us or relinquish your spot in the Upper level immediately." Several other men dart past him toward his lover as she calls to him.

"Adam, go! We can't stay in Newgrounds. At least one of us should be –" she was cut off, as they knocked her to the ground with a controlling thud.

"Ma'am, stop talking and stop struggling!" they roar at her. His heart pumps faster and faster.

"NO! I can't do this without her!" Adam wails. "Fuck!" Energy spirals throughout him.

"I'm sorry, sir. This is your last chance," they reiterate.

"I, Adam!" her words are intermittent, as her mouth is covered by oppressing leather gloves. Everything from that moment on turns to a deep gray, as Adam suddenly realizes something greater.

He stands with tears distorting his skin. A tattoo is scarred on his brain.

One foot goes forward toward the front door with the feeling of unmistakable regret, an in-the-heat-of-the-moment decision.

The memory is faded in an initial attempt to disconnect.

The painful screams clutter the air as he exits the house.

A burning sun sears a fresh set of water-sealed eyes.

A false rolling thunder consumes every other sound.

It destroys him.

Step by step he marches through tiny tornadoes of dust.

He would fight for her. He would. He had to, all those years.

His feet take him away while his tears cover his shirt.

Dreams are scary, but memories are frightening.

V

It is voting day. Tensions are higher than ever before among the valley. Over ten years of collaboration, work and effort will be hanging so delicately in the balance, the choice for salvation for the past or the present at the fingertips of the common person. What will it be? Will the Newgrounds take the majority of the vote to work with the inland and maintain a peace treaty? Will they decide that after all this time that they wish more than anything to see their families again? Is it possible that the loved ones across the border are ever so more important than the possibility of an almost different dimension? Or will human nature override the feeling for love with the survival instinct? Are they going to vote in favor of not just a better tomorrow but a better today and resurrect what could have been? Will the general population consider themselves humble in the face of change and the chance to see those lost in the war once again? Adam's mind bounces in anxiety as he stands at a vantage point from the work floor, gazing out to the roaring crowd. The classic countdown before airing begins and David's booming voice rockets into the camera.

"Ladies aaaand gentlemen, here we are today on November twenty-eighth! It's voting day, people!" he bellows as almost the entire population of the valley, now in front of the Dawne, goes ballistic in applause. "The current time is 13:03 and the very last few people are stepping off that train to join in the lines for the vote. We have decided to bring you footage LIVE from Newgrounds. Tell me, how do you feel about the vote Mr. Pottle?" David grins as he energetically shuffles over a few steps to a younger male dressed in awfully dark, ripped clothing. He has the sort of look on his face and body that says, "I don't know how to shave but I can lift three hundred pounds." He opens his mouth while flexing his fingers nervously.

"I, uh. Well I'm just glad that we are going to have this, you know? We've been stuck in shit for so long and… and this is going to be just awesome," he explains in a friendly fashion.

"Ex-cell-entay, Mr. Pottle. And what is your decision on the vote? What do you think is the way forward for us today?" he asks publicly.

"I'm actually happy with my decision. I think it should be obvious to anyone who's not a moron. We have to vote for the peace agreement. Like, duh? Come on, I know all this fancy science stuff is interesting and maybe it'll work. Who knows? Personally, I think it's best to stick to what we know and fix the world we do live in. We can't be worrying about some theory or things that don't even exist," he responds to David with a cheeky but serious grin.

"Well, you heard it here, folks. Mr. Pottle will be voting in favor of fixing relations with the inland and hoping to restore families across the world," David announces as he turns to face Mr. Pottle for a brief moment. "Very brave of you, Mr. Pottle. Go get 'em, pal," David encourages, patting a brazen shoulder. He realigns his focus to the camera for all of the people in valley to gorge their eyes upon. "We are seven minutes away from voting time, ladies and gentlemen, and the Upper level representatives are arriving at their individual stations, ready to help you make your vote count! Oh, what an exciting event!" David carries on, never wavering on the enthusiasm. Adam gawks anxiously through the peaceful glass at the mass of people. James steps over to stand beside him, placing a welcoming hand on a fiery Adam.

"Hey, whatever happens, I know that things will work out. I mean I have John, so it's alright for me. I just know with… you know. She'll be okay, man. Things will work out," James reassures him.

"Hmph, thanks," Adam speaks back with a moment of surprise. "Sorry, I'm just trying to hear what he's saying," he finishes.

"Now, folks, when you arrive at the station, in front of you there will be an enormous blue button and an equally HUGE green button! Every line-up will have two buttons for you to use. The one on the left, the blue one, will read *'peace'* and that indicates that you wish for us to follow up on the peace treaty with the inland. The other button, the green one, on your right-hand side will read *'new world,'* and if you choose this one, you'll be voting to renew the world, as we know it, not just for the families but for everyone." David smiles elegantly at a swirling camera. "Now I'm sure you all know which one you want to press, but if you're still unsure, please take time now to file yourself to the back of the line so that once you get up there, you can slap that button real fast. When you're done, head on out of there, following behind the voting station and to the right, straight on back to the train station or your homes," David rings out. As he speaks, there are several hundred people from each of the fifty or so semi-organized lines. "The faster you slap that button and get out of there, the easier it will be for everyone else and the sooner we'll have results for you," he completes his vibrant rant. There is a wave of many whispers throughout the waiting lines that accompanies complaints that fly around about why the grafts can't be used to vote. "We could have used our grafts for this. What the hell are we doing here!?" one person screams behind David's shot. In an instant of underlying satisfaction, he responds.

"Let me give you a brief history lesson, miss," he starts off even louder than usual. "In the desperate times around Reclamation Day, our previous government imposed an eternal law that stated every citizen, regardless of their social status, would receive their own graft. However, the decision was made with little time to spare before the new orders came in to separate our community. The grafts were assembled in as quickly a manner as possible. There wasn't time to troubleshoot or do rigorous testing on each one, so there are several batches of failing or unreliable grafts out there in the world. Even with that, the ones that do work grow more unreliable each day and can be hacked. It's best this way – to do things manually." His monolog of an informative session broadcasts wildly for everyone to see. The camera captures the poor woman's face as her eyes widen in a bested stance. "We are a go in thirty seconds, ladies and gentlemen!" he announces. The staff members prepare their booths and attach their masks to their faces. "And you all look very excited to be here, so let's make this a day to remember. He– HEY! The gates are rolling up and the booths are opening! So start slapping those buttons in FIVE, FOUR," he initiates a countdown which doesn't really catch on until Number Three onward, "THREE, TWO, ONE! GO! Let's go, folks. Get those votes in and make 'em count. Today, we make history." He hesitates for a second as the camera spins around to reveal what must be millions of people awaiting a chance to revolutionize the planet. The marvel of it is quite breathtaking though. The people move so quickly; they are almost running to keep up. Adam gets a good look at the screen behind him at the spectacle that runs through the courtyard below. In a spur of curiosity, he decides to take a second to peer down the front of the Dawne to see it for his own eyes. Like a ravaging colony of emaciated ants, the people dart forward in line with compliance in place of complaints, for a change. Exactly as instructed, hundreds of people get their vote in within a matter of seconds. Repeating and repeating, a well-oiled machine expulses a large volume of people as their mark among many is processed. They move forward and push the button, hundreds in a minute and a thousand in a few minutes. Without even practicing beforehand, the symphonic procedure performs extravagantly. Minutes pass one after another identically to the masses of people waiting to etch their scratch into the fabric of time. The members of the Upper level each receive a ping on their grafts with an update to inform that they will make their votes last and are required to be at the voting station out in the courtyard before 15:30. The time trickles by so painfully for Adam as he watches the endless river dwindle.

In debt to his own doing, he takes the pod to the bottom of the Dawne. The pod slips down the side of the building and slithers to a halt so perfectly that he barely notices the deceleration. The pristine glass of the pod rests mere inches from the soiled ground as it extends outward in an arched swing. Adam removes one foot followed by the other, lowering them gently to the permanent layer of dust that is so notorious for its constant existence. A minuscule measure of sand particles swirl around his foot for an instant as it connects with the ground. He exits the pod as he proceeds to follow the stone path to the courtyard amongst the dried-up dirt. Multiple minor gusts of wind blow particles of debris up from the ground directly into his moistened eyes; he squints them shut at a moment's notice. Rubbing and tackling with perturbed eyelids, he manages to remove the impurity. A tightening in his protected lungs ensues to restrict his breathing in the slightly toxic air. The dryness contaminates his lungs which launch back up a deep cough in response. Step by step, he gets closer to the voting stations, approaching from behind a smaller line of Upper Level members. The last of the Newgrounds' inhabitant voters fiddle with either their head coverings or damaged facemasks. The final few voters play their part and depart. With no one left in line, he inhales another noxious breath and steps up the station. Adam wastes not a single second in slapping the green button highlighted 'new world' in bright white lettering. He noted that the other Upper level members did the same thing. A tidal consummation of sputtering and coughing sprawls out among them continuously. After voting, they immediately return to their respective pods in a flustered sprint.

Adam, thankful for the ability to see and breathe real air, despite its burden, joins the rest of the crew atop the Dawne via a delicately smooth ride. He arrives to see David first, who is now resting contently with his elbows on the table. Each member of the Upper level perches their comforted rear ends on their respective chairs and indulge in apprehensive conversation. The orb with a small black dot in its center, in the middle of the room, blinks at David in a directional green light followed by blue and it switches to green once more. He hops to his two feet with a smile locked and ready.

"And the time approaches, people. We are minutes away from discovering the fate of our world," he speaks out. Adam begins to contemplate complexities. He hopes for everything that he has worked for, direly, that the decision will be in favor of a new world. It has almost grown past the point of necessity so much that anything else would seem simply absurd. Of course, wanting to see your family is important and understandable, but when you can have all of that and more, why not? He ponders on that thought for a moment as a deeply settled rage burns gently.

He almost had it once before, a family. There are so many things in life that he hopes for, but the opportunity for that one specifically has already passed. He looks down at the floor with reasonable discontent. Whatever happens, he decides, well, at least some people will be happy and either way the world will be improved. Regardless, it's got to be a betterment to whatever this world is nowadays. Hmph. He continues to wait patiently to see whether his reality will be orchestrated in a final harmony to create a new life not just for himself but for the entire planet. Gosh! The moments do go by so slowly. *Tick, tock, tick, tock.* Like a child's game he touches his fingers to his palm in a rhythm in an attempt to distract himself from the agonizing downtime. He glances to his graft. It's only been a minute! Can this take any longer? He begins to wonder if the whole thing is even going to happen. What's the point in having all this and holding so much tension for so long? Just give it up already!

"We are two minutes away from the reveal. Hold on to your seats, guys and girls. This is going to be brilliant," David calls.

Adam looks up. He looks down. He takes a moment to reflect on where his past has led him. Years of studying and preparation have shown him what technology can do and the day has eventually made its appearance in this everlasting world.

It is the day that will define him and glorify his achievements for the creation of a different world, or it will be the day that it all goes by almost unnoticed in the decaying landscape. Just about all of the details and problems are so ridiculously close to being solved, so near a solution. It just requires the majority of people to see it that way and the hard work will pay off for the rest of the human race.

Adam's temper can only go so far but he resists saying anything solely because of the meandering possibility that he'll have to lead an immense operation in the next few hours. He watches sharply around the room. A forcefield roof bathes in the searing sun, it all seems very familiar. The details on people's faces all of a sudden become quite intriguing. Where did she get that pimple? How long has Rory had that tattoo under his left nostril? Adam begins to notice tiny details in the dragging moments. The torture is ruining him. Like a tortoise in a rabbit race his mind paces back and forth across the sides of his brain, hoping for something, just anything! It must be the same for everyone else. Surely, the others are thinking the same thing just sitting here and biding time like it's a fucking tea party. Jeez! The excruciating mental burn intensifies. A fire that was once a lighter flame has ignited a house, spreading rapidly with each passing nanosecond. Each tiny moment drags on and on and on and on. The pain doesn't end. Will the wait end?

"The results are in! Alright my fellow valley-goers, it is time to uncover the results. Let's take a closer look at the scoreboard!" The screens that so intricately tell the story of what is being unveiled reveal a hollow and softened light gray rectangle. From either side a deep blue and a luminous green line followed by a stream of its matching color seem to spill inwards toward the center. The movement of the colors is not liquid though. It is as if two colored blocks are being pushed from the outside toward the middle. The two, although initially seeming to move at the same rate, close in toward each other at different paces. As time passes, Adam barely makes out that one side is faster than the other. Before he can put two and two together, out of shock, he stares openmouthed at the screen covered in nothing but the final results. Two bars are side by side. Each color has a number in percentage.

It must be representing the number of votes in percentile, and one is at fifty-three percent, the other at forty-seven percent. The green bar, resting on the right-hand side of the screen is sitting at a simple forty-seven percent. The new world dream is ruined, shattered to smithereens in an instant. It is gone. But how? How can this be possible? Are people out of their minds? The fact that they want to see their family so much more than allowing everyone a new chance at life is just ludicrous! What a blow-down! This is nothing more than a new form of insanity. It's just difficult to imagine a world in which all of this is wasted. The world has been improving for ten years, and for what? What grand purpose does this serve apart from reuniting one or maybe two generations of families back together? In outrage Adam flicks his eyes over to the blue bar reading fifty-three percent in a distinguishable white text. So, it all leads to this. Every ounce of work towards what should have been a beautiful moment is let down by three percent of the population. It's typical politics, but he is enraged nevertheless.

"So, it looks like the people have spoken. The technology may be put to other uses or perhaps another time but for now, the valley will attempt to reunite with the inland before the New Year! Catch us for an update next week as the inland chancellor meets with our Upper level executives to discuss details of the treaty. That's all for now, and remember, the Upper level is always here to help." David smiles fantastically as he winks before the camera shuts off and the screens across the lands dismiss. Adam can only imagine what a ruckus must be occurring on the trains home for New grounders right now. Some of them will be ecstatic and relieved because they will finally have the means to see their loved ones. Others will rage and start confrontations because they are alone and wish so desperately for a change in the waste-land they call home. Adam, along with the rest of the population of the valley, return to quarters where many wallow or jump for joy amongst the decidedly split mood. What a world!

It's funny how people act when everything hangs so brutally in the balance, even when given a fair opportunity. The world must be full of delinquents and selfish bastards. Adam returns to his room patiently in silent rage. He enters the perfect conditions of his apartment and sits down for an early afternoon meal to process the relentless wrath inside his brain right now. Emotions are something necessary for making decisions, and it would be silly to ignore them. Still, anger isn't the best, especially when it's fueled by passion. In the fiery swarm his mind wears like a belt, an idea begins to mull about.

What if he alone did something about the problem? Maybe it would be a silly decision, but at least he would finally be happy. It's not right, though, that the people voted for the peace treaty, not against it. Doing so would never be tolerated outside of his smaller friend and colleague group. There is so much anger, though. Why isn't it fair that after all this work, the technology is wasted? If he did it, would it really be such a bad thing? Hundreds of thousands of people would be happy, not just himself.

Weighing the pros and cons of decisions under stress and anger can't be good. No decision he makes right now could prove productive for anyone. But people would be happy with a new future, a new world, and everything corrected to the way it should be! A frustrated mind plays ping pong back and forth like an argument between mother and daughter. What does he do? If his work is really to go down in history or, better yet, not at all in history, then it wouldn't just be families that are reunited. It would be nations and land masses brought back to habitable conditions. Earth would be better for all life forms. Humans are such selfish beings.

Adam sighs at the kitchen table, glazing his eyes over the object in front of him completely vacantly. Wrapped up in thought, he sits there without company. Seconds turn into minutes, which turn into nearly an hour that goes by and he doesn't move. The plate before him stops steaming and sits lifelessly. His gaze is a point-laser piercing fiercely right through the sphere and outside the walls of the Dawne. That's it. He has to do it. There's no other way. A feeling of assertion without the slightest doubt overcomes his body rapidly and he dives into the stone-cold arrangement of meat and vegetables. He spends the rest of the evening relaxing and goes to bed without worry, but with stress. He gets nightmares again, the usual – her and him on that hill once again as they say goodbye for the final time before the incident of separation between the Upper level and Newgrounds. Where is she now? Oh, how he wishes he knew if there ever was anything he could do to make things right again. Oh, right.

He awakes graciously in his opulent bed space. His arms elongate and become stiffly outstretched as a gulping yawn consumes him momentarily. The golden clock beside his palatial sheets displays a time one hour earlier than his usual wakeup. In a flurry of motion, he beelines for the bathroom past the dining room, skipping breakfast. Morning routine takes only a few minutes as he hastily dresses in exuberant clothing and prepares for what may be the most flagrant event the planet has ever seen. In his outstanding suit, he huffs for a moment to focus. His eyes twist a deep wound into the luxurious mirror. There is no going back if he goes further than this. The consequences may be exponentially horrifying. However, it must be done – the sacrifice of the few for the many. He snatches the orb on the dining table on the way out and stuffs it into his jacket with haste. A swift few seconds of a jog take him right to the pod and he climbs in. Silver announces herself.

"Where to, sir?" she speaks aloud.

"Take me to Floor One Hundred and Ninety," he snaps back without hesitation.

"Work hours are not online yet, today, sir. Voice activation is required to access this floor," the machine requires.

"My name is Adam and I authorize this access." he says strictly.

"Authorization confirmed. Elevating to Floor One Hundred and Ninety," the robotic synthesis replies. The motors start up and he begins to ascend with the hum of electricity vibrating violently through the air. A few buzzing moments pass as Adam looks out to his left and his right, observing the barren land around the Dawne like it's the first time he's ever seen it. It's time to make a change to all of this. He calms his hands to prevent them from shaking and observes for a sweaty moment in the nerve-racking journey. The smell of fresh leather drives its way into his alluring nostrils. The feel of its nurturing touch is splendidly serene. Once a minute sound, the buzzing of the pod roars aggressively in the pursuit of stealth. Heightened senses get ready to alert Adam to the tiniest of abnormalities. The gears whir before slowing down to a halt. "Arriving at Floor One Hundred and Ninety. Current time: zero five one zero ours," the machination of a voice adds. Adam steps out of the movement device onto the perfectly clean work platform. His voice fills the massive room that awaits him, empty of life. The lights transition to a shining brilliance at the words of command. He sprints silently to his chair and announces his next words using his powerful presence.

"Initiate the Pangea protocol," Adam orders. Lights blast the room from the computers before they shut off again as a whirring sound stirs with sinister suspicions in the air. Clicking and fixing, moving and rotating, the control station before him begins to transform. Screens come from all over the wall to connect and attach themselves to one another in a graceful combination. Parts move in a truly beauteous manner toward the growing central culmination of technology. Many of the numerous switches and control devices amass to form three distinct panels, the first of which remains still before him while the other two swing around to greet either side of Adam. That which could be previously described as a light hum is now swaddling the room in a very noticeably deep rumble. The panels continue to move in each and every way, coming together to form what looks to be a superstructure. The controls surround his front and the screen before him is outrageously large and detailed. A great number of screens meld together and form one absolutely colossal viewing platform. From the control system around him, holograms float all around as lights flash on and off in a dazzling plethora of colors. Similar to that of a pilot's cockpit, it begins to enclose upon him, almost completely encompassing Adam in the forward direction. His seat pops off the ground, fastening on to the control panel, and begins to move with the entire device as he moves his hands back and forth. He moves with the machine as one. Like a baby in a high chair he is mounted in the greatest complexity science has ever seen. The noises from behind the console erupt even further into full-blown engine screaming.

A blindingly orange pulsating light illuminates his hand, reading out: *"Urgent message. Video call waiting."* It blinks artlessly at him. He motions his fingers to move his chair and the console but finds himself temporarily barred. Without much of an issue he quickly overrides it and holds off the message. As the final pieces of the contraption stick together, he smiles and flips an enormous green switch on the right panel. It's alive. The screens ignite the room with color and flood Adam's pupils in the same brief moment. *Boom!* A network of words and coding flies around the screen like ants in a farm as it separates itself into four quadrants. Adam has no trouble directing the specific streams of information. He types for a few seconds into the holographic keyboard, making a frolicking pitter-patter sound, which expands a bold blue message on the upper right-hand quadrant of the titanic glass display. *"Initiate Time Walk Protocol?"* It hovers slightly in front of the screen before him like the presence of Santa Claus for a four-year-old child, within reach and so warm with possibility. What surprise will change reality next? Even with the power to do so, the man in the chair does not know. Before he acts upon the tempting words in front of him, he flicks his wrist upward to investigate the warning of the urgent message. He spreads his fingers out, projecting the message to the bottom-left quadrant of his construction.

"Adam, what is this? The vote has been decided. The people want to see their families. They want to live normally! The people have spoken. This isn't what they want. Adam… please. What on Earth are you doing?" Alessia barks.

Blackened rings rest on her stormy face. Adam looks up at her, knowing fully well that she can see his face. He smiles without resentment, just full of glee. He knows that all she can probably hear is the roaring of nuclear aircraft turbines spinning at near maximum capacity. He breaks eye contact with her and pulls up two hefty wires, that must be at least an inch thick, to adjust in front of his chest. After fiddling for just an instant, he looks back up directly to her sluggish yet thoroughly displeased face. Maintaining eye contact now, his tight fists shove the two wires together as they connect seamlessly and send a gushing spurt of sparks to the roof in a horrendously loud crackle.

With the wires in place, still on the live feed, he directs his attention up to the blue message. His jaw widens while his eyes take on a more serious look as he pushes forward with a precarious index finger, the projected words push back a few inches and disseminate into the air, scattering into nothing. Years of his life were put toward this moment. Tireless hours! This culmination of millions of hours of work from a number of scientists and physicists throughout history is everything he's been waiting. However, should it fail, this could be the end of life as he knows it. A spicy shiver shoots down his spine to keep him extremely alert despite the time of day. He snaps to sit straight up and rotates eagerly to his left. His fingers close into balls as the anticipation within his very soul shudders. Four enormous robotic arms descend from the ceiling beside him to form a shape that looks like a hybrid between a circle and a tilted square. The arms connect and link together as the engine's screaming intensifies. The floor begins to rattle. The few objects that rest on the scarce shelves shimmy their way off. He looks up to the camera feed, at Alessia's horrified face, and screams at the top of his lungs above the raging clamor of jet fuel being combusted. Passion, anger, and self-concern thrive happily.

"I'm saving the fucking world!" he howls.

VI

Let me see what I can remember… I was standing there in front of the crowd. A shifting sea of content people. My body was bravely stood atop a perch that the village slaves had poured hours of labor into for a worldly benefit. A fascinating array of natural beauty peppered itself throughout the village, using nothing more than the tools of time. It was a communal area on the outskirts of the gathering posts where the women would return after a day of fruit collection. It was there they would deposit their findings before it was all sorted equally for each villager that day. I remember life was so simple and I could get by, the people could get by, and the world could get by without chaos and distrust. I must have been twenty-two or twenty-three years old when it truly began. In a village on a coast by the staggering mountains lay a peaceful town – for its time.

It was a haven where safe water was readily available from streams and the fish were plentiful in all bodies of water all across a vast and wealthy landscape. It rained often but we never thought much of it because we were the first of many to develop rain covers. I had been to so many different villages and rogue get-byers by donkey. It was the day that it all began, the day that someone invented something called currency and everyone was astounded at the concept. People were just too nervous to talk in front of crowds, so I decided to do the honors. I entertained the masses with a gargantuan grin on my face as I began to explain sonorously.

"So essentially the idea of currency is to have a common form of trade. Initially we keep it here inside the village but if we could spread this trading idea to other villages, just think of the possibilities! Admittedly, the only reason that you want some of it is because somebody else wants some of it. I know it doesn't have any material value but that's the point. It doesn't get used up, only traded for goods. For example, if a lady had collected twenty apples, she could vend them for one or more coins. Then with these coins she could trade for meat or fur, which is not as available to some people. It's sort of a reward for completing your tasks so that those who don't do as much don't get the same reward as those who really commit to keeping the village going," I elaborated on the marvelous concept, and they cheered outrageously. It must have been the first community-based event that everyone could have been happy about and that certainly brought on some joy in the village. That was the time when a basic form of currency was a coin carved from stone. Simple and easy! That's not to say it was perfect, but it was harmonious.

In the meek beginnings of civilization, it was not a mentally difficult lifestyle. Physically, some challenges would often arise during heavy downpours or floods, but we were usually able to recuperate if given some time. The village operated smoothly because everyone had a job to do. Yes, it would be based on your gender, skills, and family, but it worked. Things operated in a very straightforward manner. That was until later on that day when I arrived at my homey shelter and I went into the sleeping room where a clump of straw lay in a rather large pile that was just big enough for my torso and legs. I covered it with a rag that had taken a lot of bargaining and favors to obtain. A tiny basket sat to the side that I kept some of the nicer stones in. I had found them through the recent years. Nothing else was significant about the room normally. Each of the walls was comprised of dried mud and a grubby mess of other components smashed together to create something sturdy enough to hold a barely waterproof roof.

The hut was a little big for just me with the empty room where my parents used to sleep. My father, Erus, was just on the verge of sprouting some grays. Before I knew it, he couldn't walk. My mother didn't get to the gray-hair stage before she died. I figured it was from the startling number of open cuts from the berry bushes, but I never knew for sure. I was left alone as I blossomed into adulthood. I planned on hitting the hay for the day because I had already snatched up three rabbits that morning, which was a decent collection for the day. Cheekily satisfied, I lay down.

I remember sharing that hut with the one I loved, my one and only for life. She would always be there for me through every difficulty, but she was away during one of the most important ordeals of my life on a foraging trip across the land. They had left to another town just days before to trade goods and acquire foreign fruits. I was planning on sleeping but something began to… well I don't know exactly how to describe it because it was truly unlike anything I had ever heard before. A ringing sound tumulted at first very quietly. Snapping instinctively to my feet, I spent a mere two seconds to dart outside around to see if I could observe anything beyond the ordinary. The sound faded. I shot back indoors and once again the sound lit up the air. Confused, I began to investigate more thoroughly. I peered into my parents' old room and there seemed to be nothing unusual, so I went back into mine. I grew further befuddled as this captivating noise matured into a louder sound. It felt as though it was shaking the air or maybe it wasn't even the air. Was it my ears? Had I, too, succumbed to a nasty disease of Mother Earth's design? I felt normal when I went outside the hut so that also seemed implausible. Right then, when I was on the verge of giving up and just enduring its prolonged song, a crack appeared.

The ringing stopped dead. Like a minute in which somewhat egregious earthquake had struck the wall, a vertical slit snapped open and popped into the sheer face. What? I was utterly bamboozled. Never before had anything so strange occurred in my life. I felt reasonably hesitant to approach it. The wilderness had far too many dangers not to be cautious with new experiences. Each passing second felt like an hour as sweat beads multiplied on my brow, tickling my forehead with a sense of moisture. What was I witnessing? I stepped forward with eyes wide open to the crack to see if it was going to change again or... well, to be honest, I had no idea what to expect, but it certainly wasn't what happened next. I pushed my finger against the side of it softly just to feel the stone and mud resting together in their chilled congealed state. I moved my body closer once more and attempted a tiny push on the side to try and close it when another surprise erupted from its depths. A scorching blast of blank white light screamed from the odd crevasse, not enough to completely shine upon everything in the room, as the crack was no longer than my hand and not much thicker than a fingernail. I retracted my hand instantly in fear as the looming sweat journeyed slowly onto my nose. I backpedaled for another step as I realized something else was emitting from the crack too. What looked like insignificant wisps of azure-blue smoke gently poured out of the stretched crack. As though it were smoke from a fire, it gently exuded from the wall, dissipating into the air. The final product of its spillings was nothing greater than a foot-sized cloudlike sort of appearance. Its oozing nature intrigued me, though I knew not to touch it or dare even breathe near it. However, the next sensation to riddle my body with confusion was not from my mouth but rather my ears. Whispers, were they? It was just barely on the edge of what could be considered sound, like soft touches scraping from the inside of the crack. After a few moments of standing and staring astounded, the very same noises crept up in volume.

"Hello?" the remnants of a word made their way out. It couldn't speak, could it? There was no way it could have been alive. I almost fled in astonishment, but instead, I leaned closer to the gas. "Oh, please tell me that this thing is working. There's a damn reason we went through so much troubleshooting. Hello there, can you hear me?" a voice crept out of the slit, though it was barely distinguishable for another few passing seconds. Similar commentary continued to fall out of the strange appearance, but it sounded just like someone was on the other side of the wall. I was certain that this had to be some sort of joke and I stormed outside in fury, marching right on over to the opposite side of my room wall and I called out.

"Begone! You blasted kids, leave me alone," I told them. There was no response from the trees and bushes that simply refused to move. Whatever they'd done was seriously impressive if they wanted to scare me, but I just needed to sleep. Heading back inside with a sense of relief, I was flabbergasted to find the light source still attached to my wall.

"Ah, yes, you can hear me. No, sir, this isn't a prank!" the voice carried out. "I have a name, but I cannot tell you what it is, for your own sake. I would really like to just talk," the male-sounding articulation explained. I was baffled and interested, but instincts took over before I responded. It could have easily been a trap from something I'd never heard of. A distinct pattern of light flashes followed the voice as it increased in volume. The light's intensity would flare.

"Look, there really isn't much time and I need to talk to you. Are you still there? Are you alone?" the voice questioned me. Maybe this really was someone who was in danger. Oh, how awful would I have felt if I had left them there to perish among the beasts of wild? I decided to answer.

"Ye– yes? Hello? I'm here?" I asked. An awkward separation of silence sliced through the atmosphere between me and the wall before any sort of message came back through.

"Oh, excellent. Two-way comms are good," the voice muttered before coughing. "Ahem. I am contacting you about something that I need you to keep to yourself. Can you do that?" the message was clear, and I nodded. I realized a second later that perhaps whatever this thing was couldn't see me in the same way that I couldn't identify any body parts on it.

"Uh, yes, I can. But firstly, why are you barging into my room and cracking the wall open?" I hastily fired back.

"Oh, well, you see it's a bit tricky. Do you have time for a bit of a chat? I'll make this conversation as quick as possible for you," the flexible being told me.

"Yeah, I suppose. What do you need? I have meat and, between you and me, a handful of raspberries. Say the word and we can make a trade, or if you're in trouble, you can owe me later. I don't really need all of whatever this is," I responded with an edge of confidence.

"No, hahaha," a squeaky titter broke out, "I don't want your fruits or food of any kind for that matter. Look, I need your help with something and before I get started, I'll make things very clear for you. I am from a different realm and time. By my calculations, you're from somewhere around twenty-five hundred years ago. I can't be overly precise on the exact year but now that I have a lock on you, I can move through time with you. Yes, that should work," he explained. Some strange noise was emitted from the odd-speaking slash. They were like that of a snapped finger but quieter and more dulled down. I hadn't ever heard such peculiar sounds. It almost sounded like rain on the roof, and it repeated several times in quick succession. Pitter-patter, they popped one after another subtly behind the voice. There was also a residual low tone in the background that I was reasonably unfamiliar with, too. I was consumed with questions and anxiety.

"This is probably going to be confusing for you, but I am from the future. I am communicating to you through a form of energy called magic. You can consider me a sort of celestial being from the sky. You have no reason to worry or cry for help. Just listen to me for your sake and mine. I need you to understand what I'm about to tell you very clearly. Are you ready?" the voice inquired.

"Uh, Yes. I don't see why not. Um. Magic? I've never heard of it," I told him.

"Okay, this world is in a predicament. There are problems on a scale I don't think you could even imagine because the world I exist in depends on your world for support. I exist in the future of your world, and I'm going to need some help from you to make a few changes. You see, when society and the human race moves forward through the years, you will eventually develop something called technology, a type of magic. That sort of thing gives me these capabilities," he elaborated on his cause. "The actual reason I'm talking to you today is that despite all of this fantastic magic, the human race has reached a fatal end. Violent conflicts have spread across the oceans and almost literally torn the world in half. I have decided, as ruler of all things, that the best way to fix our mistakes would be to talk to someone like you and prevent all of that from happening," he continued with worrisome haste.

There were other voices emerging now, too, a presumably female voice that sounded deeply distressed alongside what sounded like another male. It seemed to me as though the people within the crack in my wall were having somewhat of a background dispute. Loud cursing was tossed back and forth from other parties, but the ignorance from the man I was talking simply dismissed it. I was beyond myself to understand why the female was asking him what he was doing. Couldn't she have seen for herself if she was with them? Perhaps she was also talking via a crack in the wall. It was all rather confusing in the beginning, I have to admit. The stinging light that was emerging from the wall glowed angrily momentarily before cutting back and forth between a vivid brightness and a duller effect. The vocal sounds of whoever was in the crack became hazier. A pattern must have been in play here. That I could recognize. The light seemed to pulse out much stronger when I could hear more clearly when things were being said by the mysterious man. It continued to do so for several more seconds before stabilizing back into a steady white beam through its own blue misty aura.

"We don't have much time. Do you understand so far?" he called out amongst the commotion.

"Um," I took a moment to breathe, "so you're talking to me from... the sky? Because things aren't going as planned for humans on our planet in the future. And you're doing this to improve the future, hence you contacting me? I'm confused. You know, even if any of this dreamlike scenario we have here is somewhat true, how will anything I do for you benefit the humans or you? I just... I don't really understand what role I or other people are supposed to hold in your grand plan. Is there any way you can explain this so, um, I understand what's going on?" I retorted.

"Urgh. There's too much to explain right now. You know what? I'm going to make this easy for you. You can read, can't you?" he asked me in an abrupt manner. I was not happy with his tone of voice and, truthfully, I felt minimal obligation to care, let alone comply.

"My reading skills are adequate. I can acquire a scribe from the village if necessary. Why?" I answered with a question. I waited in silence for the sentence that had the potential to clear things up for me, but no such luck came my way. The vibrant light shot out with more intensity flooding the entire room with a perfect white light. Every corner of the room illuminated as though the sun itself had entered the confined space to eliminate the very idea of darkness. Clean, bright white light completely painted everything as the noise accompanying it grew, too.

"Wait, I have a question! What, uh, who are you!?" I belted out. Among the growing white noise there was a barely audible call like that of someone speaking their mind upon a vacant hilltop.

"You can call me the Holy Spirit. Or, more simply, God," the voice rapidly diminished among the explosive, fracturing sounds. This instance erupted so ferociously into an ear-shattering roar as the room went black. Everything seemed to be back to normal with the exception of two notable features. Firstly, it would be impossible to miss the stained wall that stood boldly with an enormous split down the middle, now nearly five feet tall. Subtly odd darkness seeped from it, gripping the absence of its impressive illuminations. It must have been due to the quick change, I told myself. Such delicacy and labor-intensive time went into manufacturing the walls that kept me safe at night. Seeing them tortured in such a manner - for something that felt so false - pulled on my heart like a lost lover. Maybe a bit of an exaggeration was to be thrown about at the time, with good reason. Needless to say, I was not comfortably warm. I pondered with myself on whether what I had just seen was even real. I had heard tales of those who hunt and tales from those who gather but I had never heard such a thing as this. For hours, I lay in bed debating with myself as to whether I was beginning to go nuts. Either that, or there was a very powerful possibility that I was the first contact with the future, and that magic. I had to at least try to understand what that was. Why had I not heard of that before either? Oh, I was led to believing the world was a strange place many times before, so I couldn't really be too surprised with this manipulation of magic. Thoughts buzzed around my head endlessly until the lull of their constant swimming put me to rest not too long before sunrise.

The exact moment my chilly feet played with the floor, I shook my head in awe. It must not have been true. I had seen some incredibly odd things in my dreams on nights before, but my eyes told another story. He was real – the crack, the voice, and the light. ALL OF IT WAS REAL! The world, to me, was a vastly undiscovered place. It teetered every day on the brink of untrustworthiness. Whatever this god person had to do with me sounded a lot more interesting than a usual day in the fields or forest. For me, it was settled. Yesterday, the hole in the wall broke the integrity of what surrounded me physically, and today it did the same thing to me mentally. If I was to live in a world where a surprise like this could come out of nowhere, then why would I not want to have a say in it? Why should such instability continue to make buffoonery of our lives when a solution is finally available? It simply shouldn't. It was that day that I came to terms with the fact that I would do whatever it took to right the wrongs in this world. I would do it through this being.

Everything he said is real. It's no longer just inside my head. I'm going to help him and make things right for the human race. There would be no other way because the only way was sitting in front of me like a freshly skinned squirrel.

Everything in that moment felt deliciously ripe with opportunity and variation.

VII

Adam gazes momentarily at the computer, with mouth open wide and his hands firmly on his head as the chair beneath him rolls backward in the room one inch at a time. Spinning slightly, he stops himself by planting his large feet aggressively on the pristine floor.

"I know what has to be done next, Silver. Open the bible. Find me which page most accurately describes the reasoning that people actually believe this crap!" he commands Silver, screaming over the sound of colossal engines winding down.

"Of course, sir. Scanning now," Silver responds to him politely despite the ruckus and bombardment of messages, alerts, and notifications. The thick book resting next to Adam comes to life as the pages flip over like a magic trick. A steady beam of light warms it from above as Silver's obedient eye follows commands. Hundreds of pages a second rattle against the spine of the book. An oddly satisfying aura fills Adam's head for the tiniest moment. "Page unknown. This data cannot be found, sir. Would you like me to conduct a more thorough search?" Silver inquires. The dulling screech of burning energy sources settles at a low rumble but remain gently active in the background.

"It's either that or we need to polish off the teleportation through time technology from a few weeks ago. I have an idea, but we'll need to have that operational to follow through with it. See what you can find, and I'll contact John. Put me on the line with him," he speaks aloud in his condemning solitude. The bible beside him floats fixedly up into the air. A baby-blue laser scans through each page one by one. The book is interrogated once more, this time at a much slower pace. A ringing tone from that of an attempted call stings the air in a distinct tone before John's voice calls out.

"What in the *world* are you doing, Adam?" he launches without so much as a trickle of hesitation.

"I'm fixing the world. Now are you going to join me? Or are you going to cower like the rest of them? I know what needs to be done and some help would make this process easier for me. John, I know you want this as much as I do. I need you right now," Adam begs for assistance before John has a chance to continue his thoughts.

"I know, and I will help for fuck's sake, but I just wish you had told me you were doing this. It's not me you need to convince, Adam; it's them. Silver, display Newgrounds on screen," John elaborates. Adam's eyebrows nearly hit the ceiling as the room lights up with videos of people screaming. Even at seven o'clock in the morning the commoners swarm the streets. He immediately springs out of his chair and jogs over to the glass wall to see an army of infuriated people. He glances back at the videos to see people barreling past others, grabbing onto people's arms, legs, and faces just to move faster. Other short clips swarm the empty space around him. Folks with long beards kick children out of the way, picking up babies and throwing them to the side and ignoring the howling mothers. Many women are screaming, crying, and bellowing out loud as they trip over others' kids to get to their own, falling on the dusty ground as they attempt to snatch their kids up and away from the warpath-razing horde of furious humans. Teenagers jump hastily from one low roof to another, hurling themselves as fast as physically possible. Everyone is scrambling desperately to get to one place as one of the videos' cameras tilts up to reveal one thing in the distance: The Dawne.

"You're an idiot for installing the engines above ground. Those things are so loud. The Top Four knew what was happening almost right away, and you know how they are. Their dedication to the people led them to broadcast the whole thing. It's been only forty minutes, but they've villainized you and sent out an emergency message. There's no time to show you this but they have essentially told Newgrounds that the Dawne is doing everything they can to prevent this mistake from going any further. As you can see, though, the public isn't happy. This is some people's dream you're destroying. I hope you can live with that." John wastes no time in being delicate.

"I've thought about this for a long time. You, Evelyn, and I all deserve better than this. I don't need to see such suffering every day. I will have to live with this," Adam explains.

"Anyway, they've got people trying to crack your security system already. You don't have long. I'll get into the coding and slow them down once I get down there. I'm on my way," John tells him briefly. The communications end as abruptly as the onslaught of savage images.

"Silver, any news?" Adam echoes out into the grand room. The final few pages flip closed, snapping shut with the back cover as the book levitates calmly to its previous perch, rotating to a face-up position.

"Nothing, sir. What is the recommended course of action?" Silver requests.

"I have no other option. Put me through to the Top Four," he commands, rubbing his hands together somewhat maniacally. The line rings for less than a second before a stable connection is initialized. A video feed springs out in front of Adam. Alessia, Samantha, Trevor, and Alex are sat at a birch desk with determined eyebrows and slightly narrowed cheeks, at the ready.

"Adam, you have thirty seconds to explain what is going on before we terminate your mission immediately. Otherwise we lose the last bit of trust the Newgrounds has for us. We are absolutely beyond disappointed. The people have voted, and they want to see their families. Explain yourself before we force entry," Alessia's voice rings through the sun-pierced air like hot knives through a frozen blanket.

"Okay! Okay, listen. I've already made a connection with the past! This will work. Just listen," Adam quickly begins. Four of the eight eyebrows glaring at him raise almost a full inch. His pores transform into holes. His skin, a cliff face, and the moisture he feels is a set of a thousand well-timed waterfalls bursting at their seams, beginning to soak him from head to toe. The tips of his fingers bounce unhappily like a heart undergoing tachycardia. The pulse stands out further than ever before. Every beat is a snare drum in the chaotic band his body orchestrates through every moment. Vision shuts down to one lane and one lane only. Alone, focusing, he turns to look Alessia deep in the eye. Boring a hole through her pupils, he stands up, filling his lungs to a capacity unbeknownst to him preliminary to this second. With two feet straddled side by side, he takes one moment to take it all in. A glance outside through the immaculately cleaned glass and the world slows down for him for just the tiniest split-second.

Everything stops.

The broken glass in the street air halts in position.

He takes a breath to confirm the thoughts and let the orchestra ring out and cry.

This is it. A moment, even by surprise, will make history one way or another.

Every word needs to be constructed perfectly. He must convince them this is worth it.

Adam bellows for himself and for the several million people awaiting justice in a broken world.

Slowly, crisply, but ever so proudly, he begins to speak.

"Top Four, there are an incredible number of people out there who deserve better than what we have made for them. This. This dream, this reality that has been manufactured from the ruins we made is a long-forgotten lie. Why do they deserve this? Why do we deserve to watch so many people suffer while our lives are so simple and easy? We never learn. The human race. Always tinkering to try and get it right next time. Trying to make a better tomorrow for our children. WELL WHAT ABOUT TODAY?!" Airwaves smolder to dust under the sheer passion of his bursting lungs. The world begins to churn and move. His voice rises from its fragments and climbs in volume again. "I say that we all deserve the peace that you and I enjoy so frivolously every day. Do you want to know what's wrong with the world? It's not the dustbowl we inhabit. It's not the lack of water on our ancient, ruined globe. It's us, and the sooner we understand that… The sooner we fully accept the responsibility that comes with it, the sooner we can all be at peace, mentally and physically." The vibrant aura clutching the air allows a second to breathe, letting it all sink in. The energetic force of his voice emanates a dominating presence with every perfectly enunciated word. "So, I need your help, not your hindrance, in making this possible. I don't know, despite the vote, what reason we would have for accepting a treaty and starting from scratch yet again." A relieving sigh changes the color of the air. Adam blinks painfully slowly to inspire a change of tone. "I've made a connection with a man from the past. He says he's willing to assist. It's already underway. I promise I can make this happen. Give me thirty-six hours and I will erase every major conflict and issue we've ever had to bear. I'm talking about every global war, the Korean War, the world wars, all of it. Overt sexism and racism in the modern age, mass poverty, and frankly, unequal treatment of all kinds will all be unknown to man. That's the goal. Either way I'm going to do this, or I know for certain that I will die trying." A final breath exhales from boisterous lips with a sudden close of the connection to the feed. The holographic video call disappears with a bite into the shuddering, purified air. Adam's head repulses back an inch or so as he faces the empty glass, peering onto the fearsome streets below. An absence of confirmation leaves him to question their decision. Now drenched in a coat of pride hollowed out with despair, he vacantly and silently observes the commotion below. The orchestra plays its concluding symphony as the whir of John's pod stirs the quivering gas between them. John climbs out onto the floor and promptly suggests the first course of action.

"Okay, let's do this thing. I need you to focus. Whatever we do from here on, we do it together and to the end because if we fuck this up, everybody will know, and we'll never have this freedom again," the words echo delicately from John's more cautious mouth as Adam continues to regain his grip on the situation after an instant of raw isolation.

"Right. Okay, John, I need you to contact James and Simon. Get them down here and no one else. I'll have you upholding security protocols to buy us as much time as possible. We can only hope that people will start to realize what is really happening and change their attitude. Get James and Simon to find a way for us to send objects through time, and quickly. I have an idea that will make things easier for us. I'll stay in touch with our contact from the past and update him on what he needs to know and the premise of our plan. Sounds fresh?" Adam voices himself with a deep-rooted passion. The sense of pride and determination that seeps out from him is a type of tenacity only war-torn veterans can truly comprehend.

"Minty." John replies. A smaller-than-usual hologram appears beside John as he begins to speak. Two voices are concocted as if from nowhere at once. They speak from the other end of the line as plans are set in motion.

Adam re-establishes his posture as he peers outside and reveals to himself the wonder taking place beyond the glass. Hundreds and hundreds of inches of pure innovation delight the air outside with a stunning series of playful luminosity. The finesse of such a grand collection of light is impressive alone, but what sticks out even more is the size of the projection. Almost the size of a house, it shines brightly against the rays of the morning sun. Adam squints slightly to confirm his suspicions, and it's true. He sees the descending curls of soft hair across a face that has been so delicately crafted and taken care of. Why would that person be up there? In that holographic image? It contradicts everything the Top Four had going for them. Questions and ideas spring around the inside of Adam's mind like kids after birthday cake. Within the square projection, there lies a row of teeth that glisten in the reflecting sunlight, each perfectly aligned with one another, putting shame to that of an average citizen. It is a body that only some can come to terms with working towards and even fewer can pay for, with eyes of age and tire, eyes that have seen sunset and sunrise in every corner of the world. Astonishingly still blue, the sunrays glint off them every few seconds. Confusion is a word that would only begin to describe Adam's state of mind right now as he ponders for a few moments before it clicks. The gears turn and the gas is on. The ignition strikes within him to start a raging fire as he understands what's going on. There's a damn good reason he and the entire valley are being shown this image. The furnace inside his body sparks from a single orange flicker to a white and blue torch of unfathomable capacity. A smile smears across his face like a woman is touching him for the very first time. He remembers. Comprehending reality, he pushes himself up onto the balls of his feet. A pounding electric shock drives its way through his bones, ripping up his spine from the bottom up, cackling out of him in the form of the greatest grin ever witnessed. Whether it's euphoria or some unknown emotion, he does not care. The fact of the matter is that there is a chance now. The very essence of hope refills the supply of humanity, packing perseverance into an already happily satisfied stomach.

That's him on the big screen.

A perfect quality video of him ignites the entire valley with a flood of light. It clearly displays him just minutes ago as he so cautiously constructs his very own canticle. Another video feed sprouts in the center of the room, behind him, spontaneously, though this one differs from the one being shown to the rest of the world. Here, Alessia and the other three stand almost surreptitiously behind the raised desk. Her vocal cords inform Adam of their proposal.

"We've made our decision. To be honest, it was not overly difficult. We want to support you. We know this is an enormous risk and the majority of the Newgrounds' inhabitants will strongly disagree, which is why we need you to do whatever it is you're doing as soon as possible. Maybe we have the technology that they don't understand but the sheer manpower that they carry, we fear, may overcome our superior machinations." As she speaks, another pod arrives on the floor. Simon steps out to greet Adam. He joins in basking in the presence of the Top Four. Alessia continues without interruption, "If you can't complete this within the next twenty-four hours, we will have to terminate the project. The only way we can break this news to the public is if we initiate a definitive clause for you. Without this condition, the entirety of the society will crumble to its bare foundations. You can imagine what would happen." As Alessia speaks to them, James arrives now, too. From the outside of the glass, looking into their floor, one can make out four bold silhouettes encumbered by a curved video chat projection. The men listen to every detail of Alessia's proposition. "You, and any accomplices, will be publicly executed tomorrow at noon if you are unable to change the world as we have it within the next twenty-four hours. We have shown the people a video of you as you corrected us. It is our hope that this will assist in the process of persuading the crowd. We will do what we can to protect you from the rage that has built up in the streets, but we cannot promise anything. We will also supply you with whatever you need to get the job done. Just snap your fingers and you'll have whatever is necessary. Is there anything you need right now?" she questions the group. Everyone's eyes turn to focus on Adam.

"Firstly, thank you, aha!" he stammers for a surprised second, scratching his scalp. "I could not have asked for a better outcome. Minus the whole death penalty aspect. And yes! I need to be able to teleport objects through time. I brought James and Simon to help me with that. Just get them the supplies they need, and I will be fine," he delegates, slightly out of breath from the sudden rush and overwhelming feed of information.

"We wish you good luck. You're going to need it," Alessia states as Trevor, Samantha, and Alex all nod their heads gently in perfect synchronization, lightly shutting their eyes momentarily. The video feeds both inside and outside the Dawne cut off. Now, with everyone in the know, the crew commences. Adam rushes to his desk with cramming haste as his fingers wobble over the keyboard. His hands quiver aggressively as each button pushes down on letter after letter, intermittently dispersed by a space or an enter key. James, Simon, and John follow with equal, if not rivaled, eagerness. A grin compromises all of their serious faces as their chairs pull up autonomously, each to their own designated area. The daylight pierces sharply into the open concept room and the menacing task-takers embark on an unforgettable and unforgiving trek.

A sense of urgency plunges into the room's growing atmosphere. Whirring and clicking sounds charge the room with racing zeal as the team's train's wheels turn over with rising speed. A heavy metal 'thunk' pings from the wall in front of Adam. It is a delivery from the Top Four. Adam bends forward for a moment and pulls a piece of outstandingly blue metal from the complex machinery. It looks as though a floppy disk has been stretched and then spectacularly painted with bright baby-blue lines. After taking the object from the wall, he rapidly spins around, pushing from the back of his chair, jogging with clamorous footsteps to John's perch. "The Top Four just sent us what we need to make that teleportation happen through the bridge I made. This is it, here. Make sure you get everything. A single mistake from here on could jeopardize everything," he informs the others, mainly speaking to John, passing the object to his colleague.

"So, no pressure," John chuckles. A few scurrying steps return him to his sole sanctuary in front of the incredible supercomputer. With his back to the world his fingers dance through the air and tap several buttons as the sounds of the overwhelmingly large engines begin to spin. A machining hum echoes throughout the building before soon evolving into a much more bellicose level of noise. The four of them reach for a pair of headphones that each hold a minute hologram of a microphone in front of the users' mouths.

"Hold on, boys!" he calls out. "It's gonna get a little shaky!"

VIII

The birds and the bees flourished flawlessly in the fields at that is time of the year. The sun enriched every view with a vibrant light that responded politely to the welcoming blues of a clear sky. The perfection of it all, I believe, must have been only possible due to the simplicity of everything we enjoyed. People laughed easily. Humor was simple. Truth be told, the good times never stopped rolling. Each day, yes, perhaps, was almost a duplicate of the last, but that's what made it work. I remember such a time when you would walk outside to the delighted faces in the morning, and that's all that would've been important. We all thought that things would be this way forever, so free of violence and hatred. Everything was pure and easy, just the way we liked it, until the morning after which I had tried to convince myself was just a dream. I stood tall after a fairly disappointing sleep to stretch my limbs. One by one, they opened themselves up to the morning's embrace as my mouth pried open a bellowing yawn. As I recovered from the fatigue, I stepped over to the door of my undemanding hut a little more cautiously than I had ever done so before. I wasn't quick enough though. The crack quivered. Maybe it was my imagination. I hoped so.

"Oh, no." I whispered under an invisible breath. I knew that if it moved, or did anything for that matter, then it would all become real and my life really had changed. Oh, what a burden I thought it was! I rattled my head briefly to see, just maybe, if I really was fabricating things in my head. The crack shook once more with just a little more force this time. Well, dream ruined, I guess. Dust coughed out visibly from the wall with the second shake. A distinct sound emerged. It was a sound that I could identify only from its previous visit. 'Why,' I asked myself, 'had it chosen me?' I did not refuse to participate, however. I responded to its call as I had only just entered a state of, to be naïve, consciousness. Hallowing sounds screeched from its mysterious depths to shock me, jolting me back. My hands flew up to protect my poor eyes as the room exploded with a daggering light. The atmosphere in the room was blinding despite the immortal sun above caressing every other opening in the room with its stringy fingers of light. Dust sputtered out across the entire floor from the split in the wall face. The constructed sounds hit peak volume before taking time to simmer down to a more dull and shaky rhythm. The voice I had thought of endlessly without rest since the last incident spoke out to tickle and tease.

"Hey, are you there?" it started. The voice called out, attempting to best the deep, constant roar from behind it.

"Yes. Good morning to you, too. Why do you choose to make this entire flipping commotion come for me when I haven't even had the chance to go outside? What game are you playing at, seriously?" I retorted. 'Some things,' I thought, 'I would never understand.'

"It was that accurate?" another unfamiliar voice asked, yelling over the whirring sound in the background.

"Yes, I've impressed myself a little here, too, actually. Okay, focus," the original voice resumed. What was going on in that other world of theirs? What did they mean accuracy? Did they expect to tear a hole in another wall? It didn't matter because I wasn't given any more time to think about it very much.

"You aren't making sense here. What do you need me to do for this big plan of yours? And who's to say it will even work? The only reason I'm even trusting you is that I value my community. If things really are as you say… well I don't think I want us to end up like that," I expressed.

"Excellent," god told me. "What you're going to do is you're going to provide a reason for people to yearn for widespread peace. I need you to prevent the conflicts that the world has seen, the destruction that so violently ruined it. You will create peace and harmony among humans to protect them from themselves," he explained.

"So, no pressure," I shot back. "How is one man supposed to do all of that, to stop battles that are big enough to tear a species apart? Did you think that through?" I asked. What an idiot!

"Yes. It's not proven, but we are on our last leg here with an idea we call religion. The plan is going to sound a bit crazy. I'll be honest because it kind of is. Anyway, here goes. It's a bit complicated, so pay attention. Essentially, it's a concept in which everyone has a common belief that the universe was created by one being. The world, the trees, the animals, all of it created singlehandedly by this one being. Nobody can explain where the world came from, and that's one question that nearly everyone can get behind. 'Where did we all come from?' is a pretty big question. Wouldn't you agree?" he intrigued me, though it wasn't overly simple to imagine anything so simple with such a horrific, thought-erasing screech coming from behind the voices.

"Yes, actually. You've got me waiting for the answer, now," I told him.

"Exactly. That's where you come in. Your role in our plan here is to be the original messenger. The prophet, so to speak. The answer, generally, that you are all looking for is this: god, that's me, created the universe. I created it out of nothing through carefully crafting each animal and developing every flower and tree on the land. God is the ultimate being that brought everyone and everything into the world you live in," he described loudly. A rush came over me as if to say, 'Wow! This is actually fairly believable,' because how else would the world have been created really?

"Okay, I understand that, but how does that fit in with what you're planning?" I posed a question.

"This is it. You will claim to know my son. God's son. You will produce a text that we will send you. It will be the first book ever to be created by man because it is the overruling Word of god: the Bible. And it must be followed. You will claim order on the land and let it be known that breaking the rules laid out in the Bible will result in severe consequences. It is by having most or all of the population follow these rules that your world will be saved!" he continued, still shouting. I couldn't figure out why they didn't move away from whatever was causing the noise. That's what I would do. "This won't be easy, and there are some steps we will need to follow. We'll take it one bit at a time. Let's start with focusing on this year for now. You will be contacted at some point in the next few weeks or so and sent the Bible. There may be other things for you to wield as well, but we'll stick with the Bible for now," he kept going while still keeping some things a mystery which, frankly, annoyed the living daylights out of me. I suppose if I wanted things to go smoothly, I better had just trust the wise word rather than question it. He seemed to have things in order, for the most part. Anyway, who was I to mess with such high power?

"Okay. So, what am I supposed to do for now? Just sit back and wait for you? There must be something I can do to at least get the ball rolling per se," I eagerly jumped in.

"There is. Test it out for a few weeks, every day. Try to talk to someone new about it. Keep it brief, but don't be so hasty that it's not believable, you know? Tell people that god exists and who god is. Spread word of my beautiful omniscience. They'll ask you how you know this to be true and what will you tell them?" I was asked against a growling rumble.

"I know it's true because I know the son of god. His name is Jesus and I was told to spread his word to keep you safe." I was hesitant in my answer at first.

"Perfect. They will think you're nuts at first! Let it stir and sit with them for a while. Then, when we send you the Bible, you will prove to everyone that it's true and the plan will be set in motion. Something else to keep in mind:

we'll need a willing companion of yours with a fairly impressive beard and a close circle of friends. We won't need him for a while but be ready for when the time comes. Maybe in a year or two," he explained further.

"Okay, spread the word that god is real. Tell people I know god's son so that it's more believable. Find a man with a close circle of friends and a nice beard. Got it," I repeated back to him. "What should I do if I have questions? Will you be here?" I pondered.

"No. That's another risk I have to take. I'll check back in periodically to see how things are going, and to remind you of anything should you forget. Other than that, spread what you know as much as you can. Do you have any final questions?" he interrogated me.

"No. Well, yes. What if people don't believe me, even after a while?" I responded.

"Just trust us. Me! Trust me. I've got your rear end covered, my friend. You have to believe," the voice reiterated. Before I could get another word out, the light snapped back to darkness and the crack in the wall fell dim. The dazzle of the spectacular show had died. Suddenly I was alone, wandering a little less aimlessly through my thoughts once again. A temple of hallways and chambers unlatched in my mind and every time I dared to step foot in uncharted territory, I would always end up in the same room – doubt. As much as I would have loved to believe right away that all of this was going to work, it just didn't feel cozy with me.

I can't describe it as anything less than wandering down a hallway, of which you know what lies at the end, but there existed countless rooms on either side. Each of these unrevealed chambers had just the tiniest of spaces between the door and the doorframe that I could scarcely poke my gaze through. I felt a hammer above me, the size of another human, ready to come falling down and squash my fleeting innocence into a thousand pieces. A weight, a cloud, followed me around from the moment that conversation had ended. I'm not saying I wasn't ready for what was to come next, but I was nervous for sure. Too many uncertainties ruminated for my taste. Days went by, even then, when I would gently question the truth despite what my senses had told me. I remember my first explanation of the idea to a friend. I lacked confidence initially. I think it was due to the abundance of loose ends, although that would all soon change.

It was the day after when I first brought it up. Intriguing how the culmination of mistrust within me was flattened by a meteoric wish. The day was no different than any other. Our faces were scratched to shit. We lay down in our favorite ambush spot. We waited humbly for an innocent soul of furry meat to hop by, knowing nothing more than an inevitable future in which they cracked at our hand. With predators in a moisture-heavy forest, we hid, dormant.

"Hey, do you ever wonder why we're here?" I whispered softly, quivering, to Preston. I'd picked him up earlier that day, just as any other, by walking sixteen feet from my door to his.

"Hmm. I suppose not really. I think we're here to hunt and provide for our families. Why else would we be here?" he responded plainly, his chest pressed against a moss-endowed log.

"No. I mean, more so… Why are we, all of us, here? You know, humans, as a species. Or more accurately, every species. How did it all begin, you know?" my voice felt hollow. I wasn't an expert at spilling misinformation. The dagger in my hand wobbled mercifully. We poised together.

"I don't know, um… We've always been here, I suppose? I don't know how to answer that, man. Give me a break. Look, just in time," he informed me. He was right. I sharpened my focus to the trail, and not a moment later, the sheep's hair tripped the rabbit. Its poor face plummeted into the dirt where it struggled for barely a second before Preston pounced through the air. With an edged tool in one hand, he choked the poor thing to the ground and snapped its neck. The second rabbit attempted an escape, but I snatched it up before it was too late, like I had done a hundred times before. My fingers strangled it while my wrist brought a rather painless demise. The same thick crack snipped the tension in the air. We both stood up with muscles glowing and sweat dancing playfully on our foreheads, smiling with limp carcasses between our bloodstained fingers.

"What if I told you that I knew the answer to that question?" I proposed.

"Huh? What are you talking about, you madman?" Preston flipped back some deep black hair as we set on our path to the slaughterhouse.

"I, uh… I know where we came from, Preston. All of us," I answered somewhat shakily. I must have been giving the poor soul quite the bounce around.

"You've got me interested now. What do you think?" he asked, being my first conscript. I spoke my first convincing piece for several minutes as our feet whisked us to a decrepit wooden hut. Not much larger than a double-arms-length across, we got comfortable in front of the workbench. We retrieved the bladed tools from the rack and our fingers worked their own kind of magic to tear the lifeless creatures apart. Blood oozed too easily across half the table. As I explained myself, he began to understand. The fact that I knew the son of this so sacred god was what intrigued him the most. I can understand that though, considering I spent more time with Preston than anyone else.

"If you can introduce me to this man, this son of god, I'll believe every word of it," he explained to me. Oh, so slowly the skin peeled off the rabbit; it was almost soothing to see it tear off the hoppy little scoundrel so easily. It satisfied me. With the continuation of my story he understood that the word ought to be spread about god. I told him only as much as he needed to know. "God is real. If one is to disobey His book of rules, there would be punishment. That's how the human race is supposed to last so long," I told him. "It must be through the precarious orders of this one being." He nodded in agreement and with little hesitation. A minuscule bubble of happiness almost made an appearance on my face as the organs fell from my rabbit. Its guts and its innards that held it together fell to the dirt, to my feet. They sopped heavily with a splashing sound to the ground. With a newly found thirst quenched, I had only one question left.

"Will you help me spread the message? It's important to me. You know it gives me something to believe in. You should consider it, too. I mean, what have you got to lose? It's almost like a reward for living, something to work toward," I explained.

"I'll give it some thought, but I'll need proof first. Let me know when you can show me this book of rules or the son of this god thing," he set his demands. It followed. I told him I'd do it at the earliest convenience. Something that rocketed around the inside of my mind was the fact that despite supposedly being god's son, this so far non-existent character did not yet have a name. I'd have to remember that next time I got the chance to ask questions. Thoughts began to slide into place, creating a slightly clearer picture of what I was doing. Days flew by. Each sunrise, I would make that attempt to spread the message until my simple request grew somewhat hollow as I awaited new information. Many of the folk had a similar interest level up until the point where I couldn't physically prove any of it. They were intrigued, of course, but without a source of evidence I was without a leg to stand on.

I did what I was asked, though. I had completed the search for a well-statured man who held his own with an impressive dark brown beard. Unmistakably, it had the characteristics of a man ready to make a change, stupendous and stoic, yet mildly humble. He had the makings for great potential with a flow like that. He didn't do anything out of the ordinary for the village. He hunted, like the rest of us. He, too, was impressed with the idea of preventing conflict and had agreed to assist me on the basis that I could prove any of this.

I needed that book.

Without anything to back up my words I had to take a few moments to ponder each day without guidance. God. Hmm. When would I hear from that steering light again? Sunsets faded to a still gray rather than the usual living black with every day that I wished, no, prayed that I would hear his wisdom.

IX

"Alright, great work, gentlemen!" Adam roars into the air, taking over from the enormous turbines that disrupted their ears just moments ago. A smile smacks itself upon his face for a brief period of time before he dials in on the next part of the operation. "James, how long have we been online?" Adam calls out. Without a moment wasted, James speaks up.

"Eighty-three minutes. We're right on schedule." With this response, his hands flourish in a smooth wave of movements as he pulls up a holographic schedule that is clearly defined by twenty-minute intervals. Each time-allotment box has a brief descriptive text in it. All of them glow a capturing blue with the exception of one box. 10:20 flashes green intermittently. It reads: *'The second call ends. Teleportation testing begins.'* All four of the men take a quick glance with James' words. John seizes the opportunity to make his statement.

"Okay, boys, focus up here for one second," he states. The other three retract from their workstations while staying stationed on their butts in the metaphorical and literal hot seats. John stands uncomfortably between two metal surfaces and begins to explain.

"The idea here is to teleport this walnut, to right here," he explains, palm up with a walnut in his hand, pointing at a plate with a strange white and blue pattern across it, "in thirty seconds from now, to now. What we should get is a walnut appearing on that plate over there in a couple seconds from now. Then, thirty seconds later, we'll send it back in time by thirty seconds." As he exhales his last word, he takes a sneaky look at his watch. The others do the same. They read 10:21:10 in perfect synchronization. With common knowledge in mind they refocus to the plate beside John. Bated breath condenses heavily in the room. Each second ticks painfully. Focus and a quick dart of adrenaline in each body do nothing but make the wait more difficult. Tension rises and rises like a train steam-powered with no end in sight. Could seconds be any longer? Adam can hear the silence stabbing his brain in the back of his neck and realizes, just now, that his back is drenched with a sweaty montage of mayhem. Waiting. Waiting.

"I guess, Uh, it didn't," John comments. *ZAP!* A spark erupts from the plate, suddenly blinding the group. A crack snaps the tension in the atmosphere in two. It is a clean break. A singeing spear of smoke sizzles and fades from the newly appeared walnut. James' vision is immediately clouded delicately with a wall of water.

"YES!" John cheers aggressively. Adam, James, and Simon follow in unison. They begin to talk rapidly amongst themselves while moving back and forth in the hasty assembly of a metal cage around the original walnut on a plate two feet or so from the one that just appeared. A fairly minute contraption is placed around the metallic bars, covered in an intricate variety of purple and blue wires. As the walnut is locked deeper into the electrical mess, the other three members take half a step backward. A readout on the front of the device displays several numbers, mostly zeroes, followed intermittently by a series of letters. They can all clearly make out the '00y-00d-00h-002m-30s' readout as they rest back on their steaming chairs. John pipes up.

"Okay, change of plan. We'll need one hundred and fifty seconds, not thirty!" John perkily responds to a dazzling creation. "Also, Adam! The amount of energy we'll need for this reaction is, well, we're opening a rift in the space-time continuum. We're going to need those engines online if we're going to make this work," he instructs.

"Oh, right." Adam responds as though surprised. He spins back around to the incredible construct of a computer and begins pressing buttons. An angry bellow shakes the room. Struck by an invasive startup procedure, the massive engines begin turning.

"Did you give us max power?!" John calls out over the short distance.

"Uh. Yes, why?" Adam calls back.

"No, no. That's perfect, just making sure!" John confirms. The constant quaking becomes slightly irregular. Objects in the room clearly receive the notion that it's time to move as they start to jitter atop a slew of surfaces. John and Simon look at each other for a brief moment as a hefty realization begins to swirl through the air between them. Metal clinging corrupts the steady sounds of mechanical power.

"You know, it's not normally this rough. We'll be fine, right?!" Simon poses to the group, now yelling. The racket continues evermore.

"James!" John screams to relay the message against a rapacious rumble.

"What!? We'll be fine! We just need the activation energy! Then we can turn it down. Just hold on!" James shouts back loudly. Everything in the glass-trimmed room continues to shake more vigorously as the seconds pass. Adam can only wonder what everyone else in the building must be thinking. His ponderation is answered almost immediately as a broadcast spawns in the center of the floor. Alessia's face of thunder reigns the room.

"Simon! Deal with this!" Adam shrieks. The enormous hologram immediately collapses to less than an eighth of its original size at Simon's workspace, where he spins around to converse. Despite not understanding what was being said, Adam knows there's no realistic expectation in which it's uplifting news. Everything in sight trembles relentlessly, causing a clatter of its own. As though the world is angry with them for cheating the very laws of nature, it shivers violently. Each moment is an eternity waiting to end as they tend to the needs of the dying planet's population.

The moment arrives, and James pushes a button on the device as a screeching light erupts within the cage. Among the blue ruin, electrical sparks and a strange concoction of dust explode from the wires in a jagged and offset pattern every few milliseconds. James launches a thumbs-up into the air, catching Adam's line of sight. Adam complies and has difficulty playing around with the controls that are now bouncing up and down aggressively. There is an inaudible click, a fleeting turn of a knob, and the walnut disappears.

The whirring begins to deescalate, and the relentless shaking lets up, too. In a rigorous tapering of severity, the crew looks at the cage where the walnut was. The door swings open to reveal empty space and a wisp of smoke. They have a short-lived moment to smile and wade in a victory.

Several seconds slip past as they wait for some sort of report to be regurgitated by John. The shaking and screaming cease. There is a split second of silence. Then, in another moment of intensity, an unfounded, crisp, singular snapping noise controls their world for an instant, clean, cut, and over and done with, as if a branch was to be snapped from a tree, only ten times louder. The air emotionally curdles to a thick and swampy dread. Each set of eyes in the rooms expands to the size of oranges, scanning to see the other three in hopes of an answer to the unhomely sound.

They migrate their attention to the glass wall in search of an explanation. A quick shuffle over and they stand flabbergasted. Sharp wires and shredded metal fibers connect the Dawne and two of their, now nearly detached, adjacent travel pods. Like limp legs, they hang on to the building, looking rather helpless. Sparks toss themselves into a frenzy every few seconds. Before the team has a chance to express their thoughts, they become distracted momentarily once more. A swift object careens through the sky just a few feet from the glass. Downward it falls. Molecules of gas and dust disperse from its path as the perfect sphere cuts through the mildly toxic air. It rotates almost leisurely in the rapid descent. The object falls, revealing few scars on its perfect body, contrasting the ruinous path behind it. The previously unscathed glass and the white ball sink further. It drops through the dusty atmosphere one moment at a time. They observe as the realization of the object's origin kicks in. A proud delicacy of the Upper levelers' achievements after so long has finally ruptured. It falls out of sight before crashing to an imperfect mess on the ground below. No one dares step forward and glance down but Adam.

The pod smashes against the mediocre cushioning of sand into several cracked pieces just inches from an enraged Newgrounds' inhabitant. She raises a fist and begins to curse using every word in the book with a face full of shockwave dust. Fire erupts from its broken belly in front of a riled crowd. A bolt of disappointment strikes Adam's mind, following a toiling moment of disbelief. He can only hope that this is the first and last event of its kind for his sake and humanity's.

"The Top Four are on the line," Simon snaps the noiselessness in two. His lips quiver as vigorously as the Dawne had moments before. "They're not happy. Said if anything like that happens again, we risk the structural integrity of the Dawne. It's up to us what happens next, apparently," he cuts himself off.

"It won't matter if we have the Dawne if we have nothing left to live for," Adam barks, turning around from the horrific sight outside. "James, we know it works. We're going to start it up again and send that sphere and that book to our friend in the past."

"But she said," Simon blurts out.

"I don't care what she said, Simon, and neither should you. I don't mean to be crude but it's too late to back out," he explains to the group. He turns back to his workstation, moving sticks and pushing buttons all simultaneously. "Preparing contact once again. Two weeks following the previous temporal target. Are we all ready for re-engagement?" Adam asks as his eyes dart all around the screens before him.

"One moment." James replies. His lips seal. He fiddles with the readout on the device that once encased the walnut to match the date on Adam's display. A shudder ricochets throughout the edifice as the engines start up once more. John scrambles for the divinity sphere and the bible, placing them inside the device that James has finished with.

The other three acknowledge in their own manner that they're in order. The entire floor, buzzing and whirring, is a mad science experiment, literally. Lights begin to flash as sounds scream and tantalize the eardrums of the leading pioneers and the spawn that clamber the streets of Newgrounds. The call of the nuclear engines can be heard from miles away, yet the men continue. The herd, now at the base of the Dawne, gazes up in astonishment and turns to sprint away as two more privilege meteors come hurling down toward them. They crash not ten feet before the innocent folk into blazing balls of flaming charcoal and smoke. It's the first time these people have had the chance to see such technology up close. Many of them look as though they are really wishing they hadn't.

The heat on their faces and screaming in their ears drive them back a little further. A subtle vibration courses through the ground and they can feel it.

Terror and hope have never been so closely related.

X

It had been so long since the first contact. They told me it would be just weeks until I would get more answers. They were wrong.

I waited five months to get an answer to the mounting pile of questions. Hundreds of people at this point waited with me for the proof. Where was this sacred Bible? When would we meet the Son of god? My curiosities were taken care of on an unsuspecting night when I was within days of letting it all go.

A painful thump startled me. A crashing sound haunted the night for an instant. My dream shattered and I sprang up, ready for action. Was there a creature of the shadows lurking beyond these thin walls? I had to be sure that my survival was guaranteed before anything else. Hesitant, I moved closer to the door. Silence pierced the blackness. Only the moon dared to donate its guidance at this hour. In a stiff and achy state, my fingers fumbled around against the wall where I would keep my tools. Oddly, a clinging sound vibrated through the rod that I grabbed. It sounded like metal, but in that moment, I thought it impossible. I glanced to the floor and an interesting sight flared by my eyes. Before investigating, I thought it best to confirm my suspicions of an outside threat. The wind picked up for a moment and a streak of my hair jostled up and down against my forehead while most of it remained behind cover. I scanned the outside area with accusing eyes. My breath expelled with relief into the sinister darkness, as nothing out of the ordinary was to be found.

I returned my attention to the object I had clattered the rod against on the floor. After bending forward to hold it within my clutches, my senses heightened. It wasn't silent. A noise joined the moon to decorate the humble scene. It was a hiss, a sizzle. It was rare for the times I lived in then but was still very real. That was the moment that it clicked for me. I felt a primal surge shoot across every inch of my young body. It was not easy for a man of my intelligence at the time to comprehend. The aging crack in the wall was smoking quietly. Any other time in my lifetime, I would have thought it was about to catch fire, but I managed to put two and two together. I shuffled over to catch the moonlight through the door to reveal the object so that I could tell it apart from the dense blackness that stirred indoors.

My breath ran away, as I was taken aback. They did it. They actually managed to send me something from the future. 'How absurd!' I thought to myself. With my mind running rampant with theories, I examined the object. It seemed circular in shape but not perfectly spherical. No, it was carved in and out with some scripture of sorts. I took a moment to cringe because whoever had attempted in writing clearly did not know what they were doing. Either that or it was a combination of letters I hadn't seen before and had yet to understand. Regardless, I felt befuddled by the obscure markings. It was just small enough that I could hold it in my hand, though large enough to make the hold sort of uncomfortable. A clean and smooth stone-looking band wrapped around the middle to break the carvings. There was a hole in the top and the bottom, too. For something from the future, it sure wasn't overly exciting. I was sort of expecting some strange coloring or movement to accompany such an object. With dismissive thought, I walked back to my bed in hope of understanding the strange item.

I felt a rush of rage command me as I tripped and fell forward. Just for an instant I could have screamed. With a face of disapproval, I looked at my feet to see a vaguely square-shaped object. The vial within me containing thirst for the unknown was utterly insatiable in that moment, and so I grabbed it and ran over to the doorway. I swung open the door quickly and sat down. The lunar effulgence engulfed my front side entirely as I perched my bottom on the doorstep. I had no need for a torch or sconce, as I could see perfectly clear with nature's gift of light. Two sweeps of the back of my hand cleared any leftover dust from the front cover. This is what I'd been waiting for.

'The Bible.'

It read in oversized text. Moonlight shimmered delicately upon the first page as the book turned open in front of me with a smooth motion of my fingers. Despite the brightness of what I thought to be another planet up above, I felt as though I was in a monotone world. The grayish beam from above me drowned out the color of the world. I jumped in feet–first, eyes focusing, hands gently trembling, and veins pulsed with excitement, as my curiosity was deeply satisfied. I felt, for a short time, so alone on that doorstep. Everyone else's house was there but no one dared step out at this time. It was just me and my lonesome sinking further into this spiteful and dramatic tale of a man named Jesus. I must have sat there listening to the content chirping of crickets and caroling croaks of the frogs in the forest for some time. My ears and eyes gorged themselves. Moments like these were rare, but I remember falling in love with them, where I would get so lost in a pattern of thought or an idea that

I could sit and stare at the moon and not even see it. One of nature's beautiful melodies grabbed hold of me and tore me deeper into the night. Word after word after word plunged me through a whirlpool of new information. The book was much larger than any I'd ever seen before, but my goodness was the story fascinating! How they could have produced something like this was a miracle, but somehow it seemed like just my kind of thing, the kind of thing that only I could have made happen. I continued to very happily enjoy the sweet touch of the moon as I delved further through the calamitous chapters. Very well written, though! I had to admit that I realized just how believable this was. My eyes dashed across page after page like a daily routine on repeat. They coursed over and over until I reached my physical limit.

The surroundings were too relaxing despite the adrenaline pounding away, as an answer had fallen at my feet. I managed to pick myself up off the floor, grabbing a nearby stick to place in the book, marking the page I was currently reading. My bare feet carried me to my cot where I lay down. Without barrel-loads of information being funneled through my pupils I could begin to wander and investigate my thoughts. The way the story came together was impressive.

This whole religion concept could change the world simply because people will believe tradition. There'd be no realistic expectation in which everyone would have the chance to read the entire book. I thought quietly to myself. It was likely that a majority of believers will simply accept what they have been told. It was easy to believe that their sole reason for committing wholeheartedly to this cause was because there was a book with 'rules' and because everyone else believed it, too. Social pressure is a powerful thing.

The puzzle pieces slid seamlessly into place. Humans are animals, too. We are a part of nature's grand creation. We would move in herds the same way as any other creature, for a common cause. A way of life canderive from a common belief. 'An interesting thought,' I would think to myself, and I knew it would not be without controversy.

You know, with the horrific scenes of human sacrifice and genocide, it was still an outstanding read. Those sorts of parts made me want to puke, truthfully. I braved the harshness of it, though, simply by overlooking it, hiding it under the dirt like it didn't exist. As long as you'd only focus on the good parts, it was perfect. Of course, that only applies to religion. As long as we could all agree to do so, it would be acceptable. Social pressure is a very powerful thing.

I lay alone in the cot as ideas mingled around me, gently melding together. This was the way the world would remain peaceful, because of me and because of what had happened here. The soothing conception blinded me as I rested my body in preparation of the next day. 'What was next to come?' I would think to myself. This was ecstatic news, yet I still awaited instructions.

I believed it all, though. I had to.

The remaining hours of darkness passed quickly. I woke to the harsh streaks of sunlight slicing through the minute holes in the ceiling. Immediately, my hands reached for the Bible, pulling it close to me. It wasn't a dream. It never was. Nevertheless, I had a job to do. After dressing myself with the rags we used to wear, I burst outside into the warm embrace of the world, the book in one hand and the sphere in the other. My feet swept me along the dirt path to the entrance of the forest where I would meet Preston each morning. He noticed me sprinting and I caught the movement his eyebrows made as they twitched upward. I slowed down to a light jog before halting, a little out of breath. There was a stump beneath him rooted to the ground that he would always sit, waiting for me underneath glorious sunlight. He shot up, greenery enveloped the backdrop, and he stood with one arm outstretched.

"Haha, hey!" he chuckled at me. "So, this must be the famous Bible we've all heard so much about?" he somewhat jokingly asked.

"Yeah, this is it. God is real. All of it, man. There's a reason we're on this planet and it's because of god. Don't tell me you can think otherwise," I said, handing the extensive body of text over to him, feeling an excessive weight leave me as I did.

"It does exist. Oh boy, you weren't kidding. Hmph," he scoffed lightheartedly as he flipped through the pages in a frantically excited scan. He focused for a minute or so, getting a quick grasp of the first page more than any of the others, before turning back to me with another question. "So, if this is the Bible, what... what is that?" he questioned, pointing to the sphere I held cautiously in my left hand.

"I, um... I don't actually really know," I had to think on my feet. "All I know is that it's some kind of tool, you know, but I don't quite understand it yet. Something to help spread the divine message," I concluded.

"Interesting. So, what's the plan then? You gonna come hunting today or now that you *finally* found your book, do you have other plans?" he asked me. I thought I would have been sure that I would know what do next, but I was wrong. I didn't.

Just like when my lady took that apple, I thought I'd know what was coming next, but I had no idea.

"I think I'll play this one by ear until I know what I'm really doing with these things." I responded in hopes that I would be contacted once more from the mystery man. He nodded firmly in response.

We continued our day in the forest, as usual, searching for prey. Once we'd found our spot for that day, we squatted down for respite in the leaves and ferns. My vocal cords began, for the first time, to speak the word of god as I recited some of the crude content in the Bible. I read several pages to Preston intermittently and I truly felt like I had a purpose. I felt as though I was finally fixing the mistakes of my past, the debt I owed to myself and Mother Earth. Maybe they weren't personal mistakes, but it didn't matter, did it? The book tortured me into believing I had sinned, shoving falsities down my throat until I began to enjoy it. It was all a hardship worth going through. Though, from an outsider's perspective, it would have seemed... manipulative? It wasn't though, I told myself so I could bare it.

It was a short day. At least it felt like one. The sun began its descent behind the mountains much faster than I would usually have expected, so we returned via the trail we instinctively knew with a couple of squirrels and a rabbit between us.

After some tiring conversation with a good friend we returned home. A flooding red wave of light cascaded perfectly over the mountaintops to infect the sky with veins of color. I walked with him in the crimson glow to my house from Preston's. I could hear an obnoxious noise from outside the hut. The screeching bellowed out from the front archway of the house. That was them! Answers, I thought, and Preston needed to witness it firsthand.

"Is that normal?" he asked me as we walked by my house. "I've never had that noise come from my house," he informed me.

"Come on, buddy, I've got to show you this," I instructed. "This is where the magic happens, the real show, g," I finished, darting inside. We stepped out of the light of the dying sun and into a space between my four walls to bear witness to the anomaly that started it all. Sure enough, it sat deep in the bones of the shelter and oozed an odd mist-like gas.

"Hey! It's me, um, are you there?" I called out over the destructive white noise.

"Uh," Preston spoke, "who are you –" he was cut off.

"Ah, yes! Almost thought we'd lost the time zone. Phew," the voice said quietly. "Okay, let's hear an update. Tell me you got the Bible and the divinity sphere," God spoke with convincing might.

"Yes, yeah, I got those last night. So that's what it's called? Divin– divinity sphere," I struggled. "What? Why do I need this? Also, you told me you'd be in touch in a couple of weeks. It has been three months," I inquired so curiously with a stern tone. Preston stood there as though a lightning bolt had struck him solid. His eyes blew up and his mouth broadened rudely. Sheer surprise riddled his boggled mind.

"That object, the divinity sphere, has the power to influence minds. Keep it with you when you speak the word of god and it will perk the interest of more people, get more of them hooked. It uses magic basically. Just hold on to it every day without fail. It will convince people that they ought to follow the divine word to avoid the post-mortem consequences," he explained, avoiding my question entirely.

"Oh, cool." An overwhelming feeling seeped into my bones. My body became drenched with thoughts of the responsibility to come with such power. "So, with that, what should I do next? There are a lot of people now who know all about this whole religion business, but they need proof. Oh, and I did what you asked. One of my friends with a beard is willing to help. I don't mean to be pushy, but what's next?" I demanded humbly.

"I'm going to assume that you've done some reading, so stop me from talking if I what I'm saying isn't making sense to you," I was told. "Your friend with the beard will be the one they call Jesus. I know that sounds a bit farfetched, but you can validate this sudden change of identity fairly easily. Because the idea of religion is a made-up fairytale, you can say that I, as god, wanted him to stay hidden as my son until now. And, of course, anyone who dares question the wrath of god will face the outlined post-mortem consequences," he explained.

"But I thought –" I attempted to interrupt.

"I know what you're thinking. The big ordeal about Jesus being born from a virgin mother in a stable. Yes, well, unfortunately we're going to have to make a couple of compromises. You need to remember this is all made up. People will believe anything you tell them as long as you tell them the right way. That's what religion is, my friend, a fictional story. Don't get lost," he made it clear. With every passing moment I tried to wrap my head around the complications that could arise. Every time I got new information, it felt as though the task grew even larger and more frightening. Toiling thoughts fluttered through my mind. 'If it was made up, then how was he real?'

"Uh, yeah, Right." I replied, hesitant because I knew even I was falling for the trap.

"So, you've read what needs to be done. Crucifixion, resurrection, all of it. You need to make it seem as real as possible. Do whatever you can to convince people that this is real. You have time to plan, but we don't. You have all the time in the world. This religion is going to take over the world one day. I want you to make it so good that even you would believe it," he commanded. "Tell them anything. In fact, tell them you have spoken with god himself. Anything to make them devote their lives to appreciating me as a deity." My eyes dropped to the ground for a second because I knew that it didn't need to be that good for me to believe it. The idea of having someone out there watching me, keeping me safe, kept me nice and warm inside. A flickering change of heart began to work its way through my intestines with passing moments.

"Okay, I'll finish getting together my group of 'disciples' as one would call them. We'll pull off each part in accordance with the Bible. I'll make sure that they believe it. I trust you, God." I felt as though the ground underneath me was trembling, though it must have been the adrenaline of standing before such an important being.

"That's all I have for you, for now, I believe. Be ready for contact again in about three weeks. I'll want to know what you've accomplished thus far. Goodbye." The voice cut through the crack a final time as the light faded along with the disturbing background screeches.

"I, what?" Preston mumbled. His eyes were scanning in all ways possible in an optical seizure. He bound forward to the wall and began an inspection. With knees pushing against the ground, his ear sucked itself to the crack. His breathing became impossibly quiet for a few seconds before he looked up with desperation scribbled across his poor face.

"It's gone," his breath spilled out.

XI

The turbines affixed to the opposite side of the once-so-prestigious Dawne start revolving slower as the connection with the past ceases. In the control room, Adam rolls backward slightly in his chair, grinning, as his aged knuckles crack amidst commanding fingers. He scoffs lightheartedly through his nose with a gaze that floats deftly to the floor. Nobody else knows, but they will. His heart pumps just a little more powerfully.

"Okay, simple tricks, boys. I'm just relocating the wormhole to three weeks in advance of the previous jump. Is there anything else I should be aware of?" James calls out over the dying engines.

"Oh, you mean other than the fact that pieces of the building are literally falling off because of how much energy we need from the engines?" John responds. "No. Not really," he finishes with a cheeky lift-up. Simon chooses to chime in.

"Yeah. About that. I'm still on with the Top Four. They're going to send someone our way to shut us down if we don't stop. They said it's too unstable. We could risk losing the whole building if we keep this up," Simon relays. Adam turns around with James to look at Simon. The looks on their faces alone dictate respect. Adam stands for a moment, happy to share his opinion. Simon's eyes peel backward to the hind of his head with a face that can only wonder if the dark clouds above Adam are real.

"Well, you tell them this, Simon. If we *do* stop, we could risk losing the ENTIRE world. How about that, huh?" Adam rages to his colleagues. "Why don't they understand? I mean, if this doesn't work, we're all long gone horsemen anyway." He furthers with a sigh of mild anxiousness. "Simon, you're killing it. Just keep feeding them bullshit to buy us time. John, be ready to activate the maximum-security protocol. I don't want to be nervous when I do my share of feeding the bullshit –" he trails off. The sweat glands are certainly activated now as he takes a seat once more to face the grand console beside him. His back can compare to the dew on a morning-crested leaf if any are still alive to this day. With hope in his heart and determination in his mind, his fingers pounce to the elongated keyboard to begin an intricate series of button-pushing.

"Let's talk to Jesus, folks," Adam snickers.

"Activating engine turbines again," James calls out to the team. "We are good to go. Full power is enabled –" His voice breaks off as the overwhelming machines turn over.

Like a skyscraper sized monster coming to life, the entire building vibrates aggressively. Everything bounces again just as it did before, jittering up and down. The team's focus drowns toward the enormous screen which lights up to eradicate every possible ounce of darkness using a surge of baby-blue hues. Their faces become splattered with the same color as the massive amounts of energy shines radiantly from the screen. Eight eyes, in synchronization, scrutinize their own brilliance. A remarkable array of noises explores the air between their ears.

"Hold the fuck on!" James screams.

Moments pass and the engines ram up to maximum capacity. Each of their hands grab tightly to anything nearby as the shaking refuses to end. Objects are sliding off shelves to the floor which is now becoming quite the ruin., a situation which spells misjudgment at the beginning of an apex of power and mayhem. From an uninformed perspective one can say it looks like true madness has embodied itself into a single scenario. A piercing crack sound struggles little in making itself known amongst the havoc. A screen on their right-hand side expands to reveal a view of the back of the Dawne by its base where the engines are locked in place. The engines spin, but there is an oddity that catches their eye. A concernedly large spray of rocks and dust just explode on the right engine from where it connects to the Dawne.

The engine is off the center from its original position on the Dawne. However, its ability to produce millions of joules remains unhindered.

With an edgy amount of anticipation, the four scientists await their disciples' word. What will they have for them? What events have transpired over, what for them are only a few minutes, the past several weeks? Anxiety and excitement are too close for comfort for these four men as they undergo a ground-shaking experience, literally.

XII

"I don't know when he'll choose to show himself! I don't question the Lord," I told the others. That's another name we had decided to call him – the Lord. It made sense to us at the time simply because we felt so minute before such an incomparable being. I attempted to speak firmly as the organizer of this group, but I knew that our newly found Jesus was the real center of attention.

We were all gathering for the first time, and I had to say I was rather eager to begin. It had felt like the longest three weeks. Trying to pick and choose exactly who to be Jesus' disciples was quite challenging, but if the lord wished it so, it would be done. Fresh summer winds blew the grass around us just enough to allow a calming rustle to fill the air. After a season of such warm weather, we weren't unhappy with the cheeky chill that lingered against the sun's presence. We sat in an oval sort of shape in a clearing within a tall field, hidden from view.

"So, we all know why we're here. Am I right? Is there anyone that needs another rundown? Get us all on the same page, you might say," Jesus alleviated social awkwardness with a common topic. Several hands popped up in minor confusion.

"Okay, well, it's not too complicated. As long as you can remember your job, we'll have no problems," Jesus began. 'Believable.' I thought it must be believable. It must work for the Lord, for our savior. "By now, we've all read the proverbs on what happens. I will spread the word of my existence to prove to everyone that religion is real. It does exist. Now we know that there are some people who disagree with the idea. Once we make it socially unacceptable to break God's rules, and some people will disregard them anyway, we hope that others will step in and enforce those rules. We need to make sure that we do this, too, to show people that it's okay to speak up in the name of God. Defend yourself against those who choose not to believe in the answer to your problems. The all-seeing beauty," he elaborated for us. "Mark, nobody in the village really knows who you are. You will come to me and claim to be blind and I will act as though to heal you at the town's gathering next week. You will act surprised and grateful; the people shall be convinced. Should they ask me to heal somebody else, I will explain that I, Jesus Christ, am only able to heal at God's discretion, when and how He deems worthy." The circle nodded in unison, happily drinking the milk of lies. "Judas," he said. Everyone present was given a new identity for the whole process. "You're going to die."

A short breath of air accumulated simultaneously among the group. We'd all read it in the book. We knew what was coming. I wasn't surprised, since I planned the whole thing with Jesus, formerly Bob. Each set of eyes switched immediately to Judas, formerly Fred.

"I, uh," he coughed with his hand over his mouth before regaining traction, "I know, sorry, I've been awfully ill recently. I don't think I'll make it much longer. I just want my life to mean something after death. I'm hoping I can do good at least once, even with the event of my death," he sputtered. A toxic sensation shuddered among us mentally, though we were all truly grateful to have found someone to fit the role so well. It's not that we didn't care for him; we did. However, it was more important that god's word was spread than one life spared.

"Exactly, we appreciate it, seriously." We all smiled and comforted him in the thought of his own demise. "To recap. Jesus will announce himself as the son of god and prove it by healing Mark in front of a crowd. As word spreads and the minor population of disbelief grows, we will address that we acknowledge some people disagree. Jesus will command that he is above all and, in rebellion there will likely be a small force of people that attempts to remove, or even kill him. Meanwhile, Judas will claim to have kissed Jesus. Because homosexuality is a 'sin,'" I air-quoted the word sin. "Judas, here, will feel guilty for betraying Jesus and God and thus kills himself. In response to those who wish to kill Jesus, we host a public crucifixion of him to satisfy these people. Seeing Jesus dead should satisfy their cruel tongues. Through the power of God, whom I will contact shortly, Jesus will be resurrected and ultimately prove to everyone that God is real and that following his ways has its benefits." I felt like I had just spat out the shortest and most vague summary of the Bible possible.

The group nodded as they understood. The plan had only just begun. The discussion didn't last much longer, as tasks were distributed among the group to set the plan in motion.

"In order to confirm that I have your full conviction, your one hundred percent commitment to this task, each of you will make a vow as you enter my home as we attempt to reach God." They responded each time with a nod or a quiet 'mhmm.' "You will pronounce your love for God so that He does not smite you in His presence. In doing so, you accept that should you fail to comply or complete any part of your taskings that God will take His toll on your life. Are there any questions before we go?" I asked the group. Surprisingly, there was only one question. A hand shot up from the middle of the humble group amongst the clearing in the grass.

"Yes?" I questioned.

"You keep talking as though God is real. Is He actually up there watching, as the creator of our world, or is this an act? What are we really doing here? I just have to know. Is god real or not?" he so hastily asked.

"More than you could ever imagine." I told him. "Rise now, followers. As we walk to my house in search of the Holy Spirit," I instructed. They joined me in a standing position and followed both Jesus and myself out of the field. A mere four minutes drifted by as we walked in an obedient single file to my place of dwelling. God's first hearing. As each person entered the doorframe, I had Jesus demand that they repeat the following phrase after him:

"Lord, help me not lean on my own understanding of the world but in everything find You and only You so that You can direct my all of me. My words, thoughts, and actions. In Jesus' name."

A haunting sentiment of fear encircled with faith and uncertainty rocketed about my stomach. The world's most dangerous butterflies ran amok. I followed the final follower through the doorway and into my room where those horrific background noises lived freely. The mist that I had so readily been prey to seeped dexterously from the wall. God was listening.

"It doesn't seem like much, but in order to hear his voice you must seat yourself correctly. Two columns of six, split down the middle, please," I spoke, and it was like an invisible hand grabbed them and plopped them into place. There was zero hesitation. Once in position, it was oddly pleasing to the eye. Having a column for me to walk up and down in the center I found was very appetizing. We were lucky there that we had enough room to squish people in. With all organized, they sat patiently. A short smile escaped for a second before I regained control. Things were finally stirring past the torturous wait, and I was beyond pleased. A sermon began. It was god's turn to speak now.

"God, they are here for you now. The disciples of your precious Jesus Christ are waiting for your voice," I meekly exhaled. The tension soared. Everybody's eyes were fixated passionately to the blue and steamy substance that seeped into the air. Waiting. Waiting. What could have been no longer than a second or two bore the weight of hours. Excruciating, you might say.

"Good day, ladies and gentlemen," he spoke slowly, mightier than ever before. The voice thundered through the air. An otherworldly presence had entered our realm. The tension, cut with a knife, gushed across the floor. It was so deeply satisfying. Eyes widened as jaws dropped. The truth was revealed to the followers for once and my heart bounced with grace.

"I am God. The ruler of this world and many others. I created everything you see around you, even yourselves. As you can tell, I'm more real than you could have ever imagined." Several sets of eyes darted my way, catching an unintentional similarity. "And I need your help," He mandated perfectly. "Your world is in danger, and I know by now that the only way I can prevent such danger is to ask for your help. As the creator of everything in your world, I have the power to choose where you are sent to in the afterlife. Should you choose not to play by the rules, you will not only be excommunicated but also get rid of your society and left to rot in hell. Join hands, and may you pray for the gift of salvation!"

God dictated to the small mass of people.

Jesus rose from the front and led the folks in a prayer.

They must have memorized it from the Bible.

The faith was beautiful, unionizing even.

XIII

Adam speaks with ferocity to the unwavering crowd through the open time portal that sits open, steadily swirling before them. The very same blue mist that entered the atmosphere on the other side of the communication thousands of years ago now seeps into the control room. An odd aura that they continually try to understand flutters in from behind the colossal monitor. Gently layering the room with light hints of blue and mild purple, the mist sets and hovers. With his last word, echoes of footsteps pour through the speakers followed closely by an instant of silence. This silence may be the very last one before things begin to make an impact in such a broken, twisted world. Among the silence there is the sound of a droplet of water dripping. It happens once, and from the complex portal drops a small blue and leather backpack. A few moments pass. Another dripping noise breaks the silence as a tiny handbook pops from the portal. It reads 'Handling Eternal Life for Dummies.' Adam scoops them up hastily before the other's notice. The delicate rigidity breaks with a soft, peaceful speaking of several people.

"No way! It's actually working," James whispers to Adam just loudly enough so that it can be heard over the idling engines. Adam turns slightly and nods to the slow rhythm of the prayer in agreement with James. As the words flow through the portal ever so graciously, they smile. For once, in this insane world, the steps to a proper future, a secure future, are in place. A sentiment of minor completion tingles through his spine. In a flash of surprise, his graft beeps loudly from his hand. That's not right.

It is now, in this moment, that Adam remembers the realities of the current world. Forgetting the dream, he tremors with his eyes closed for a brief moment. In his mind he can see the people screaming and hear their tormented voices. With fists raised, they chant for change, all of them innocent. Masses of dust swirl around the Dawne from the wasted legions of land around it, swooping back through the city under an unforgiving star.

These people, more than any, deserve salvation.

Adam regains control of his mind as the prayer comes to a smooth stop.

He opens the message on his graft with disbelief. Lacking the ability to fully concentrate, he grasps his forehead with a flat grip for a second. There are so many things to contemplate.

"Simon!" Adam mouths across the room so as not to be heard. "Take this," he adds. Simon gives a rushed nod across a room drowned in sweaty patience. A bluish white light snaps through the air between them, landing on Simon's graft as he begins to analyze the odd encryption. Adam turns back to the portal, resetting his mind for the game.

"Excellent, my followers. As the disciples of Jesus, you will carry out what is necessary. Listen to your brethren," he speaks with an absence of urgency, taking time to powerfully launch each word through time and into the past. "You will follow every word of command from your leader, the prophet, and Jesus. Should you fail to adhere to these simple rules, you will face the consequences. I guarantee you that hell is the last place on your bucket list. You want a happy afterlife where your dreams come true. Do not fail me, and make sure I am known to everyone as the divine ruler of all things. You'll be happy to know I work very hard every day to ensure your survival and happiness. I am the only thing that matters to you, and you will do everything in your power to spread that idea. Good afternoon, all. I bid you farewell. Remember, I will always be watching," Adam finishes. A quick glance is exchanged among the four of them. The turbines continue to howl from the other side of a coronium-coated barricade. The eerie mist rests undisturbed amongst the tribunal. The connection remains open despite a cease in communication. Adam looks upward, almost behind him, for a moment and raises a single finger pointing upward slightly above stomach-height.

"Listen." Adam says.

They each take an instant to read his lips. In compliance, their ears pick up a little. Words of compulsion emanate from the past.

"Behold, my followers. The Divine One. Our Lord. God. The One Being," the voice ends and, with it, the bridge that holds up the connection to their time. The oozing mist disperses hastily into the air, swirling counterclockwise faster and faster in a vortex-like fashion, sucking against the wall before sealing completely.

"Oh, wow. They are totally buying it. No question. Ha! If I have to be honest, I'm pretty impressed," Simon gushes. "Although, this message is scaring me, here, come take a look at this, guys," he says. They scamper over to the right side of the room to see what Simon's talking about. He enlarges the message for everyone to see. "Look!" he exclaims. A few hesitant seconds pass.

"Wow." John says in response.

"A– How would they?" James stutters. They stare dumbfounded at the message hovering idly before them.

"What you are messing with is more powerful than you could possibly imagine. I know things don't make sense right now, and they shouldn't. It's best that way. Just be careful with the sphere, Adam. Just remember what's most important. For me."

Adam mutters something under his breath, inaudible to the rest of the group. He whispers further to himself, "It must be her."

He continues, slowly, "The only logical explanation for this," he pauses before concluding, "is that somebody else knows what we are doing here. And my guess is that it's somebody from the future."

"So, what does that mean?" Simon asks.

"That means it worked, Simon. That means it freaking worked!" A smile smashes into his face. "The only reason anybody would know anything about what's going on in this room is if they were present, or it's somebody from the future, so… So, so, so!" He grins with relief. "It must be one of us!" he bolsters. "Or her," he hides under his breath. Looking around at the six eyes daunting over him, he questions. "Well, what do you have to say? You must be thinking something with an expression like that on your faces." he demands.

"Adam, this message isn't good news. It can't be. Read it again," James tells him.

"Whoever sent this message has seen failure. They've seen the reality in which things crumble, Adam. Why else would there be a word of caution rather than congratulations or celebration?" Simon chirps in. Dread swamps Adam's heart immediately. They're right. Why else would somebody suggest being careful?

"Oh, fuck," Adam murmurs. A second to process even this information is all he needs to formulate a response. "That… I suppose that makes more sense. Ah, shit. Okay. I guess we have more work to do, boys," Adam assures them. A vast array of emotions controls his every thought with each unstable moment. The sirens in his mind cause a racket. It would make sense, though, he thinks. To someone from the future they're just the past, a thought, a common memory.

James turns to Adam with minor discontent. His eyes lock with Adam's in a moment of horror. "Adam, you need to tell us exactly what you know about the divinity sphere. If we aren't on the same page, things are going to be a lot more difficult for us. What is so ultimately special about this object? Where did it come from?" He hesitates for a moment to break the stare. "We need to know," he requests.

"I… The divinity sphere is an object that was given to me by someone I used to know. I've had dreams about it. I even talked to one of the school professors during my bi-monthly inspection. I'm scared that I don't know as much as I should about it, but I do know that it has the power to persuade people into believing things they otherwise wouldn't," he lies, knowing fully well that it could have the capability of ensnaring the beholder in a perfect universe, given enough energy. "I just thought it would be useful for our experiment." Adam says.

"But if it's dangerous, then we need to be careful." James tells him.

"Okay, mhm," Adam admits. "On the next transmission I'll tell them something, uh. I'll have to come up with something. I think that, at this point, they'll believe anything. I'm hoping. Ah, I'm just praying," Adam answers.

"I'm glad. It's important for us to be on the same page, buddy, so we appreciate this," James reassures. "After you."

"Right, it's time to get back on the air. Let's make sure we don't accidentally destroy everything we've worked for over a poor choice of words," Adam commands. The air grows raw with tension once more, ripe with anticipation. "James, set the clock three weeks forward. Let's find out if they managed to do this," he says.

James' fingers fiddle around with a dial for a few seconds before he gives an enormous thumbs-up to Adam, who isn't paying attention to him.

"Ready," he calls out to him.

"Let's fire up those engines, gentlemen." Adam instructs.

XIV

I was swaying in the crowd as our newly crowned Jesus stood atop the podium in his corruptly beige rags and mighty beard. The air was light and aroused as he spoke with passion and heart in every word, existing in solitude slightly above the standstill gathering. It had taken some time to accumulate such an amount of people. An agglomeration of strangers passing by would each stop one by one. It must have been nearly an hour into the prophetic speech before the most interesting and convincing event took place. An aching voice boomed across the plentiful village square.

"I am Jesus, the son of God, our lord whom hath created this world with his very hands. I am the prophet, the one who speaks on his behalf to communicate with mankind. It is me! I speak for God!" he continued after hundreds of other words before somebody in the crowd cut him off.

"Listen, man, you're no more special than the rest of us. Ged 'own from there and get back to work. Stop wasting everyone's time with this shit," he cried, at first alone. Several moments later, though, he was backed by a cluster of supportive calls from elsewhere in the crowd. The rumble grew explosively and in a matter of seconds there were people seemingly outraged by the idea. Jesus had earned his chance to shine and prepared to embrace it. You could see it written on his face. Reveling in the riches of screams, he howled above all.

"I AM THE SON OF GOD!" he shrieked. "I will prove myself of such stature. I will need a volunteer! I need a blind volunteer!" The command silenced the mass. An eerie moment haunted the town square briefly as the population stood struck, without a word. The intensity simmered in the air before a man I knew too well shot up his hand.

"I'll do it," he spoke out as hundreds of heads turned in a way that got under my skin like foul breath. I shuddered as the mechanical operation of each person turning in unison completed its invasive maneuver. "Oh, for God's sake, people, what have I got left to lose anyway? I can't even fucking see," Mark belted, moving forward with his arms outstretched. Gentle whispers passed around here and there. Very little commotion occurred between the anxious spectators. An infinite number of beady eyes gawked at his every step as he marched flavorlessly over the dusty stone toward Jesus.

"Ah, you have been blessed this day, old soul, for you shall see the world through your own healed eyes by the power of the Holy Spirit," Jesus concocted. As he spoke, a few more whispers grew with the unstable impatience among the crowd. Mark climbed the small steps to stand beside Jesus on the platform. The audibility of the words between the commoners increased as Jesus went on further. "Yesterday, you were a man without sight. Today, you will see." He placed his hand facedown above and in front of Mark's face as if to pick up a circular object. "Lean forward, brother. Place your skull between my fingers." Jesus instructed in front of the mass of people. Mark complied. With a sluggish yet smooth movement he

gravitated headfirst toward Jesus. The prolonged fingers sucked up Mark's skull. Movement ceased. "With the power invested in me by the Lord, God, the Holy Spirit, brother, I deem you worthy of sight. You Will SEE!" He wailed, deconstructing all else. The whispers grinded to a sudden halt as my senses heightened.

The gas was in the air, primed for ignition.

It was as though the world was anew as people stared.

Jesus steadily removed his hand from Mark's dome.

"You are welcome, brother," he states.

Mark lifted his head to face Jesus and opened his eyes to see. As everything seemingly came into focus for him, he screamed.

The spark went off.

"I can see!" Mark cried.

A wave of roaring fire emerged as gasps throughout the masses of spectators. Disbelief, ruined by false evidence, disappeared from the horde. I stood behind the conglomeration of people in awe. The glimmer in their eyes ricocheted out to illuminate the sky and create the heavens. Explosive intrigue settled to dust as a newborn passion to serve. The dream was becoming a reality. Everything that had been told to us by god transformed in ways nobody could have ever imagined, besides me.

It felt rather quaint knowing the reason for such a change was a lie and because of this, I felt I had to believe it, too. I couldn't evolve into a modern world with the pressure of knowing it was unreal. It couldn't be. How could he, our Lord, have communicated with us to tell us any of this in the first place? This idea, this religion, I told myself, could not have been false.

It hurt me to no end to ponder that it may be untrue so much so that I chose to believe otherwise, to avoid the pain, and become livestock.

"It's real! I can finally see!" Mark screamed once more with his arms stretched out to the crowd. "Whatever you have done, it is incredible. The work of the Lord is upon us. Thank him for me, Jesus. Please," Mark bellowed.

"The Lord is upon us, people. I am Jesus as the son of God. I have proven to you now. God is real!" Jesus called out.

An earth-trembling clamor fusilladed into the air. Unfortunately, not everyone was entirely convinced, but many average people were beyond words in their current state of screaming. A smile crept onto my face and I joined in for the extensive cheering. Jesus went on for a few more minutes to explain the meaning of our religion. He introduced to them the idea of the heavens and the laws of god. Jesus made it real. He made it real for them.

"I don't believe it. Heal my ma!" a stranger shrieked out.

"The power invested in me by God is not to be messed with, and only at God's discretion. I will try again another day, but miracles do not happen so often, my friend," Jesus explained. Like fish on a hook, most people attached themselves without a second thought. It made sense though. With nothing else to believe in, we were simply wandering around the planet in search of personal gain and happiness.

I could've only imagined a world as painful as that, alone.

The following days were ripe with gossip. People talked, and they talked often about what had happened. Everybody wanted to read the Bible, and so I collected some scribes to create copies for everyone. It must have been months, then, without contact from god. It grated on me just a hair more each day. Every morning, I would argue with myself about whether it was real or not. One day, though, it clicked. My body filled with an aura of transcendence a little more each day. I was not only convinced, but addicted. It was then that I realized salvation was at hand. Praise be to God. Slowly but surely, everyone interested was given more than enough time to read and study a copy of the Bible.

It wasn't too long before questions arose, circulating throughout the community like rats. People had begun placing things under scrutiny in search of the truth and more answers.

As the group that started things from the beginning, we had come to the conclusion that Judas' time had come. His part of the play was ready to showcase. We had to give the people what they wanted if religion was going to be the way of the future for mankind. Sacrifices were necessary to appease, because whatever the cost, God must be cherished.

The wind shuffled the field's elements with a light breeze under a gifting sun. We had planned to meet in the fields one day to discuss exactly how things were to play out, and we did. Rather, most of us did. I counted the heads within the cut-out circle between the crops. Eleven bodies sat patiently, including my own. Where was the twelfth? I had to ask.

"Has anybody actually seen Judas? He kind of needs to be here," I inquired to the knowledgeable group. There was no response. A heavy pause sat damp in the air. I waited, hoping that somebody would speak up. In a moment of breathlessness, someone rose to the occasion. To our dismay, however, they were not from our group.

"Help! Anybody, help! Someone, anyone!" a voice screamed. We all stood up hastily. I motioned with my fingers to follow and they did. We bolted down the dirty grass route toward the primary pathway that the field connected to. With every thundering step, the gears inside my head turned autonomously. Judas was missing. There was a cry for help. What was going on? My breath began to run dry by the time we'd reached the main path that led in and out of the village by the forest. I had very little time to let my imagination begin constructing the unthinkable. Damn it, I let it run wild without me. I didn't want to bear the image in my mind, but I had a horrible feeling that I already knew what had happened. I wasn't alone. By the time we'd been running for nearly a minute, the path was within view. We continued to dart forward through the rough grass, over the beaten path, until we hit stones. Thoughts gathered in conclusion as we rested our eyes in the tiniest bit of relief that we'd been right in our assumptions. The image became so horrifyingly real. There he was, stopped and dead.

Judas kneeled, motionless, on the cold pebbled pavement. Two abnormally large sticks protruded ruthlessly from the back of his blood-ridden, palm-down hands. His chin was tucked deeply into a blood fountain of a chest. A merciless log plunged right through his fractured back and displaced heart directly into the ground beneath him, holding him in place like a crimson-glazed ragdoll. The clothes he adorned were thoroughly saturated with wine-red coloring. Several organs that had crossed ways with the invasive lumber spilled around him in countless pieces. Penetrating wood that he had so happily accepted his whole life was now the very reason for his not-so-endearing ending.

Personally, I could never understand a person like him. I found breasts to be far too amusing. Never before had that sort of decision been an influencing factor on anyone's lives. I had to believe that after this, it wasn't so safe.

Thin, dark blood oozed from the lifeless corpse into the thirsty cracks between the stones. It traveled further down the trail toward the town center on its own freewill. The street flourished in deep red, coming to life under a blessing sun.

Rich with a righteous vengeance, the ground suffocated the thoughts of all who bore witness. The very beginning of religious domination had begun with the ultimate price – the sacrifice of a man's life.

It was with this sight that we all stopped with a crushing sense of togetherness to ponder who could have caused such a thing. In the following moments, Jesus took it upon himself to seize this opportunity despite how others felt in the situation. Their thoughts didn't matter to him as long as they heard, understood, and practiced his message.

His worn brown flip-flops carried him toward the demonic sight. He held the divinity sphere I had given to him in his hands. He spoke boldly with a power that reverberated between our ears.

"Ladies and gentlemen! Witness the plague of homosexuality. The raw energy of God has surfaced to our planet to smite the unworthy!" he shrieked madly.

There were nearly a hundred people gathered at the opening. People had been screaming for help without a drop of care for anyone else's eardrums. Everybody looked around at one another, bewildered. An urge to triumph over something so minor, someone's sexuality, riddled the crowd.

"What the fuck is this!?" One man stepped forward out of the growing circle. He stood with arms raised and a face of pure hatred. He became struck with the gaze of over a hundred people all at once. A tension slipped into the air between the two vocal men.

"Tell me, brother, why does it bother you that a man is punished for acting against what is written in the holy book? Surely, you must agree that he is worth damnation," Jesus responded carefully. Several beastly whispers clawed out from the bushes of people in agreement. Breathless from waiting, the mass of people stood in a cesspool of anxiety. A few of the looks on the surrounding faces turned to anger. Some remained unchanged.

"I'm gay, too, but that doesn't mean I should be treated any differently, does it!?" the man screamed at Jesus.

Instantly, the crowd began to move. All around this strange man, people were starting to inch away from him, backing up into nearby viewers just to steer clear. It was as though he was sick with a contagious disease. They spread continuously until there was approximately a ten or fifteen-foot gap between him and the nearest observer. The stranger turned to notice what was happening.

"Alright, then riddle me this, 'son of god,'" he pointed his fingers upward imitatively. "If contradicting the Bible is so bad, then why does nobody choose to shame Timothy and his crew for fishing and for eating shellfish? That's one of your crazy sins, but nobody seems to care about that," he moaned. Silence hung in the air as people shuffled away from him once more. "Or, or what about all of us who eat pig's meat every so often, huh?" he continued to no avail. The conglomerate of humans stared at him, fixated on one fact only.

"God works in mysterious ways, fellowman." Jesus answered him loudly, the sphere still in his hands. The crowd chose not to speak, assumingly so in agreement. I was taken aback that nobody wanted an answer to the question this stranger had just posed. Why were some sins okay and not others?

Everybody was absolutely fine with it, picking and choosing as they wish. It was horrific.

"You have sinned, but I may clean your soul and body if you so choose. Join me, brother. Cleanse yourself of these horrible sins," Jesus offered. His blanket-like dressings covered the sphere from view as his arms remained lowered now.

"And if I don't?" he retorted.

"You have seen the consequences for such practices. They lie before us. Set yourself right in the world. Come forth," Jesus told him. The man hesitated for a few seconds, looking back and forth across the sea of judging faces. His head dropped down for a quick moment. His lips separated hastily as he shot his words to the ground with a response.

"I'm not joining your ridiculous clan. These ways are savage and inconsistent. It will never last, and you'll be sorry, Mister Jesus. Why don't you just go and fuck yourself?!" he screamed.

The crowd campaigned toward him in a rapid shuffle, avoiding catching his eye as he raged at the bearded man before him.

"Salvation and cleansing are within your grasp. Just say the word," Jesus called to him.

"No, fuck this. I'm out," he retorted. Jesus turned around to face away from the man in acceptance. He faced outward of the surrounding horde of humans, ignoring reality.

"Ha! You really think so?" A man, backed by several other women and men, pushed him toward the center of the ring. The gay man's eyes hit his hairline like a spring. Befuddled, he caught his step and turned to the strangely aggressive man.

"Back off," he told the crowd member.

"God works in mysterious ways," the scruffy man said before winding up an arm behind him. The poor, innocent fool had less than a second to respond to such an escalation. Before he could raise a limb to defend himself, the power of a horse's hoof concussed him to his rear end. He skidded a couple of inches across the stone with an angered and worrisome look writhing through his every muscle in his face. After brushing off the dirt from the odd man's hand, he pulled himself to his feet.

His hands swung gently by his side, lowered.

"Okay, you know what? That's it. This has gone too far. I'm leaving," he voiced.

"It'll be a cold day in hell when I let a gay man walk the same streets as me!" a lady called out from the now-hundreds-of-entertained people. An overwhelmingly intense roar of 'yeah' and 'woo's spiraled from the agreeing circle of villagers.

The leader of the religious movement, as the son of God, remained silent, facing the opposite direction.

I stood only ten feet away from him, refusing to admit what was happening. I saw pride glisten with a growing passion in their eyes as the explosion of noise increased. I couldn't watch what must have happened next. I heard an impressive amount of cheering followed by a series of painful shrieks. In the corner of my eye, limbs flew all about. The tremoring screams of torment pierced right through the monotony of the barbaric yelling. They didn't last long, though. After less than a minute of stitching my gaze to Jesus' denying eyes the racket slowly suffocated through a brutal battery of fury. The agonic suffering rotted to provide a means of humor for the remainder. Laughter gently decorated the putrid air as a tear broke its way free. It snapped off from the same eye that was still fixed onto Jesus' unrelenting focus to look away.

I had difficulty breathing for just a moment, yet I did so slowly, in disbelief. Religion was supposed to bring peace. It had brought unity. That much was true. The dead man was right; these ways were savage. But there was nothing else to follow.

The hordes of people gravitated back to the village nonchalantly, I noticed, as their disgusting voices began to fade. This wasn't how it was supposed to go. Fading out of earshot from the main group of people, I walked up to Jesus with anger crawling desperately within my heart. My voice quivered with raw, very real fear. If things weren't in motion before, they certainly were now.

"You just – you just stood there. Why? Why didn't you do anything?" I questioned. "You knew exactly what was going on, and you just stood there. How could you do that? This is your religion! We're supposed to be spreading peace and you let them kill him? Why!?" I screamed at him. I yelled, despite being inches from his face. He retracted an unbroken tear as his mouth opened.

"The question you need to ask is not why I didn't stop them, my brother. But rather, why didn't you?" he said.

"Oh, and this works," he finished, stretching his arm out and handing me the circular object.

I took it, feeling the power course through me. He was right. A feeling of uncertainty flashed through me and I shoved the sphere back against him, and he grasped on to it. The responsibility was corrupting.

The wind skimmed across the grassy field beside us, fluttering by without an issue. A soft rustle joined, breathing simultaneously with the deceased tension in the air. Birds called out to one another in the distance as the flexible trees housed them so delicately. We were encircled with a natural beauty that I knew was important to our home, our planet. I would have given anything to bring peace to it. I should have stopped them. I feared that if I had tried, they'd have only pummeled me into a corpse, too.

I felt utterly controlled by a numbing dilemma in an otherwise carefree world. I stood side by side with Jesus looking out to the growing greens moving on the horizon. 'There must have been a way,' I thought, 'for us to conquer this challenge.' I was always ready for something to be difficult, but not when it meant people were dying.

That was the first moment in which I doubted whether I wanted to continue, but it was too late. I saw the way those people walked away without any issue like it was business. They were truly committed with heart and soul. It wasn't right. Religion ought to be a haven for all and sundry. I knew who would have had an answer, but I didn't know how to consistently talk to him. He was unreliable, just like everything else, it seemed.

"What do we do?" Jesus said, dispersing awkwardness.

"Wha? – Uh, what do you mean?" I asked him.

"About the bodies," he whispered.

"Wolves'll take them probably." I told him.

"Should we have a funeral?" he asked.

"Yeah. Spend a couple of hours cleaning this up to make a funeral no one will go to," I responded.

"Listen," he said my name, "they're worth it." Jesus said. I knew he was good on the inside.

"I just can't. I'm an organizer, not so much a doer, sorry. I need to fix this. All of this. You can either help me or do the dogs' work. You know the wolves would clean this up by the morning," I told him.

"Maybe you're right, but we can't leave them here," he said.

"No, this… this is on you," I said. "I'll see you tomorrow."

In my doubting state of mind, I bid Jesus goodbye for the day and walked home with a bloodshot-red mind's eye. A rite of disappointment flooded me. I arrived home within a few minutes, passing the animal-attracting trail of blood leaking down the main road. It was at this moment that I missed her more than anything. When would she return with Preston's girl from their traveling trip

102

to tell me what to do? The idea of dragging her into this petrified me. I looked around my room for an answer. My gaze wandered with my mind for several seconds before I looked down to my hands. There was something extraordinary about this thing, beyond what I had already seen. I knew it, but couldn't put my finger on it.

"Just show me something, please. Anything," I whispered. I hoped. I prayed. I felt embarrassed to be a part of the chaos that had just caused another man's death, but I needed an answer. I wanted to believe in something greater than me and I followed that thought through anything.

Even if it steered other people in a different direction, I knew it was different for me. It had to be. At the time, I thought I was so much wiser. But I was blind.

I waited for a few moments, and then a few moments more. I racked my brain. Where was the answer!? In my doubts and thoughts I tore myself apart just thinking about the responsibility that came with such power. I was afraid that I couldn't do it alone. The door to God's guidance never opened when I wanted it to. It only presented itself when it was absolutely necessary, and that drove me up the wall.

I remembered what Jesus had said earlier that day. 'God works in mysterious ways.' The words bounced around within me. It seemed like such a blatantly obvious way to cover up any imperfections or inconsistencies. If anything steered off the path to safety or even sanity, one could explain it all with that lie. It got to me, though, because what if it wasn't a lie? What if it all really meant something greater than us and the best ways of expressing it were through rarely crude actions. I tore my investigating eyes from the sphere in my thick hands. They found themselves begging at the mercy of the crack in the wall, drawn toward despite my willingness to abandon my destiny.

I didn't want to have to think for myself anymore. My thought pattern began to rely on someone else, and I craved that euphoric feeling. It was so much easier to be told what to do rather than make decisions for me or rather than actually be someone. I would have so much rather been a pawn in the Lord's game than an individual person in my own world. I think now, perhaps I was.

I longed to make the dream come true of preserving the world through peace, given this new and interesting idea. I really did, but in that moment, there was no answer. I waited and waited.

XV

"Let's fire up those engines, boys." Adam instructs. The men turn the necessary dials and engage the proper mechanisms as per usual.

"Let's see what they've got for us this time!" Adam calls out to the group, grinning greedily.

The roar of the turbines shatters any remaining peace in the air as they lose track of what everyone else is yelling out for a few seconds amongst the raw, ear-splitting chaos. The smiles on their faces put a kid in a candy store to shame. Not that candy stores are even a thing anymore. The peak volume of the engines continues for a barely a second longer than it should, and Adam stands up immediately, holding on to his chair to stabilize – grumble, sputter, and cut. The deafening pounding, rather than curving out to a smooth purr, snaps to a sudden halt. Like an elderly spine being snapped in half in an instant, the noise cuts out. Few sputters follow as the building ceases to shake. Adam remains standing in the unexpected near-silence.

"Uh, what the –?" he mutters. The clamoring of failing engines grinds to a complete and utter end. "Fuck!" he cries. Immediately, he swivels his head to look at Simon, who looks back with his jaw open.

"Adam, why are you looking at me?" he jolts.

"Because who else is going to have an answer for me?" he demands.

"Oh, uhm. Right. Just give me a sec," Simon pauses. "Aha! Oh, shit! That's it, right there," he continues.

"Well, what is it? What's wrong!?" James chimes in.

"It's the engine blocks. One of the supports has buckled! Look," he states. His fingers whiz around in a flurry of motions over the control surface to enlarge a moving image of the rear end of the Dawne. The video feed of the outdoors shows several thick arms keeping the overwhelmingly large engines secured in place. The camera zooms in close to the second motor on the right. Four impressively large steel arms hold up each engine, which are fastened tightly to the back of the Dawne. The image zooms in further to reveal a cracked support beam that has bent beneath the right engine, quivering as it keeps the colossal weight in place.

"Fucking shit, man. What are we gonna do?" James asks.

"Send out a drone, NOW!" Adam's words blurt from his mouth. "The Top Four will know what happened. We need to get out there and fix it before they make sure it stays like that!" he commands.

"I'm on it!" James responds. A decorative whirl of fingers and limbs moving across the control screen encourages a startup sound from two of their travel pods.

"Silver, we need you to stop the Top Four from causing any more damage to the engines. Use one of the drones to start fixing the support and the other to defend its brethren," James calls to the delicate air.

"Yes, sir. Pods engaging now," a robotic voice replies smoothly. The men watch the pods disconnect from the building with their own eyes, intrigued. An expulsion of visible gas from the pods' previous resting place shoots out from the Dawne and into the decaying air outside. Each of the men resorts to a screen the size of the wall to monitor the automatons' progress. Two hopeless metallic meteors scream downward rapidly. The four of them stand entirely still apart from the trembling in a few knees. For the first time in their brave endeavor, they find themselves unsure of the certainty of their plan.

Machinery's whirs fill the room and flicker across the outside of the Dawne as the pods hurl toward the ground. Now, only thirty or so feet from the surface of the Earth, their spinning comes to a halt. The uncontrolled shakiness ceases, too. In just half of a second, four overwhelmingly long stannic rods spring out from each of the spheres' undersides. As though perfectly planned, they extend their legs in the last few milliseconds of descent.

"For fuck's sake! I told you guys the extra airflow wasn't worth suspending the engine!" Simon screams at James.

"Well, it worked!" James retorts.

"Oh yeah, it's doing a great job!" Simon repels.

The men jump into a hurricane of childish insults and dismembering responses. Bickering back and forth, they fail to notice the display on the screen as the two objects connect with the ground.

Dust rises in a blanket around the eight spines that dig six inches into the ground. The central bodies sink a few centimeters as the legs catch them from the bloodcurdling fall. A perfunctory hiss emerges from each of the spheres, eliminating excess stress. In unison, they begin marching hastily around the side of the tower, one cold foot after the other. Nearly ten feet tall, the machines move without a single moment of hesitation around to the back of the impressive structure. With their movements, two more appendages unfold from the center, revealing metallurgic arms with a thousand unconceivable fingers on the hand. They have no hands, but rather levitating blue balls with a mesmerizing number of fragments. A harsh sun scorches the hind of each pod as they finalize their march to approach the engines at the base of the tower.

"It doesn't matter now because it doesn't work anymore," words pound against the wall back and forth between the gentlemen.

"You can't be serious. It doesn't matter now? We aren't done yet! Do you SEE a better world out there?" another voice requests. A limb from the corruptive mess within their argumentative chamber gestures strongly toward the screen.

A hesitation arises, and they stop. Pure fear infects them. With spines like tree trunks, they cower in front of the images. Their trains of thought buckle over and cross paths in a savage ruin. They stare hopelessly at the screen.

The first pod uses its mammoth-sized arms, leaning forward now, to support the structure. It pushes against the Dawne to compress the beam and lock it back into position. Several metal claws extend from the base of its powerful legs, gripping deeply into the roasting sand to lock the machine into place. The second pod rotates to face outward and backs up into the supporting member. As it grows closer to its partner, they each create a series of silver tendrils from their mid-regions that extend toward one another. The two touch and the spawning vines ensnare the opposing masses. Dust swirls in a frenzy of withered natural surroundings. An episode of hissing and locking pushes the powerful mass right against the engine block as it begins to generate a current. Blue energy swirls through their parts and rockets into the restored engine. A sound audible from the control floor shakes the building violently with a rocking start.

"Oh, fuck. For a second there, I thought it was over," James said. A moment of caution resides among the group. The screen continues to display the bot duo at the base of the building.

"Don't get your hopes up." Simon replies. Not a moment later, an immense blue beam soars down from the sky to encompass the supporting robot. Like a ray of light reflecting from a sea-sunken star the beam pierces the air. Each of their eyes moves upward to track this odd heliograph to its source. A minute pod floats peacefully beside the tip of the Dawne. An overwhelming, sweltering sun sits behind it. A voice booms across the land, lifting the top layer of sand several feet into the air.

"THIS has gone far enough."

Adam knows that voice. They all do. The beam flourishes brighter in the already-near-blinding daylight.

"You will not ruin a world we have worked so hard for!" the second voice commands, unsettling the ground.

"As one, we unite," a third voice calls.

"To bring you your reckoning," the fourth and final voice echoes upon a dried wasteland. An impressive level of volume emits from an ominously small pod. Adam ponders. Maybe he thought too soon? They watch the pod of fooling grandeur begin to descend. What starts as an innocent levitation soon becomes an eerily fast drop from the sky. The pod begins rotating as the others had done not a minute ago, and sure enough, two autonomous arms explode from the sides of the pod, followed by four monstrous legs. They poke out in an instant to unfold, with one enormous metal hand in front and one behind. The impeccable machine collides aggressively with the ground. Simon opens communication and speaks boldly with little hesitation.

"Top Four, what exactly are you going to do? It's too late to go back, isn't it?" his voice carries out from a powerful speaker across the deserted land, the hind of the Dawne.

"Not if we can help it!" Alessia's voice booms, raising miniature sandstorms as the fallen robot rises steadily to a grand, stoic stance. Its gracious feet begin moving in a fashion to encroach upon the supporting mechanism. Simon pounces from his seat in a flurry, throwing his gear to the ground.

"Woah! Where do you think you're going?" Adam immediately questions.

"Where no one else will, and where I have to." Simon says. "I wouldn't put it past them to waste no time in smashing the two pods we sent to smithereens. If that happens, there's no more future for us. Maybe I'll die, maybe not. Either way, it's better than doing nothing," Simon explains, hurrying off.

"Yeah, you're right," John chirps in. "I'll come with Adam, James. Take care of it all. I don't really see us coming back from this, to be honest. If anything, we can hold them off for a while so you can get the job done," John says.

"Your sacrifice," Adam replies, "will be remembered." The four of them take a brief moment to exchange exit pleasantries. "Goodbye, old friends." Adam waves softly to his colleagues from the center of the command construct.

"Silver." Adam calls.

"Yes, sir?" the room responds fluently.

"Take care of these men," he finishes.

Perhaps it's the tension in the air that lies dastardly close to being destroyed by a ruinous blast of energy, or the love they have grown for religion and a god. Regardless of the motive, they hope desperately for an answer and a change.

Two men desert their four-member family in the hopes of creating a world they thought could exist only in their imagination.

"Safety protocols deactivating. Would you like to engage combat mode, sir?" the smooth voice requests. Satisfied in their air-conditioned seats, they both reply in unison.

"What do you think?" They each turn to look at one another through panels of mildly tinted glass and a meter of toxic air. A smile finds warm freedom for just a second across both of their mouths. As the lock between their eyes disconnects, they extend their right arms forward.

"Graft fusion in progress," Silver says calmly. The doors behind them close one final time with a subtle hiss and click. Metallic prongs jet down from the rounded ceiling and slide quickly into the back of their hands. Gasses expel from the connection between the Dawne and the pods as they levitate away from the building and make their way to its rear. They drive with haste and soon find themselves almost directly above the unholy machination that marches steadily toward their last hope. A harnessing mechanism folds across their torsos and secures them deeply into the chair. "Preparing to drop in three, two, one," Silver informs them.

A hesitant moment passes after she speaks, leaving the two gentlemen enough time to grip tightly to the controls before them. They fall immediately, hurling toward the Earth as the pods begin to rotate. As they advance closer to the sandy surface below, an ear-shattering clanging rattles their cages. The limb-like extensions protrude from the sides with a sudden decrease in rotation speed as they land on all-fours with an impressive expansion of sand. With cockpits facing down, they pause in synchronization. The Top Four halt. Clicking and whirring fill the air briefly as the body of their construct rotates to face them, glittering in the sunlight.

"Silver, make sure to keep the comms open. I want to be able to talk to them while they're out there." Adam demands in the control room.

"Yes, sir," Silver responds.

As though well-rehearsed, in the wilderness, the two-stand upright to face their opponent in the barren arena. A conversation across a hundred meters of wasteland ensues through earth-shaking speakers.

"What makes you think you can stop us?" Trevor boasts from behind the thickest of protection. He'd just barely be able to make out the figures of Simon and John, sitting in their pods, from his position. "We are the epitome of power," he states.

"If we don't, no one will." John calls across the dust-ridden air. "Look around you. No one deserves this world for a home. Not even you," he tells them.

"You have little respect, young man, for what we have created here. Do you know why the world is the way it is? Do you have ANY idea as to what has really happened?" Samantha trembles.

"Yeah. We know. The wars and the –" Simon attempts to make a point.

"NO! Not the wars, damn it!" Trevor revolts. "The wars were just a lesson," he sighs excruciatingly slowly. "The stories of the wars, yes, they're true, but the reason we had those wars in the first place is that religion failed," he continues. "I have tried before to resurrect this world. As have my brethren three."

"What are you – What do you mean?" Simon requests as the earth beneath them shivers.

"I for Buddha, Samantha for Hashem, Alessia for Allah, and Alex for millions of them in the Hindu manner. We have tried to save this world from damnation by using religion as a tool of peace. We've done this before, but every time, the world is bound to end in self-destruction. The safety protocol has always been to reverse time to mankind's earliest footsteps on Earth to prevent the extinction of our species," Trever elaborates, knowing there would be questions, so he allows Samantha to delve further.

"We had high hopes for you guys, though. You did something none of us had ever thought of before by using that artifact in new ways. We were impressed," Samantha continues. Alessia picks up where she leaves off. Simon and John make what they can only hope is eye contact with the opposing four in their mechanical armor.

"But this time, it's time to break the cycle. The suffering must end. Once we saw how quickly this was turning sour, we knew it had to come to an end. Now, the only thing left to do is to break the supports behind you into submission or to dust," she concludes for the weary men. Their pod turns back around to face the Dawne again as a simultaneous walking motion initiates from its four legs.

"It's a somber story that is true," Simon tells them through deafening means, "but I'm afraid I can't allow that. Not today." He booms upon the mischievous terrain. Silence responds from the furthering machine. Simon smacks his fingers against an image that reads out *'toggle microphone'* as he breathes out dauntingly. "For God," he attempts, under his breath. The saliva dashing from his lips accompanies the sweat dousing his brow. The two of them begin moving toward the Dawne and the opposing figure with increasing velocity. The pitter-patter of incredibly large claws slicing subtly into the sand is soft with their advance.

In the control room, Adam's face lights up with joy as two of his best friends distract the problem.

"Just keep them distracted long enough so that I can get through," Adam relays to them through Silver.

"Are we ready to go?" James asks him as they both watch their brothers careen forward over the barren wastes.

"Uhh," Adam stutters as he sifts through information to locate the answer. "Yes, full power! We're ready! Hit it now, James! Our time is limited," Adam quivers.

XVI

The moon glared down at us with vengeance, jealous of our progression. I was left praying. I knelt in front of what had become an altar for a concept I thought I understood. Why was the bloodshed so paramount in this grand concoction of a journey to world peace? With a list of questions longer than the seconds that went by, I knelt, convicted to serve. I waited that night. I could not move before an answer revealed itself. Puzzles in my mind crossed paths as often as pain struck my heart.

After hours filled with the absence of God, I felt abandoned. Did God care not for the lost lives? I had to pursue my faith in the hopes that I could right the world.

A sliver of my imagination leaked into my conscious thoughts to tempt me into leaving this idea of religion for someone else to follow, in a fraction of a second of true doubt. I couldn't have been closer to damnation when it sprang out at me.

The light consumed my room entirely just for an instant, nearly blinding me. As the baby-blue light dimmed, its remnants shone beautifully from the crack.

Finally, I could see the light.

"Hello," I cried out softly. "Is anybody there? God? We need you now. I need you," I spoke, trembling. I was impressed at the response time this went around. It wasn't often that a reply was so quick to come through.

"Yes, hello. I'm here and I need you, too," God spoke to me. I was mildly confused until he continued. "It's time to crucify Jesus. I need you to move on with the plan and execute the remainder of the Bible. The resurrection of this world cannot wait any longer. Do you hear me?" His voice thundered through the walls.

"Yes, my Lord, uh, absolutely," I strung on from His rant. "I have some questions, though." I heard a disgruntled 'mhm' echo faintly beneath the noisy background. "There have been some… mishaps along the way. Some people don't agree with some of the specifics laid out in the Bible. A recent event actually ended up with two people dying because of a disagreement about how you supposedly feel about gay people." I explained to Him.

"I'm stopping you right there, my friend." God commanded.

"Anyone who disagrees with me or the Bible is not worthy of a peaceful world. They can burn for all I care. What's important is unity of a majority. If you can get everyone on the same page for me, I'll be happy," His voice vibrated viciously through the delicate structure. "Even if it means," His voice slowed down eerily sluggish for the next word, "excluding... those who disagree," He ended abruptly.

I couldn't think of anything to say in response. I didn't agree, but if it was the will of God, I dared not argue. I knew, inside, what I believed. Though, strangely, I was morphing. Physically, I remained unchanged but every other tangible aspect of what made me human folded over and warped around me, spinning me in all different directions. Who was I, really, if not a knight for a kingdom that I did not understand the contents of? Each sunrise taught me that another purpose existed for me, but the reward was held elsewhere. If, as a person, I was once a statue, I had become silky magma in the powerful hands of God. Content and ripe, I obliged to commands with the racing excitement of one day rising to heaven and meeting Him face-to-face. My ways of life were changing, and it was without a drop of regret that I embraced the evolution of my soul.

I thought I knew my purpose, but I was just another brick in the wall. In that sense, I think I did.

These thoughts combined themselves to become the hammer to the forge that would one day deliver me to what I believed to be a greater purpose.

"The divinity sphere. The ancient artifact that I gave to you is how you will convince them all to join hands and eliminate those who dare to retort. You must keep it safe and make use of its full potential," God decreed.

"Where are you at exactly in the timeline of events? I have noticed, still, little change in the world for your efforts," I spoke with confidence despite the Being's dissatisfaction.

"Judas' life has been taken. We aren't far from convincing the rest of the non-believers that the magic of your powers is real with the resurrection of Jesus after his crucifixion. It should not be too much longer, my Lord," I rambled slightly as I closed off my sentence.

. I prayed to impress in any form. I begged for forgiveness through my thoughts in an attempt to forge those thoughts into actions. I needed the Lord to see me, not for me though, just as what he wanted me to be – angelic and flawless, which I was not.

Without defining it clearly, I would mentally grovel in the hope of becoming someone worthy of His grand, intricate plan.

That's all I wished for.

The voice came through once more, though this time it was evidently muffled as though it was not directing its words toward me.

"Ask them what they would do differently, Simon. What would they do to prevent this cycle from happening again? What hope is there for our world?" it called in stray guidance.

"Uh," I stuttered, "sorry, pardon?" I inquired.

"Oh, nothing. You needn't worry about that, precious follower," He dictated. I respected the rather odd command.

"It is with haste that I will have Jesus crucified for the world to see what the power of religion can do," I was quick to inform him.

"Excellent. We will talk again soon when there are no people left to doubt the exuberance of my perfection," He spoke strongly. He followed his divine direction with a short speech to instruct me on something incredible. "One final note. If you wish to manually control when to speak with me, and override my time targeting, you must press the orb on the button that lies within the smooth band, at its center. Hold it for ten seconds, and I will be there. There will only be enough energy for you to use it up to three times, so you must be careful. Use your wisdom with such responsibility. You are still unaware of its true power. Follow these directions, and you will be one of the first to ascend, my good friend. As long as all is in order, you will have your taste of our realm," I stood there, flabbergasted. With a delicate ending to a riveting concept, the connection between our voices reduced to nothing but a gentle sway of yellow ash falling from the crack. I didn't want to waste any time because things had to be done, but it was far from me to see what their realm could look like.

I stood for a moment in awe as I imagined the possibilities of the future. Will they have trees, still? Will the birds still call in the morning to wake the people? Whatever the reality, I felt responsible. I had so much difficulty visualizing something beyond my scope. Every day for so many years had been so similar to its counterparts. Why should that ever change? The answer to that should have been obvious, given my situation. I failed to see it at the time probably because of my blatant and blind obedience. After accepting a mild mental defeat, I took a stab in the dark at trying to sleep. Perhaps I got a few minutes of true shuteye, but it all felt like a blur. As much as I tried to clear my mind to rest through the sinister night, I could not. I had decided to give up and prepared myself for the following day, running through the plan in my head. After communicating with God once more, I felt ready to tackle my mission. I needed to retake the sphere and get to work.

I had to improvise slightly because of previous unplanned events. It was important that I didn't worry, and I didn't because I knew what had to be done. A sort of sophisticated harmony came from the fact that we all believed in the same thing, regardless of the reason. After a short while of contemplation, I rose up to exit the minute building, stepping into straightening sunlight that glinted off the blood-soaked stones before me.

I stepped delicately onto the pathway so as not to smear red across the underside of my feet. Despite the early hour of morning, it took little effort to group together a certain kind of man. As I reached the village square, I saw them crowding and yelling with more energy than I could have mustered. With a rowdy ambush to a kind morning, they called out to the opposing conglomeration of people. It couldn't have been more than thirty or so against what looked like the rest of the village folks, several hundred nearly.

It was mildly difficult to pinpoint one phrase or sentence over the next as they bombarded the peaceful air with statements like: "Jesus has no power!" or "This man is a fake!" or my favorite one that I found kind of amusing: "Where is this 'God' person anyway, and why doesn't He show His face?" The slew of comments aggravated the more popular crowd who clearly disagreed but seemed as though they had little to back up their beliefs. Pecking at the ears of many, the retorts came back with more ammunition than the larger group could keep up with.

As I walked closer, I could identify without any issue that the smaller aggressive group was huddled in a circle facing outward as though in some kind of defensive stance. They were trapped in from all sides, like the bull's eye of a target, by a larger ring of people. I had to push past a few people to make my way close enough to the front to see exactly what the minute group had encircled. I have to admit that in some way, I almost wished I hadn't done so because I had seen enough bloodshed. Despite their grit, the angry faces of the few unsettled men and women weren't distracting enough to take away from the gem that sat defenseless in the center of their cult-like circle.

Jesus!

I had to rinse away the shock for a second before I could produce any sound.

"Jesus!" I yelled out. He caught my eye and did not let go. Between a wavy mess of arms and legs, our eyes held a stern gaze. He and I held a connection for another few seconds until he lowered his stare to the object in his hand – the sphere. He nudged it forward by a fraction of an inch in a quick gesture. My brain clicked, and I knew what had to happen. I scrambled forward to make it to the front row of the outer ring amongst the encircling humans. From that point we waited. We waited despite the harassing calls and torturous comments. We waited through the threatening and arguing. We waited in what seemed like forever but could not have been more than a minute or two. Right then, we saw the opportunity and took it. His eyes lit up, as did mine as a window of time opened in which he rolled the potent ball toward me through the legs of his capturers. The barely audible scratching against the sinister stone caught my ear. I followed it with my eyes cautiously until the unit landed firmly between my clammy fingertips. I rose to my feet and pondered. The thoughts I had concocted overnight stirred into motion. The gears grinded to create a smooth function in my mind as the plan blended together. My eyes glazed over the intricate object frivolously while the final pieces snapped into place.

I shuffled my feet into the crack of open space between the center group and its encircling crowd. As I prepared to speak up against the majority, my hands became damp with sweat. My grip strength against the sphere increased. Images of a carcass screwed to the ground flooded my mind's eye. I remembered what happened the day before to those who spoke out against the beliefs of God. The intensity of the pump in my chest grew in outrage. My throat tightened. My senses heightened. I began to fill my lungs through an airway that felt almost sealed to the outside world. With immense strength I shot my arm up with the sphere in hand and I boomed above the catastrophic bickering commentary.

"Yes! Okay, so maybe they have a different viewpoint. That's okay! Isn't it?" I screeched at the top of my lungs. I remember the searing pain writhing through my throat with every word.

The disruptive chatter refused to simmer, and I took it upon myself to try once more. My clutch drilled into the sphere as my lungs prepared to launch.

"HEY!" I screamed into the craziness. The first thing I noticed in the corner of my eye, besides a slight reduction in the noise volume, was the sphere changing. It wasn't exactly a change but more like a vibration. I almost dropped it! My grip loosened for a moment before squeezing tight once again as I lowered it to investigate. The noise level still made communication relatively arduous. I looked at the sphere after lowering it and it vibrated once more. I focused with deep intention. In a loving astonishment I adored a gentle flash of blue light emerging from its dusty crevasses. The patterns that marked the object glowed for the littlest fraction of a second. My pupils bore rigidly into the sphere. With fingers wrapped cautiously around it, I loosened my tight hold for a second time and held it in both hands. I waited for something else to appear or move. There was nothing. But then again, there was something. It was not the sphere, though. In my deep focus toward the mysterious object I had become blind. Or rather, I had become deaf. Backtracking several seconds,

I realized that the moment the sphere had shaken and turned blue for an instant was the same moment everyone had gone silent. Not a whisper floated by in the stony silence. I looked up for a moment as an off-putting number of eyes paralyzed me. 'It was one thing to ask for attention,' I thought. It was another thing to get it.

"Right." I coughed out, "Ahem! I mean, right. Listen here!" Why did I think I was ready to orchestrate something like this? I could feel my voice ready to crack at the push of a button I couldn't touch. I searched for the words and it was as though by magic they appeared at my tongue. "These people have the right to a different opinion than you. Even if they do not agree with you right now, maybe one day they will. And it is possible that even that does not come to fruition, but you must accept that these people also have something they believe in. It's good to have faith in something, regardless of what that is!" I spoke proudly with a confidence that came from God knows where. A detonation of disagreement consumed the larger outer crowd. So, I spoke out loud again to calm their nerves.

"Listen to what I have to say before revolting!" my vocal cords called. Initially there was little effect, but I waited for a moment. The sphere I held strongly in my hand vibrated eerily and turned a faint blue momentarily. The strange, repeating change occurred in synchronization with a hush from the gathering of people. It amazed me. "Perfect. Why don't I offer up a solution that ought to please us all?" A buzzing excitement kept them quiet. "I have an idea that I think will entertain both sides, here. If we were to, say, kill Jesus, should he not return to life as the son of the true deity, the Lord himself?" I proposed. There was instant outrage. As I continued to speak, I did not hesitate for them to be quiet to assert dominance. "This argument, whether our beliefs are true or not, will tear us apart as a species! It will make or break us and divide us. We cannot continue like this, especially with such bloodshed so early on," I finished for a moment. The sphere vibrated again to shut them up. From the vast collection of heads and hands, one stood out to yell.

"Okay. So, what? We just kill him and hope for the best?" he questioned loud enough for everyone to latch on to the thought.

"No. We let him decide. He'd be the one dying after all. If he continues to breathe after death, then it must be true. There would be no explanation other than that God is real. If his death is permanent, we drop it forever, no longer to be questioned. This debate will cease to torture mankind in this village," I commanded.

I saw hundreds of nodding heads. An unclean ocean of hair bounced together as the folks decided in harmonious unison. The center circle lowered their arms and straightened their bodies upright in mild agreement. A collection of tension emptied suddenly from the air.

The pressure of what felt like thousands of eyes piled upon me. Despite the urge to cower, an inexplicable endowment conquered my fears for me. I shuffled to the group of people that surrounded Jesus, urging them to move closer to their former opposition. They obeyed with mild reluctance. Jesus rose from his keeled position to one knee and then to his feet.

"I accept this proposition," he said with a convincing disappointment, "on the premise that my death is honored," his voice echoed across a barren atmosphere.

"But how exactly?" I questioned. We really did put on a fascinating show. Fiction from what I knew to be magic, science, and acting.

"I will die on the cross at high noon tomorrow," he called to the crowd. "The method of death may be however you choose, but I shall die with my arms outstretched to show grace and the image of a warm embrace to those in need." He hesitated for a moment, sighing gently into the thin air. "If there is nothing I can do to appease the aggression of the non-believers but die, then I will," he paused, looking up to the sky. "But may God help me! I will be restored! I will return and walk the earth with greater lavish than before. If I fail to live beyond certain death, then you may bury your devoted acts to my father, God," he finalized.

It was settled. There were no questions. Luckily, everybody seemed to agree and understood the risk. It was impressive to see so many people have such blind faith, as though they knew the outcome without a sliver of doubt.

Much like ants from a hill, a small portion of the group made haste. Within a few hours a tree had been fallen to begin the construction of something we were all still wrapping our heads around. It all went by rather quickly in a blur. I assisted, too. A shining sun cast its oppressive rays down on us that day as we worked to the end of our wits to put together a piece our masterpiece for our hopeful savior, Jesus. I assisted, too. All I really remember was running back and forth between two places for a short while. That and plenty of time spent cutting wood. A lot of precision went into something so quickly planned. You could honestly tell that these people were putting their heart and soul into this. They, too, begged for an answer to the question I had so often been asking.

Shortly after most of the work had been done, we had little left but to transport the wood. With numerous beads of sweat pulsating against my brow, I helped lift one of the two pieces of weighty lumber above my shoulder to the final site where we were to combine them together and erect our creation, all in a day's work. Most people had vanished back into their lives for the afternoon with an eerie, almost sinister, insouciance.

We arrived at the town square for the second time that day to begin constructing atop the speaker's pedestal. It was delicate but dirty. It was fascinating and cultured, with a grand cross nearly ten feet tall. With boards no thicker than a fat man's thumb and as wide as his torso, the two pieces of wood were bound together in the shape of the letter *T*. The top bar, though, was lowered a few feet. We had to leave room for him to rest his head, even in supposed death. Supported by a few smaller beams, the structure stood with mighty splendor.

We chatted amongst ourselves peacefully for a few minutes to revel in our achievement for a short time before returning to bed as the sun kissed the horizon goodnight.

I wasted no time losing sleep because I knew I had the ability to communicate with God at my call. A little payoff was harmless.

XVII

Adam dictates order and instruction to the mass of light before him using his commanding presence. Words peel from him like a godly being as he controls the events of over two thousand years ago. A rush of adrenaline surges within his veins and his hands stop shaking with a build of confidence. Each phrase he forges can change the world forever. He knows it. He controls it like turning the page of a book. It gets easier every time. The conversation comes to a close with a final word from his worldly, dominant existence.

He finishes his talk with an ancient voice and his eyes open to connect with the screen as he watches the bravery outside unfold. With very little time needed to accelerate, the two heroes steam forward. Now, only ten feet or so behind the Top Four, they link their powerful robotic arms together. The living metal at their fingertips folds and rearranges itself to slide elegantly together to form something new. Now, they fight as one connected colossal unit. Their legs carry them right up to their newfound enemy and they attempt to make a dash forward, lowering the bar that is made of their connected appendages. They prepare to pounce forward in an attempt to sweep from underneath and render the pending threat immobile. Miniscule rockets unfold from the back of their conjoined limb and initiate an explosive propulsion forward.

Sweat emerges from Simon's hands now as he crosses his eyebrows. A dastardly sensitive machine needs only a sneeze to buckle or move in the wrong direction. A mistake would not be easily forgiven.

The target bewilders its enemies with a jump barely high enough to clear the smashing obstacle. One of its four adeptly crafted legs lightly scrapes across the arm-bar and gives birth to a spell of sparks. A light chuckle flies the air from the Top Four. Now, with a position of advantage from behind and above their two attackers, they levitate for a moment. At the end of each impeccably sheen arm a cluster of frazzling light blue energy launches away from the metallic mass toward each opponent. Before the two knightly men have time to react, the bolts of energy sear through the metal on their hulky bodies, tearing away both of their enormous left arms.

"This world deserves salvation if nothing else. Surrender yourselves to us and end your suffering," the Top Four belt out in unison. Still levitating twenty feet above the surface of the dying Earth, they rally up for another shot and take their chance. This time, John and Simon know what's coming and manage to dart outward to leave a trail of blue scar the sand between them. In an attempt to not waste any momentum, they run opposite directions and soon circle back toward either side of the Top Four's devastating machination. John's bot's right-hand transforms almost magically into a whip-like mirage of blue. He flings the whip at the Top Four, ensnaring their bot's feet together, mid-air. Simon speeds around from the other side simultaneously with a series of loud metal clanging, and he leaps forward with one arm cocked back behind him, prepared to attack. In a frenzy of panic, the Top Four stand frozen in the heated environment torn in a dangerous dilemma. Simon's battle machine swings down with its massive arm, fist-first, to instantaneously shatter the protective cockpit that hides the Top Four. Not a second later, John rotates his entire colossus to snap the whip into forcing the Top Four to barrel into the sand with an unheavenly collapse. A haze of sand corrupts their vision for a moment as John retracts his whip and Simon levitates slowly to the ground as they encroach upon their common enemy.

"This is judgment, you bastards," John bellows to their decaying husk.

"I guess you could say you've been deserted," Simon cowls. He snickers to himself behind the powerful microphone.

"Simon, that's not –" John speaks but is cut off by a ruinous blast of force, striking them where they stand. John feels the tremor to his core as every inch of his body rattles like a bag of bones. They soar in opposite directions nearly a hundred meters. With their metallic legs up in the air and shimmering in the sunlight, they skid backward through the mounds of sand. Behind the whirring of their machines and the whisper of the desert, they can make out the call of rage. The voice of reckoning drowns out all else. The searing hot air they take in with every breath becomes irrelevant as their bodies attune to a pulverizing shout.

"You cannot prey on the vigilant!" Trevor roars with prowess. "For this, you will suffer. This ends now!" After a moment of recollection, Simon and John stand using their one arm for support against the brushing winds. They have little difficulty noticing that half of their opponents' protective hub has been smashed clean off.

"You know what? Fuck this guy and his petty friends," Simon communicates in private to John. With almost practiced precision, they each raise their right arm forward. Stern claws shoot into the sandy ground from the bottom of eight total straddling legs. A building, climbing noise emits from both of them with increasing intensity. Rising and rising, the volume grows. The cadence increases indefinitely until John breaks the cycle.

"Agreed." John tells him in response. An ear-splitting explosion fractures the air as they each cast a football-sized missile at supersonic speed toward their target. An instant later, the missiles slam into either side of the belligerent carapace, sending it spinning like a bullet a few feet high through the air. The Top Four's prized possession struggles to react as it slides against the disturbingly smooth terrain. Small vines of dust cough up from the aftermath, but soon clear before the two men approach, encased in armor. They stand tall above the cowering metal carcass, ignoring the deafening ringing bouncing throughout their harassed ears. From the ruin's top side, one can make out several limbs emerging as the sand surrounding the wreckage dampens with red stains. Fingers followed by hands and arms scramble hopelessly from the smoky mess. Severed dark metal scraps lay strewn about carelessly like distraught scratches against the sandy earth.

Simon and John watch as the Top Four struggle to breathe properly in the dusty confusion. A melody of coughs spills out into the quiet arena as they take in the reality of their world through their lungs. The intermittent moments are disturbed by distant calls fueled with rage from Newgrounds. With All Four in view, Simon takes it upon himself to make the first statement. He hesitates, waiting until Samantha and Trevor stop shooting wine-colored streams of fluid from their throats onto the sun-scarred metal.

"I thought you were the glorious leaders of this world," he scoffs. "Faced with imminent death and defeat, what are you now?" he questions his desperate and insect-like victims. A feeling of misguidance stirred gently with victory fills the tips of his fingers, his spine, and his mind.

"Now, we are free," Alex tells him, wrangling with his lungs. "The cycle will end. Whatever you've done now will change the future of our planet," he explains with difficulty.

"This will not go without," Samantha adds on through her blood-soaked lips as an eruption of clotted damage snorts out from her nose, "consequences." She crawls a few inches further forward against razor-sharp shards of disorganized chaos.

From the control room, Adam takes his chance to yell over the engines' disruption through a line of communication.

"Ask them what they would do differently, Simon. What would they do to prevent this cycle from happening again? What hope is there for our world?" he interrogates himself. Simon happily obliges. He shifts some controls with nimble movements to transform the end of his right motor-driven arm into a hand with humanoid fingers.

"So, Alessia, leader of the Top Four, ruler of the broken world," he summons, moving forward with an uncomfortably large extension, "what would you do differently to change the course of humanity? How in this disaster can humans become what they should be?" he demands. The bulky finger pushes against her fairly limp body as she rolls over. With her chest exposed to a glistening sky, she speaks softly.

"The artifact was designed by a power even greater than you can imagine, with powers unseen by our kind. If you can use the divinity sphere in the correct manner, it may be possible for you to restore the human race," she pauses to take a slow breath of mildly toxic air. Her mouth expels a deep hiss for several seconds before she continues. "Therein lies just one problem," she states. John chirps in immediately.

"Which is what exactly?" He shifts forward to tremble the earth and the calamity before him, driving his finger into her side. Squealing in pain from shuffling across the thorny wreck unwillingly, the Top Four cry out. Alessia elaborates after they seize a moment to recollect themselves.

"The amount of energy you would need to open such an artifact is beyond our capabilities–" her voice fades slowly with corrupted inhalations. "It's going to need one hell of a miracle." The final letter falls from her trying lips into a chilling silence.

"Adam, she's gone," Simon relays.

"Yes, well, they made these sacrifices necessary. Just keep the others alive. We're not savages. I'm sure Silver could help!" he answers with haste. John extends the tips of his robot's arm into a smooth car-sized spoon crafted from a billion miniscule shards. Gently, he scoops up the remaining three bodies, softly shoveling them into his cockpit.

"Silver, I know it's tight in here, but I need life support online for the four people. Do what you can to save their sorry souls. If it were up to me, I'd kill you for what you've done. Then again, you guys feel the same way," he talks to the robotic assistance and the three unresponsive bodies with a worrying pride.

"Of course. Life support systems enabled. Oxygen at seventy percent and decreasing. Sir, I recommend getting them back as soon as possible if you are to live," she says calmly. As her words come out, so do several small tubes to stuff up the noses and down the throats of the damaged bodies. A wire comes from the ceiling of the small capsule for each of them to connect to three frayed hands. They fall asleep with seconds. Adam and James are each presented on screen with a facial identification and heart rate of each of the suffering members. With their eyes closed, they fail to respond to any attempts John makes to wake them.

In the emptiness of the aftermath, the four men wait in a breath of relief. They sit tight with their pupils scanning around in a peaceful lack of sound. In a relaxed manner, they each wait for someone else to say something, hoping for direction.

James takes his chance to say something to John and Simon over the microphone.

"Uh, boys," he says.

"Yes?" they both reply.

"The engines..." He waits another second. "They're not happy!" Four beady and somewhat tired eyes dart over to look at the Dawne.

"Fuck!" John calls out.

"For fuck's sake." Simon says quietly as they both observe the supporting pillar formed by the previous robots as it quivers with an unfamiliar uncertainty. The two connected pods, now combined as a beam to hold the massive engines, shake as they come closer to buckling under the pressure. Two of the four men react on impulse as they shoot over there without a moment to think. Spiked metal claws for feet whisk them to the Dawne in seconds, despite it being nearly a kilometer away after the catastrophic combat. A trail of dust puffs up in their wake as they slow down to a halt at the building's base.

"You tired yet?" Simon asks John through a softened blow over the speakers.

"No shit, I am. I thought that would be the end of it!" John responds to him with shallow breaths.

"Well." Simon says with a turning tone of voice, "you thought wrong!" He tells him as the feeling of determination shoots down his spine.

They poise their machines to stand at either side of the newly formed support. In unison, they raise their right arms upward. Forming the image of a vertical pole with their robots, they shove the ends of their arms forward several inches. The swirling mass of mystery on the end of their limbs morphs into a star-spiked plate, sinking its many teeth barely a millimeter into the metal flesh of the engine. As a lock and seal is crafted from the flexible weaponry, they strap in for some time. John and Simon frown as their bodies shake rather violently from the rumble of the engines. They grit their teeth to the thought that the machines they manipulate have become nothing more than stable objects to rest on. Metallic tendrils protrude from the abdomen region of the robots to bore into the somewhat-new center pole between the two of them. From top to bottom, there must be nearly a hundred miniscule attachments that emerge from the two active hunks of machinery as they combine with the support to create a more peaceful use of the pods. Finally, the dangerous feet of their bots extend their claws deep into the shifty sand until they hit something more stable – soil.

"Haha! Isn't that refreshing?" Simon jokes to lighten the mood.

"It would be if we weren't underneath a several thousand-pound nuclear reactor, buddy. If I wasn't literally holding the future of humanity in my hands, I'm sure it would be," John says cheekily and out of breath.

Their attention turns upward again as the rumbling slows down and grinds to a low simmer rather than a bolstering roar.

"Adam!" John seeks action. "What's going on, man? Why are the engines shutting down?" he asks in a heated disagreement with the situation.

"Don't worry, ah, just changing the time-zone lock. Give me one second," Adam reassures them, holding the word 'one' a little longer than he ought to.

"That's alright. We're here now. There are four bots holding the engines, so we should be stable for some time," Simon confirms to the anxious group.

"Perfect. Alright, my fellow gentlemen, let us see what the world has to offer," Adam hesitates for a moment, consumed with hope. "Here we go. Three, two, one," he says with clinched eyebrows and focused facial muscles. Moments after his words enter the air, Simon and John feel a rough vibration writhe through their bodies as their stoic machinations stabilize the enormous turbines.

They smile at each other with a wandering sense of glee that had easily been lost in the battle.

XVIII

Rays of sunlight crested my rooftop as the clouds parted ways for their raw brilliance, revealing an astonishing sea of blue above us. Birds chattered with harmonic joy amongst a soft backing of leaves brushing faintly in the wind. As my head emerged eagerly from the poorly put together doorway, I caught a couple of squirrels hopping inattentively across the main road of the village. With every morning, a smile sneaked onto my face that I could not hold back despite the ever-changing circumstances. The critters seemed happy, too! They passed by the fading stains of coldblooded murder as though they weren't even there. The ecosystem remained consistent as the chords of wildlife danced senselessly about our eardrums.

For nature, this was just another day in the cycle, unordinary.

I can dutifully assure you, however, that it was nothing of the sort. That was the day, I believe anyway, that things were slowly beginning to come together, another highly critical landmark in the map of history that forged our world. I had forgotten all other tasks amid protecting the way forward for our species, for the Lord.

I knew I had become driven solely by a purpose higher than me. To be a piece of such a larger puzzle was enough motivation. I arose later than usual for the morning, though. 'Most likely,' I thought, 'due to such a lack of sleep recently. Good thing, too. I would need my energy to be ready for what is coming next.' I waited for a short while before midday to make my way down to the town square to our divine creation, an orchestrated tool of peaceful passing.

It was almost like a form of mutually assured destruction because we knew that at least one side of the argument was doomed regardless of the outcome. I felt the fear in the air, of that reality that no situation could occur in which both Jesus and the future of the human race could remain perfectly intact.

Even if Jesus survived, what is then left of us? Were we herding husks of meat or carapaces of carpenters and couriers? Had we become decaying minds of the meek and merry? It seemed too good to be true that everyone could walk away happy.

I prayed that the Lord could make it so.

The almighty star was failing in its continuous task of piercing the clouds. The air grew with tension like rabid roots under a young, careless forest. A ball of fire bigger than we could have ever imagined rose to the tiptop of its perfect and repetitive arc, nothing could see clearly through the encroaching fog. Daylight became mystified and gray as the time drew near.

They came by the tens at first. It seemed that the population of the village was doubling minute by minute. Sprouting like trees edging from newborn plains, they appeared. They herded forward to get closer and closer to one another to observe the coming sufferance before them. The calf was left alone. There was this baby squirrel that knew no better. The hunted was weak here under the scrutiny of so many watchful preying eyes. Natural selection had come to take its course as the fit thrived on outclassing the weak. Humble and alone, Jesus arrived at the square.

You could tell outright that the eyes in the settling mist were here simply for the spectacle, a show put on by a 'willing' participant. But what were to be the tools of his destruction? The watchers stopped their movements to observe his. Lonely footsteps echoed across a damp and stone-cold arena. At first, it sounded of two rocks being gently smashed together. It changed as he monotonously and steadily creaked the wooden steps to the altar. Most gawked angrily, a pack waiting to pounce.

There was one thing that needed to be clarified before the moment of his death, though.

"How will you kill him, then?" one absurdly hungry member called out.

"I don't care. I just wanna see blood," another voice claimed almost discreetly.

"Hey, fuck you. That's our leader up there. He'll come back. Just you watch!" an active crowd-goer yelled. A participant of the crew that helped to build the cross rose to the altar with me and reached behind to pick up some spare nails that were left unused.

"We will nail him to the cross with these dirty leftover nails. If the penetration does not kill him right away, infection will soon have its way," he said. With this statement, many eyes winced at the thought. All the while, some of the bloodthirsty continued to bare dull, uneducated teeth. Now joined with us atop the stand, Jesus spoke softly.

"I do this for you, father. I do this for the sanity and safety of our kind. May God bless your souls!" he ended his final call. The last five words were much louder and carried far through the valley for seconds after. The humbled animal had no more actions to take and no more noises to make other than to die. He took his fingers and held two of them upright.

He tapped his forehead. He tapped the center of his chest. He tapped above his left nipple. He tapped above his right nipple. It must have seemed meaningless to the slaughterous crowd, but I noticed, and so did a few other believers.

The cross.

He formed a cross in the air on his body as though to protect him, as though all of this was real. It was becoming a way of life. It was breathing a normative culture for so many.

A small stool had been brought to the altar for Jesus to stand on so that he could be more aligned with the enormous cross. This was, for too many, nothing more than a show. He placed his feet on it and pushed upward and turned to face the crowd. His arms rose to become parallel with the floor and he looked to the side in pure embarrassment. He had rosy cheeks and was somewhat naked. He was picture-perfect. Excellent! It was better than I could have imagined. I tried not to smile but mildly failed.

I locked eyes with the man I'd met yesterday as we each stood with rusty nails in one hand and a small hammer-like creation in the other. We nodded toward each other and placed a nail in the palm of the poor man's hands. With little regret I pushed forward with one hand and began to hammer relentlessly with the other. They all watched as the suffering started.

Initially, it was just a deep wince in an effort to handle the pain, but it soon grew far from a tolerable range. The village and its outskirts for some miles were consecrated with the screaming of pain. Every contact was an event that lasted longer than the moment of force. The echo was followed each time by a cheap gasp from the herd. But soon enough, a wince wasn't enough as he howled. He screamed louder with deeper penetration. The sharp point was driven deeper through the flesh. Blood began to spurt out in regulated bursts all over me and the wooden support. It started to get in the way and I was annoyed. I had to start twisting it to get it to go through the bone. I heard a crack and almost paused, but my devotion to the Lord kept me focused. I thought I knew the pain I was causing him. I kept hammering without remorse. The pain mattered not because there was a goal, a purpose. Thick, familiar streams of color fired off mercilessly as his body began to wish for a swifter death. It was done again and again. *Smack, smack.* There was endless crunching and juicing. I slammed the rock harder and harder against a squishy and reluctant opening. Each pulse spread more of the liquid across my hands and his. What had begun as a series of isolated events had become one continuous utter cry for help. Agony tore the flesh from his bone as we dug further and further. We ripped his hand almost in two and I felt the resistance of the wood behind it. I had made it. 'It can only get easier,' I thought.

I had never been more wrong. The seeping fog decided to clear a little with the final few pushes of rock to nail, revealing the entire audience to us. One final thrust sank the entirety of the nail through his helpless flesh. With a waterfall of blood leaking from either side of him, he hung there lifeless. The mist continued to clear. We watched it evaporate slowly as the mass of people stood expressionless before a truly wretched sight. Dripping blood filled an awkward yet disgustingly fulfilling silence. Why did we feel satisfied? I had no acceptable answer. Perhaps I was afraid to admit to anything. I watched as the last of the crowd members were revealed with an outward brush of nature's blinding vapor. I had to wipe my eyes from the bloodstains because my vision was blurred with tears. As my eyes cleared, I had to be sure of what I was seeing. I thought it impossible.

She had the fairest face for miles and miles. She wore true beauty. It had been so long. I felt hopeless without her. I looked across hundreds of people, but there was only one who concerned me. With hair that trickled down her shoulder like a blessing from above and with eyes that would make the moon jealous of their sheen, she was completely incomparable. The love of my life walked into town with a minute posse of other women. They had returned from their year-long venture safely and there I was, holding a stick with a rock on it, coated in the blood of a hanging corpse, a corpse that every person we knew was staring at. You could say I had some explaining to do.

The screams were immediate, likely because they were the only ones who didn't know what was happening. It made things very awkward for the rest of us. The small gathering of females danced about, frantically shaking their hands and crying out for help or an explanation. I felt like I had betrayed her. She stood steady among her brethren and looked me dead in the eye. The confidence that woman exuded took my damn breath away. In the period of time that they had been away gathering exotics our world had been turned upside down. I looked an absolute fool with my mouth wide open, with hands still sopping wet, dripping with thick clots of blood, but I yelled anyway.

"Silence!" I ordered. It had little effect on the squabbling group. "Bring the ladies this way. An explanation is due to these fine women." I called. Within minutes, the bountiful harvest they had brought was taken to be sorted. I took a minute to rinse my hands off with some water and picked up my precious orb as I waited for the collection of alienated women. They were given water and food to calm their nerves as much as possible. Following myself, the envoy of ladies was escorted to the field where I could explain everything in a more peaceful setting. We pushed through the village to the other side. Marching upon the center trail, I held a dark silence. Footsteps clicked through streets they thought they knew, now stained a ruined red.

A few shrieks were let out as we passed the tattered remains of Judas' speared corpse on the edge of the field. I brought them to the clearing and sat them down and began spinning and weaving the tale. I dared not speak to my lover separately from the rest of them in the case that any drama was to appear within their group. A glorious sun blessed us as we talked. I unpacked everything, everything from the strange crack that started it all to the voice that was behind it. I unveiled all I knew about the object it had given me, more specifically the Bible. I neglected mentioning the divine-like sphere, for I feared it was too powerful, and I still did not understand it yet. I went on further about the beliefs the book held and what God had promised us in return for following His orders – peace. There were some tears and angry shouts as I delved further into why bloodshed had been so hasty to appear recently.

As I went on, I had begun feeling as though so much more had happened than even I had realized. It was a rush. It was consuming, but so lovable. I could understand their disgust. However, I did not agree with it. A transformation I refused to acknowledge was already deep underway and with each beautiful second in this tunnel, I was ecstatic to dive further in.

It must have consumed over an hour of our time before I stopped talking. I was relieved and somewhat flooded with a sensation of personal pride that I had been able to introduce relative newcomers to our religion, to our God.

"… And that's why we had to kill him," I paused. "It wasn't murder. It was a test and a sacrifice," I explained.

My lips conceded to the end of the story to date as the final pieces of information were put together in their minds like a puzzle being finally fit for once. A spur of hesitation came about me as I awaited a collection of questions to fall upon my weary soul.

"So, I get it. You had to kill the Jesus guy to see if God's magical powers are real. That, to me, makes sense. What is it, though, that you are actually believing in? Is it the existence of God? Or the belief that you can use His powers to exploit for your own good by 'pleasing' Him through rather unusual practices?" one of the ladies fired at me.

'Fuck!' I thought.

I wanted to tell her honestly that it was simply the existence of a higher being and purpose to follow. And peace, right. I wish that I could have told her it was for more than personal righteousness. A slimy spear of shadow was stuck in my throat. As I attempted to remove it, I could feel its cursing touch contract the muscles in my throat. I was trapped in a verbal cage. As the silence grew longer, I felt that they knew something was up. I had to think of my feet. I simply wouldn't have had it if they weren't totally convinced, not after everything we'd been through already. I caressed the orb in my fingers lightly.

It brought incomparable confidence to my meekness. My brain was writing a response while my throat tried to clear the clumpy obstruction. The milliseconds evolved, coming closer and closer together. Then, in an instant, I had found the perfect response. It flowed through my fingers and dashed to my mind to form concrete thought.

"Ladies, what we have discovered here is for the good of all of mankind. We believe in a being that gives us direction to unify people and encourage peace, the sort of peace that will extend through the ages and protect us from any further conflict," I explained as calmly as I could.

"Be honest with us. How well has that really worked so far?" another one of the women fired back. I had to appease the aggression. Back pedaling was not an option.

"There have been... necessary sacrifices. You must understand that nothing good comes easily. We had to ensure that everyone was on the same page and that rebellion wouldn't be tolerated either. It breaks my heart, too, to see the life drain from innocent eyes. But I would rather witness that than massive internal conflict in the future," I attempted to elaborate deeper.

"Alright," my lover spoke among her feeble follower group, "so what or who has given you this idea that we are bound to kill ourselves in the future? Why do we need extraordinary measures to prevent it? I couldn't imagine that happening, not with the people we have here. It seems a bit farfetched, this whole thing. We have no proof, my love." My heart pounded louder than her words could have for a second as she spoke. "Give us something, and we will believe you. I will, at least, believe it all with a little more concrete evidence," she requested. Her herd of humble sheep quivered silently behind her, nodding slightly.

"Okay, then." I didn't want to show God's presence around like a trophy, but admittedly, it was better than yet another round of bloodshed. "You want proof? Follow me," I barked rather rapidly. Several legs rose up from the patted ground. They obliged and followed me as we marched single file. It was a much shorter distance this time, though, as we came to a halt in front of my house.

"You've just taken us home, my dear," she said flatly. "I thought you said the crack stopped?" Her eyes widened. I knew I was in trouble. I could see it writhing through her face as she said sternly, "What have you done?"

"Well, umm, there isn't *really* a good way of putting this. It's probably better I just show you," I said, infested with a little fear.

A sinister shiver sauntered down my spine as I entered the place I called my own. A sense I had become thirsty for heightened. The knowledge that I would have the chance to please the Lord once more filled my naughty little fingers with joy. We entered my sleeping chamber and I rearranged a few things quickly to make room for seating as there had been before. I moved the ladies to their appropriate spots for them to enjoy the most beautiful sight of their lives. We formed an empty column down the middle, with people in rows on either side, just like last time. Nearly twenty new faces presented themselves to the currently empty crack in the wall. A few looks of confusion were exchanged throughout the room, but there was one pair of eyes that held strong. The time had come. It was now or never. I squeezed my fingers on the orb exactly how God had taught me to establish a connection and my eyes widened. I prepared myself for the rush. My fingers released their squeezing grip somewhat from the sealed button on the impressive object.

A faint whisper began to harmonize in the air. The noise emanated from the crack subtly at first, but it soon dilated to something much greater in stature. My ears smiled for me. Instantly, I was happier. A few seconds passed by. The sound thrived, reaching a more stable state. I recognized its perfection when it peaked, a plateau of utter stillness. I was ready for him.

"Ladies, this is God. The architect of our world. Our supreme leader. The One Being," I spoke with a pride I knew was dangerous.

The bold blue mist oozed gently from the wall, satisfyingly filling the room little by little. It took a few seconds to process what I had said. Not long after, His divine voice echoed as music to my ears.

XIX

Adam stares at his marvelous construct, confounded with confusion for a moment. Why must he introduce himself once again to more followers? This isn't how things are meant to be, he thinks to himself. Regardless, he must play along to prevent even the smallest sliver of suspicion.

"Welcome, ladies. I am God, the fabled being," he introduces himself kindly. "I must say I'm surprised you haven't been introduced to my religion. How exactly have you found yourselves lost in a transforming world?" he ricochets. A light gasp can be heard through the portal. His vocal cords reverberate with a certain essence of foretelling power. Adam considers himself fortunate to have such a flexible presence. He thinks to himself, given that everything he knows and does is a construct of his own doing, perhaps he truly is divine.

A pauper speech comes back in return.

"They have been traveling, my Lord. Forgive me for not cultivating them to your practices earlier. These kind women here have been searching for new places, foods, and plants. An exploration team, if you will. They've been absent for some time, even before my first encounter with yourself," a male voice says.

"So, what are you then? This must be some sort of light trick. An illusion or trap even. Are we being hunted?" a higher, more panicky voice trembles through time.

Adam needs not pause for reflection. He already knows what he is, through and through. He had no doubts and was ready to prove that they shouldn't either.

"To put you at ease, I am also of human form. I created man in my image, and I contact you now to encourage the spread of belief in my existence. For unity and, ultimately, peace. I created all that is around you – the trees, the fruit, the birds, and the bees. I can tell you far more about your world than you already know. I have seen alternate futures. They have the potential to ruin an entire species, entire worlds even. I'm here to prevent that. This is no trap or illusion, just your creator asking for cooperation to create a better world, a better future, for the human race," he explains relatively simply. With every time-altering word he delivers, the spark inside him dances happily, evolving further into a self-sustaining fire.

A pause hovers closely in the air for a short time before words extend from the other side once again.

"Okay, so you just existed this whole time? You never intervened when people we knew were dying, or the crops failed to flourish. Why? I'm not convinced that you are who you say you are," a stern female voice pounds through the space-time continuum. That voice, Adam thinks, is oddly familiar. No, it isn't the same. This lady speaks with inexperience. It can't be. "All of this is very impressive, but if you are so incredibly powerful… why exactly do you need our help?" a solid question stings the air as he stares into a swirling abyss. He knows that he has his own concoctions in mind, but they are far from fruition yet. Still, in the back of his mind, he questions whether he knows that voice.

A chill sneakily strikes the full length of his spine. Brewing in his mind are the many reasons he should request help and he takes a few moments to carefully select the right one.

"I don't contact you purely for protecting the future of your species. I also aspire to create a world where people have a reason to act appropriately and kindly to one another. It has to start somewhere," he delivers. "Any further questions you have can be directed to the young man before you once you have read the holy text. Waste no time, and if you don't mind, I'd like to talk with him," Adam instructs. Little to no change in sound haunts him for a moment until he speaks up in finality. "Alone!" his lungs burst out. A meager few seconds scoot by as the sound of several people hushing one another, rushing to escape, emits from the collective mass.

"Tell me, my child. Where are we? Tell me you have made progress," Adam says with a fleeting condescendence.

"Yes, Lord. Jesus is being moved to a chamber for his death as we speak. He was crucified earlier today, exactly as instructed in the Bible," the manly voice responds. "The task at hand requires something from you… We need to bring him back to life now. I don't really know how to do that…" the voice pauses and then whispers, "without you."

"Understandable. Give me a minute to prepare something for you," Adam says calmly. He swings his body around. "mute us" He mouths to James A swift swish of his companion's nimble fingers orders the computer to materialize a hazy glasslike barrier between themselves and the mystical whirlpool.

"James, I need the planet souls now," Adam's throat contracts the tiniest of measurements as he attempts to rest easy.

"Already on it, my friend." James says as he walks over to Adam, holding a circular veil with two gently cusped hands. Adam places his in a similar manner beneath James' bowl and James separates his fingers, allowing the mystery to slide through his fingers and into Adam's.

"Look, buddy," James lets a minute blast of air release from his nostrils, briefly looking to the side, "we don't know a lot about where this came from... All we know is what the messenger told us about another dimension. This puts another variable into our already-impossible situation. Are you sure you're okay with this?" His eyebrows rise as he shoots a horrifying gaze into Adam's experienced eyes.

"I am," he replies. "Let's pray it works," he adds, chuckling at the vanity of succumbing to prayers over science. James looks at him again, narrowing the center of his eyebrows toward his nose. Adam breathes in quickly as the object slides completely into his hands, giving him full control. A gooey mess of guilt and fear finds a momentary home in Adam's heart but is quickly repressed. James waves his fingers once again to remove the translucent wall.

"This is," Adam peers into cupped palms, sighing under his breath, "an object forged by the angels of heaven." He rolls his eyes. "It has the power to restore life and reanimate a corpse," he speaks slowly, barely convinced even half of what he said is true. "You must be incredibly careful with it. It is the definition of fragile. Dropping this object could alter things in a way that even I cannot understand," he continues as beads of sweat make an attempt to spawn on his forehead. "You will take one of these objects and place it on Jesus' corpse and soak it with the hottest water you can find. You must not be seen, though. It must be an act of God. I will give you two, in case you... lose one." Adam hammers back down on himself, knowing all too well the complications of emotions and human error.

"Okay, so, don't drop it and hot water. I can do that," the voice echoes back through time.

"Cup your hands in front of the portal. I'm sending it to you now," Adam guides. A several-seconds pause sits heavy. "Are you ready, my child?"

"Yes, I am ready for your gift of life," he says with a bright passion. Adam opens his closed hands to reveal two miniscule cubes, dark but blue. Their color changes similar to that of a chameleon, but faster. They sit in his hand as though being wrapped and unwrapped simultaneously with black and azure-blue ribbons. The surface appearance of the cubes demonstrates an ever-changing display to a world so much grander than itself. A constantly evolving sheet fails to stop as though it actively conceals a more important entity. An energy of unknown origin simmers delicately through his hands. Adam wonders for a second how they arrived in that backpack. The orbs simmer with a vibration but more alive. It is as if they are of an otherworldly design. Adam stands up and shuffles directly beside the impressive concoction. He proceeds by shaping his hands into a plate, sliding the object into the portal without the need of a nudge. The mesmerizing cubes drop together from the grip of his hands and into the mixed mesh of varying blue energy. They greet the impressive gateway with the sound one would hear from a droplet of water meeting a still pond. A satisfying plop pads the taunted air for an instant of childish joy.

"I'll make contact with you again once you've resurrected my son and truly convinced every one of my power." Adam shivers nimbly. Both men in the room perform some waving magic with their hands and close down the bridge through time. The delicate haze evaporates from the room. Eyes rest to look toward the floor with a thankful and hopeful moment of silence.

A setting sun fires off tepid beams of light to shred through the glass, warming the back of both of their necks. With a pleasant run of sunlight caressing their rear sides, James speaks up to break the moment of weakness.

"Hey, Adam. I know we planned on being able to work through the night, but we've got a problem." He clutches to what remains of a moment of deep social energy. His fingers skip across the holographic keyboard in such a way that illuminates the darkening room. A bright amber message clings to the molecules of air around them:

FUEL REMAINING: 93L. 100L/hr = 0.93 Hrs run-time remain.

"We don't have enough fuel to make it to the morning, especially if we continue communications this often. We have to take a break and figure out what the fuck we're gonna do. There just isn't enough fuel to keep up comms for so long, Adam," he elaborates on a pressing issue, swinging his chair around to face the bent-over figure. Adam pauses briefly, thankful.

"Okay," Adam breathes out with a clenched face. "I am SO tired of shit going wrong today. Every time we fix something or try something new, another problem pops up." He feels his muscles tighten. His body, in tune with his mind, contracts, synching up any loose slack. "Why can't we just have a series of events that goes smoothly, for Christ's sake!?" He gyrates to face outward and begins a wrath-ridden path to the flat wall of glass. His distorted face soaks up a ginger tint of sunlight from a raging outdoor scene. He notices, among other things, the extended channel of human figures rooting itself at the lowermost section of the tower. "And you little shits!" he screams, allowing a deeper voice to run wild, "why can't you just be grateful for this opportunity like normal fucking people?" His boisterous lungs propel. With a mind on the loose, he watches a scrambling mess of members attempting to break in. A few deep breaths ricochet from the silky glass. "James," he calls, watching the sun fall in the same manner as his grasp on control, slipping away so slowly that he won't notice until he does.

"Yeah, what's up, man?" James asks.

"I don't know how much longer I can do this," he vents. The faintest notion of a tear surfaces on his right eye. "I just want her back. Fuck. It's been so long without…" a voice crack spikes.

"Let it out. You can't keep this bottled up." James bounces from his chair to join him. "We've got some time now to relax for a second. Maybe we can breathe without having everything shoved down our throats for a minute, hey?"

"I know we've only been working for, like, less than a day," Adam spurts. He leans forward against the glass with one hand. "But I feel like we've been here for fucking ages, and still, nothing."

"Adam, I know you wouldn't have dared to take this on if you knew you couldn't," James explains.

"Yeah, but I –" Adam tries to get in. A tear comes to life in his other eye, as both seem decently glazed and starved.

"No. Buddy, listen to me," James takes over. "I understand you lost your world to the system we now dedicate our lives to. I don't know that pain, and neither do most people. You lost everything, but look at how far you've come," James continues.

"Wow!" Adam breathes. "Thanks, James," he says.

"I'm not done." James assures him as they both watch the sun sink into the ground. "The emotion and reasoning you have behind this are both so much greater than anyone else. Your life has pretty much been created for this. I believe in you. And if anyone is to be 'god,' per se, it should be you." James places a comforting hand on Adam's shoulder as they observe the ensnaring orange glow. The remnants of a sun's path fill the sky with a delicacy they enjoy for a few moments amongst the spewing emotional remarks.

Adam attempts to bring a halt to his emotion, bearing the weight of a guilty conscience. He thinks of nothing other than how wrong this is and what his friend is doing for him. The second greatest companion of his current life has such trust in him. In a state of falling powerlessness, he feels a tinge of power in one aspect of a desperate situation. What little fire burns within him, after an internal downpour, connects to ignite a spark. A consuming wave of deeper emotions shudders throughout his bones. He holds himself back from acting on them. Like a broken record snapped in half, his mind twitches. Thoughts careen through his complicated mind, thoughts that race like horses, but those horses are being poked and prodded with scorching hot sticks only to make them run faster. Adam prays to himself that he can hold back from betraying a brother. A conversation stirs within him as he looks over his elbow to the dying sunset. 'Do it. Don't do it. Just fucking do it already.'

The colors combine and dissociate rapidly, every heartbeat and every pulse. The oranges and browns swirl to a culmination of aggressive red and hate-bearing black.

'He's been so nice. Don't hurt him. He's gonna help you finish the job! No, there is a plan and it must be followed for the construction of a perfect world. NO, his loyalty has served too well.'

A linear collection of explosions triggers within him one by one. Like naval mines left dormant for too long they rocket into a cataclysmic chain.

'Leave him alone. He's done nothing but good by you all this time. If he survives until the end, he'll stop you from making things right with Evelyn, which can't happen. AGH!'

"Ughh!" he cries out in agony. "Fine!" he screams into the smudged glass. In a moment of self-retribution, he wipes away the tears. His elbow lowers from leaning on the window as he uprights himself, turning to face a smiling, innocent James.

"You can tell me anything, man. Come on, let it out," James reassures him. Adam's gaze focuses on James' face, but it matters not. He has already made his decision.

"You," Adam mutters, barely audible. He takes a small step forward, closing the distance between himself and the lanky man.

"You are the best friend I could have ever asked for," he sniffles. "Thank you," he reconciles, extending his arms in a strange entwinement of relief and disappointment.

"Of course." James replies to him with the honest belief that the physical embrace is out of thankfulness.

A small de-escalation commences between them as the two negotiate and resolve for a few short minutes. The final beams of the sunset's light vacate the room, but not before the evening lights turn themselves on. A grand show of mainly white bulbs cast an art form of light into the room, making it seem like daytime once again inside the Dawne.

The seizing chill of the night strikes as darkness falls. The threadbare trail of angered citizens reduces in size significantly. Many of its members return to their residences for the night, but there remains a sizeable group of nocturnal powerless arbiters. The last trickles of hopeful folks scuttle back to their homes, or a nighttime shelter, for the evening. The overnight fighters ignite torches and collect blankets to keep themselves fueled for vengeance. Their attempts at belittling such a stoic structure fail to cause any damage or real commotion. Their clanging voices die off in a black distance. They are nothing compared to the godlike blacksmiths that lie high in a warm, well-lit room.

XX

In a dashing display of blue and black ribbons, the small cube-like things were constantly changing in my hands. I gripped firmly to the delicate pair, fearing subtly for my life. As my fingers soldered themselves desperately to the complicated set, I nodded in mellow content. I exchanged final words with the holy voice. My heart trembled in a minor episode of separation anxiety as the connection with God faded to nothing, as per a growing norm. I was alone in my room while the ladies were waiting outside. I found the loneliness somewhat regenerative. It did not compare, however, to the nights I waited. I did so with painful endurance longing for my one and only fair lady. I was careful to place them underneath a burlap sack by my cot so that it was stable enough for me to leave alone. As much as I tried to keep my hands still, they bounced gently with unfounded energy that I could only assume was nervousness.

With an overwhelming sense of responsibility resting invisibly on my shoulders, I left the room to confront the awaiting posse. Our feet tackled the mulchy ground between links of a cold and stony path with soft crunches as we discussed the odds and ends of the situation. Walking down to drop people off at their residences one by one, we ensured each of the women had their proper share of the plethora of resources they had brought back. The day was beginning to collapse, and I escorted my love to our dwelling for the evening, informing her that I had some important matters to take care of. I'd only been gone for just under a couple of hours from the plaza but had forgotten to give any instructions to the other of my disciples on what to do with the body. With urgent strides, I darted back to the square as the sunset caved in. I returned to find several trustworthy members, Preston included. They were making efforts at keeping people from gawking absentmindedly at the bloodstained corpse. The feet of the corpse must also have been taken care of, I saw, as they too were masochistically sewn to the wooden boards. A crown of thorns lay atop his head. The complete image the Bible had described for us was fulfilled.

"Right, fellas. Where to, then?" Preston asked as we made humble attempts to protect the privacy of our savior. I wasn't as grateful this time to be by his side again.

"Everyone on one end, tilt it flat. I'll lead," I confirmed. I told the others they could leave. 'Four able-bodied men,' I thought, 'would have little trouble moving the rather abstract shape.' "And! Lift!" I shouted through the darkening evening. Initially, after lifting the cross, we marched in silence. I admit I was definitely wrong about the estimation of the weight of that thing. Regular conversation soon struck about as we hoped to pass the time faster. We did, however, take a break every five or six minutes to rest.

With legs aching through the obfuscating sky, we panted in a moderate state of breathlessness. We'd trudged on for over an hour out of town. I was lucky to have them trust me as much as they did. The last few hundred meters crippled me. I could only imagine the others felt it too – the pulsating muscles, the vibrating beads of sweat, and the dry feeling that came with each numbing breath. We were going delirious on an overnight journey to a site I knew would be just perfect.

We arrived under a lambent moon that cast light and shadow alike upon the eerie forest. The colors of the mournful scene had faded to little else than a binary pattern. To me, everything was black and white. Wiping a hovering sweat from my brow, I lowered the carcass with the rest of them. We stared for a blank moment at the cracked, imperfect circle of stone. It stood before a jet-black cave opening almost equivalent in size. Each of its chips, dents, and other deformities were highlighted in breaching white beams from above. A small nook was to be found to the right of the enormous circular rock, thanks to God's gracious gift of flooding moonlight. With an illuminated path, our feet treaded over the mud and messy gravel toward the tight opening.

"We'll have to, uh, tilt him on his side." I ordered. We counted to three, twisting the falsely dubbed culpable carapace a full quarter-turn. Blood oozed from the spikes that tore between his dead skin and the wood. It dripped onto the dry ground, unsettling the cadence of our shuffling feet. I could feel them wincing with each deafening drop. The ticking of the toll of fatigue constricted our limited movements as balls of bloody liquid fell to connect with a smoothened surface beneath us. The haunting echoes of his wrongly caused suffering manipulated the sounds of the night until we made it inside. A staggering impression of darkness rapidly consumed our pupils as all senses of direction dwindled. We moved a few feet further in as the blackness encompassed everything.

"That should do it." I spoke in an echoic whisper. My shoulder muscles strained, bubbling with the tiniest molecules of sweat. The carved log lowered to the stone-cold ground with a group effort.

"So, we just leave him here? That seems a bit wrong. Don't you think?" Preston questioned. I had to think on my feet again. Why would we leave him here?

With some practice I had grown better at such a cunning skill and piped up through the dark and dreary emptiness.

"It's probably best that he has an open space, free of earth-crawling insects and preying birds, for him to decay. I pray, though, that he will resurrect and bring a purpose to this life, to our lives. Come on. We best leave him be," I answered with an instruction. With a final taunting comment, we disappeared from the uncanny chamber.

A scandalous amount of grunting, puffing, and shoving between four seemingly powerful men managed to get the stone to roll over the opening, sealing Jesus in from the outside world. Little was to be said on the hike back. What took one hour on the way out required only forty or so minutes on the return journey, but even in that time, I had noticed the difference in the atmosphere. Without the guidance of Jesus, the moonlight glowed one shade dimmer. The colors of foliage and rocks were one shade darker. As if the black and white of a lifeless world could get any darker, I feared that it would all slip away to black. I developed a crippling bone of dismay within me. As it slithered through my spine, I asked myself over and over whether the world would emerge safely. If, somehow, this plan crumbled, what would be left of me? What would be left of us? This feeling of requirement was satisfying with the presence of something real, but rather hollow without a material answer. It was so hollow, in fact, that the only clear and logical solution was to make up for the lack of materialistic support. The idea of preaching was born in that sense.

Every aspect of this religion became something contrived from a coincidence or a whim. I knew the faith was doing me well because I felt like a better person for it. Maybe, perhaps, just maybe there was a destructive tendency hidden within. 'It is irrelevant,' I thought, 'because I have belief in something so much purer than myself.' However, my spirits were defeated in the absence of Jesus. A knot in my core felt battered and ruined knowing that he was dead. It wasn't the fact that I had to carry the weight by myself, but the further lack of evidence that it could all be real.

I would sit at the corner of streets with people in the evening as the rare non-believer would pass by and we'd shout at them for disagreeing, for having a different viewpoint. We'd follow them down the road screaming about how not believing was a sin and how they'd suffer for it. Our voices would echo the words of the Lord in combined chorus, informing people how their choices were judged, and they will always be under the scrutiny of God. It wasn't perfect. None of it was, but we thought it was okay.

I got back home that night after some small talk with the boys. I arrived in the early hours of the morning to a wonderful woman lying on the floor, sprawled out. I wished to lie with her as I had done so many times before, but I knew that God wished against it. I slept by myself that night, in minor pain, knowing I could not hold my fair lady through the night. My eyes closed. I was shattered. My faith slithered further around my pinky finger.

The moon sank through the remainder of the night to trade places with a crispy morning sun. My investigative eyes opened to her sitting beside me. A creation of her hair's own making sat atop her head in a frazzling display. Still, I found her alluring. I noticed her hand sailing up and down my back as my eyes opened fully, and I smiled at her. She smiled back happily. A perfectly placed beam of sunlight broke through the doorway to light her gorgeous face. It made the messy nest of hair look like a heaven I had yet to reach. Relaxing and satisfying, I lay there calmly as her warm fingers kept me comfortable.

"We need to talk," she said. A spike of anxiety nipped my heart.

No man ever wanted to hear those four words from his lady. Luckily, she spoke before my mind had time to frantically shake itself apart.

I lifted my eyelids and eyebrows and I was fairly sure that even my forehead moved up a little in attendance.

"Why didn't you sleep with me last night, honey?" she inquired. I had to hold back my immediate thoughts and ponder for a second, debating to myself on the right choice of words.

"Darling, I love you, and always will, but the Lord controls our world. We cannot lie together until bound by marriage. You are the best thing in my life, but I'm afraid of what could happen if we disobey his word," I explained slowly. Her hands trickled up and down through my hair. As relaxing as it was, I waited for a response. She spoke as the birds began to sing in the distance, chirping away the morning stillness.

"I understand your passion and deep-seated love for this newfound God. The stories check out, for the most part. I just don't want this to get in the way of us, you know?" she paused for a moment to peck my forehead with her perfect sweet lips. "I will support you, but I don't want to lose you," she said with a suffering smile.

"I know, sweetie, and I know that it's probably a huge change for you, with being away for much of it. You'll soon see. When I prove to the world that this isn't just some ruse, we can all rejoice. Once Jesus comes back, arms wide with forgiveness, we will all owe our lives to him," I delivered gently. She looked into my eyes the same way I stared into hers. I could feel, as our hands linked together, the syncopated heartbeats. I moved my neck up to kiss her, and the world melted into calming images. My mind flooded with a consuming sense of love I knew only from one other source.

As the next couple of days flickered by, a dreadful pressure wedged itself between those who chose to believe and those who were still not convinced. There was a simple cycle. It went sunrise, sunset, repeat. I made every effort to continue the concealment of the odd objects that I had been given by God. The curiosity within me begged me to examine it. I knew, however, that my fear of the unknown was not as important as saving my species.

On the third hallow night I made myself mobile in the direction of the cave. I scooped up one of the mysterious cubes in the sack I had covered it in, leaving one behind, and set out for the man himself. On my way out of the village I acquired a pail for some water and some small fletched sticks for firewood. Pushing through the dew-ridden branches and plots of mud in the path by myself was far less entertaining than with my friends. A rigid sense of loneliness blanketed the journey. I marched on, regardless. After every few footsteps, I began to wonder, as my mind had nothing else to occupy itself with. It ran off on its own adventure. The crippling chill of being alone was beginning to ease its way into my life far more often than I would have liked. I must have been granted a pot of gold's worth of luck to have been entrusted with a lover. I feared for my life that had I not had her, I would have been much more enamored by this mission. I was peacefully content with having her to guard me from this consuming aberration. I wasn't too invested. Of course, that was what I thought. Thinking of the conversation I'd had the other morning, my thoughts began to churn to a boiling agitation. I wasn't falling. I wasn't losing myself. I knew that, and the more I told to myself, the more real it began to feel. A consistent falsity, with enough practice, could become a reality. Case in point: this.

An alpine moon put me at rest with a deepened lack of colors for my surroundings. My heart pumped wildly as my hands grew slightly damp in excitement. The world was about to finally realize the true power of the Lord. I pushed on to the clearing before the cave and stared at its decaying glory, riddled with a form of ecstasy that was mediated by hope. My mind was jumping and bouncing around like never before and I could feel it intensely. The excitement was soon quelled, though, as I stood before the enormous circular stone wondering how I was going to get through to the other side. Bathing in a rich, but subtle, moonlight, I ogled aimlessly. What was I supposed to do? In my momentary defeat, I decided to use the time to fill the pail I'd brought with water and start a fire to bring it up to temperature. Not twenty minutes later, I was standing beside a crackling source of illumination and warmth. With another hefty stick I'd found from the forest, I suspended the water for some time as steam showed the faintest of appearances, unfolding from the still bucket. My arms started to ache several minutes in, but the pain was worth it. I didn't know it would have taken this long, but fuck, I wish I did. The muscles in my arm cramped to accompany my solitude. An agonizing sear of pain jolted through me occasionally. It found a fiery home in my shoulder and I winced, sweating from heat and exhaustion. I forced myself not to call out to the wilderness in pain. It was important to remain strong and silent in light of Jesus' sacrifice. Every moment was utter torment.

Finally, the evil-looking liquid was beginning to come to life. An agitation on its surface evolved into a constant simmer and, after what felt like hours, a bubbling beauty. While I was enduring the cackling call of that taunting bucket, I had time to think about how I was going to get through the door-like covering in front of the cave. In the disturbing fire of anguish, I had considered a few possibilities, quickly dismissing one after the other, but I became very fond of one idea in particular. After putting the pail of boiling water down, I rushed over to the wall-like rock.

I took the oversized stick that I had been using to hold the bucket with and lodged it between the ground and the underside of the stone. Wrenching heavily with already-sore muscles, I rammed the wood deep into the space between the two and then pulled perilously on the end of it, hoping to dislodge the stone just a few inches for me to squeeze through. With the broad length of wood stuck in the right spot, I put my body weight on it, hanging like a monkey. I held tightly with closed fingers to the end, bouncing in an attempt to lift the other end and roll the flat boulder. With several raging attempts, I managed to get some movement. I groaned and grunted, pulling even harder with my entire body now hanging from the edge of a powerful piece of wood. Yanking down with my arms, I felt a change in the consistency of my movements. It wiggled out of position. An instability surfaced and I regrettably tore down with a final pull. An explosion of wood chips rocketed into the air as I fell an inch or so to the ground. A deafening snap swaddled my ears in a pinch. As I came to from falling over, I immediately inspected the damage. The rock had moved several inches, though I wasn't sure it was wide enough for me to get through. I picked up the remnant stick to carry the steaming pail. After I dropped it carefully through the hole, I scurried back to the fire for another stick. I grabbed one carefully, still aflame from the fire, so I could see once inside. The hole I'd pried open wasn't big enough for me to get through while standing, so I had to crawl. Snakelike, I lay on the ground and crawled through mucky gravel until I popped out into the cave's opening. It was a moment of relief, just a moment before my lungs almost expelled the entire contents of my body on the ground in disgust. A putrid stench slammed its way into my nostrils, creating a deeply sunken unwelcome home. The smell forced my eyes to swell and curl backwards as my entire face squinted forcefully. My muscles seized up, cinching my body shut for a second in fear of what I may find. The darkness gave way to the flickering flames on the end of my burning staff as I forcibly peeled my eyes back open. Covered in dirt and sweat, tickled by burn marks and aching profoundly from physical labor, I arrived at the body, or at least what was left. I felt in my heart, somehow, that there was nothing I could do. My natural instincts told me to run, to hide, to flee. I kept down the vomit from desecrating the deforming body. Shoving the bottom end of my torch into the ground, I took in a deep breath. All I could think was that it was time to make history. With a deliberately slow motion, I unraveled the cloth from the morphing object. Its pulsing vibrations ricocheted through my fingers, encouraging the row of sweat on my forehead.

"Okay." I whispered to myself under stifled breaths. The echoes of my words shimmered through the empty space. With great caution, I transferred the strange cube above the bucket, now beside the lifeless body.

"AHH!" I screamed into the innocent night, dipping my fingers into the scalding water with the sphere in hand. "Fuck!" my voice pelted through the quivering blackness as the skin on my hands felt raw and weak. After realizing how little I'd thought it through, I scooped my hand back up from the aggressive double agent. My mind was racing with the thought of how I'd be able to keep it up for much longer than a couple of seconds but was quick to notice the change in the sphere's complexion. With its outer layer doused lightly with calescent water, it began to drip as though pieces were falling off. The ribbon-like appendages that held it together, almost like a band of rubbers, began sloping off the now-curved surface. My hands instinctively took it above the body. The lengthy noodle-like slices fell off one at a time, ranging in colors. It transformed from a heavily controlling black to a free-roaming blue and purple hybrid. Then, in a moment it stopped. Its temperature, shape, and texture were returning to normal, as normal as it could get, I mean. The sphere returned to its cubic anatomy, and rather than falling, the pieces of a whole continued to slither around it once more.

"Ahh, okay." I assured myself I had begun to understand the pattern. My lungs filled with a generous amount of burning air and stale cave odors. In a state of haste and determination, my fingers grasped a little tighter as I plunged them several inches into the menacing bucket. My face was awry with tightening expressions. The intense sensation of pain caused me to squeeze even harder. I could barely feel my fucking fingers. My head felt like a log cracked in two, a daring naturally insane endeavor and a lustful sentiment of fulfillment. I managed to peek through my squinting eyes and was taken aback. In shock and fear of permanent damage I finally removed my hands from the boiling hot water, raising the object above Jesus' body. Lengths of the strange substance peeled off like before as it unraveled. The odd vine-like attachments fell in an elegant manner, perfectly vertical. Satisfaction had never been so easily defined. As they collapsed onto his body, they began wrapping around him, just as they were doing with the object I held still.

Beautiful, calm, and gentle, all the things my hands were not, this image became. Once more, the temperature of the ball returned to normal and I was ready to continue. And so, I kneeled there for what must have been four or five hours. I would sink my hands into a painful bath of the unknown without even thinking, diving right in every time without a second thought. The water would cool, and I'd reheat it and continue. Every few minutes, the diameter of this delirious object would shrink the tiniest amount as its infinitesimal number of densely packaged parts dispersed across Jesus' body. As time passed, my numbing mind grew vigilant. I finished the job as the final few strands disassociated from my empty fingers, recombining to flourish around the vibrating corpse.

He looked like something from God knew where, like the cubic object itself had taken a human shape. I couldn't see his skin, his face, or his clothes. All of him was consumed by God knew what. Luckily, I believed, God did know what. With the task complete, I left my work behind, grabbed my torch and bucket, and squeezed out of the cave.

The walk home was an interesting one. A self-reflection occurred that transcended the physical world. My eyes had been opened to reality, to sacrifice. My actions, now, could not be undone. Satisfied, I smiled. I could finally see what I had already become.

With everything considered, I retired my beaten body for the night. Sore muscles and scars on the skin sent me swiftly into the sunken ship they call sleep.

I woke rather disgruntled to some aches the day after, but I remained content, knowing that my actions were in congruency with the Lord's. Maybe, somewhere deeper, I was a little naïve to say that everything would work out perfectly for everyone. I wouldn't have admitted it at the time, though.

XXI

Sunday. Do you know why they call it that? Why, of all things, is it denoted as the day of the sun? There must have been thousands of other options, you might think. But why Sunday?

I'll tell you why.

The day after I had completed what was asked of me was, by all accounts, the best day of my life, bar one. The day the birds' call was more rejuvenating than a loved one's kiss. The day the wind blew through the air to waft a sense of delight our way we only ever dreamed of, not too powerful, but not so still to be eerie. It was the day that the human race came together for the first time on to bring peace to the age of man.

It would last, too! But we'll get there.

Let's continue.

The world was anew that day. Perhaps it was all psychological, and I recall it differently through retrospect, but it was definitely something to behold.

When I awoke, I went through a short morning routine as usual, with a smile on my face and with thanks to the gleaming beams of sunlight blessing my every move. It flew by as I greeted my miss with a cute peck on the forehead with her waking. After a few charming minutes, we were ready to tackle the day just as any other. 'The only difference is everything,' I thought. We strolled together toward the town center, exchanging a few words.

"I look forward to it all, you know, the finished project." I dazzled her with a rainbow motion from my fingers.

"Me too, honey. It'll be good for all of us, I think." She smiled, swaying her hair through the finely tuned breeze and glorious sunshine.

"Alrighty, let's see him then. I can't wait to watch the minds of the non-believers turn to God for their answers." I had to stifle back a giggle as we sauntered down the path, the same path whose shade of red was now fading along with the worries of the world. Another set of minutes ticked by. We arrived at the village square to find the same group of people who waited there every day with high hopes. Some people would say they might have been a little obsessed or crazy. They were just eager is all.

It wasn't just the normal crew, however. Each day, a few more people would show up, but rumor had gotten around that he was to return this day. There must have been seventy or eighty people sitting on the sides of the flat stretch of land in a meek attempt to bear witness to anything spectacular. As I turned the corner, hand-in-hand with my lover, I saw him.

Flawlessly atop the pedestal, he stood stoic and bold. Happiness surged through him with arms outstretched. His face glared against the brush of sunlight. The entirety of his body glowed in a manner I would deem angelic. His clothes were made from a heavenly gold, pearly white, and the finest beige cloth in the land. He stood proud but humble, content, and forgiving. The subtle, cheeky breeze lifted his lengthy locks a little as he breathed in the air of retribution. A dazzling brilliance overcame every sense of my body. I noted, too, that he looked as though he had lost years. His skin was flawless and heavily decorated with a beard of great splendor. As I finally grew aware of the reality formed by his impressive restoration, all the colors of the world became alive. The trees were more vibrant than ever before, shimmering as millions of voluptuous bulbs. The air carried a lovely breeze that smelled like clean grassy fields with a mystical hint of seawater. My skin felt more sensitive but more robust. As far as I could tell, everything was better.

"And with my return," he called to the growing crowd, "there will finally be unity and peace." My heart melted almost as much as it did every day when I looked into the star-crossed eyes of my lover. The crowd was growing rapidly.

"Now, if anyone is in disagreement, pray tell," he soothed our ears, standing in an image of perfection, "but this day, every seven days will be named Sunday. Sun as in the circle in the sky, but also in reference to the truth behind my relationship to God. It will be the day of peace, of relaxation. It will forever be the day of the Lord. May we owe him our lives! Amen!" He shouted softly. Through the practices that had been occurring throughout the town for some time, people instinctively knew what to say to conclude and vow to Jesus that he had been heard. Hundreds and hundreds of people were congregating to witness a new world being born.

"Amen," we all repeated back to him, the weaponless army. Physically, we were weaponless, but we still had our voices. Then it hit me! I had to reunite with the Lord Himself to inform him of our progress, oh my. I would have hated to have kept him waiting.

Jesus dictated to us the meaning behind the newly named Sunday. And just as he did, a small pocket of people I specifically remember being a part of the non-believing resistance spoke up. One burly rather unappealing man ruined the façade with a destructive tone.

"Alright. I've seen enough magic. I know a trick when I see it," he claimed boldly. "But this, this is something impressive. I'm not saying I believe it, even now, but I will spread word of your story. And I'll be sure to connect with faraway lands about your ideals. Thank you for your kindness, Jesus, but we'll be off now." He surprised the mass. "Come on now, wee willikers, come with me. the Scottish-like accent called." He gathered several younger folks as they turned around, heading from the town square. There couldn't have been more than thirty of them marching together against a clearly beating sun. Sacks of supplies surmounted their backs as they walked further down the path less traveled. As everyone was distracted with the rogue group's exit, I hopped onto the lower step of the pedestal to quickly meet and greet my great work.

"Hey, Jesus," I whispered loudly. His head turned toward me. "When you're done here, I need you to meet me at my place. As soon as possible, please," I urged him. I saw him nod powerfully. My body swung around half a turn as I galloped past my lady, picking her hand as I went. It was high noon and I'd just arrived to my humble abode in preparation for updating God on the progress of my work. My lips met my ears at the thoughts of being at ease and God knowing that I had made His dream reality.

I could hear some heavy footsteps plundering their way through the dusty outside and I didn't have to second-guess their owner's identity. A quick nip on the right spot of the divine sphere I carried with me initiated a magical connection with the wall I begged so often to hear from. Miniscule particles of blue dust emitted from the crack on the wall. This phenomenon amazed me every time. As per usual, I waited several seconds until I heard the voice of the one true creator.

"My Lord, are you there?" I gently coaxed. "I have Jesus here with me. He's back." My heart trembled as I hoped that my actions would please him. My fingers shook mildly with every moment. I knew there was no going back. I stared blankly at the delightful swirl of colors before me. I could feel the omniscient presence creeping its way into my veins and filling me up. My insides were wet with devotion and I was thirsty for more.

XXII

"Thanks again, man. I wouldn't be here without you. I'm just worked up about this… It's just getting difficult to picture it all coming together. There's just so much hanging by a thread." Adam's words strike through an emotional dissipation looming in the air.

"Well, let's make sure it's the strongest damn thread in history." James tells him confidently. Adam, however, is aware of something else that stirs within his mind He ruminates with reasoning for his previous aggressive actions and the truth behind the plan, really.

"Alright, enough sappy shit. We've got work to do, boys," he replies as he opens communications with the men still supporting the engine at the base of the Dawne. "Let's get this bridge opened up and see what we've got." Adam commands.

"That's the Adam I like to see," James bounces back with innocence.

"You ready down there?" Adam speaks up into the microphone as the audio transmits to John and Simon.

"More than ever." John says.

"I sure am. Let's get this going!" Simon replies.

A flurry of chatter occurs between Adam and James as levers are pulled, knobs are twisted, and buttons are pushed. The once-humble rumble of the engines ignites to become something far more powerful. The whirling noise screams through the moon-blessed atmosphere of the valley. The building shakes angrily for a few moments before settling to a cool and constant vibration in the arid air. The eyes of two very determined men, perhaps now with ulterior motives, are mesmerized as the portal expands from nothingness. In mass manipulation, they stare.

An array of sounds begins to emerge from the bamboozling aura as their ears match the focus in their eyes.

"My Lord, are you there?" the voice kindly asks. "I have Jesus here with me. He's back."

"This is excellent news. So, the people are in certain agreement, then?" Adam wastes no time with pleasantries.

"Uhm, well, almost entirely," the voice emits. Instantly, Adam's hairs stand up on the back of his neck. 'Surely,' he thinks to himself, 'there cannot be another complication with His plan.'

"And what news have you for me?" He utters with a hasty fire in His throat.

"There was a small group of people, more insignificant than before, that decided not to believe. They didn't leave in vain, though." Adam's ears, growing impatient, clutched tighter to the story. "They said that they would spread the word of what we have created. I imagine their view to be impartial, however. It will only be a matter of time until people create their own ideas around our religion. Their own judgments of Jesus and God. It doesn't matter, though. Everyone who stays here now will pray every Sunday. I've made sure of that," the ancient voice proclaims through time. Adam sits back with the most euphoric grin on his face. In the enjoyment of the moment his facial muscles pull back toward his ears and he lets out a silent breath.

"You've done it. The beginning of my divine rule has been established," Adam speaks intentionally slowly, repressing the absence of trepidation.

"Yes, my Lord." A quivering and happy connotation is poorly hidden in the words of the mystery man.

"I would be happy to say that the bulk of your work is done. However, that is not the case. Your task will continue for years to come." Adam releases a sigh in a tranquil mental task, just heavy enough for James to hear. "For an indefinite number of years, you will yield to the Bible. You will spread my name in utter glory and defend it with your life. Jesus will pass and become a part of history. You have a much more important role in the universe than you may have thought. Yes, there will be people who doubt my powers, still. You will not bend to the sinners and the will of evil. I need you, my friend and follower, to be the ever-changing and adapting voice of reason for my purpose. To keep humans safe from themselves, forever." Adam breathes in and out with serene grace as the final tendrils of emotion depart from his cold chassis.

"God, I am beyond grateful for this opportunity, but I must ask how I am expected to live for so long?" the voice shakes from behind an evolving void.

James leans forward with an elbow on his knees, raising an eyebrow. Adam catches the movement in the corner of his eye but chooses to disregard it. Consistency is all too important now.

"The sphere you have been using is more powerful than you imagined. Within it is the ability to prolong life, slow down the aging process, if you will. In exchange for unwavering loyalty to my cause, despite any and all complications, it shall grant you the gift of immortality. Become one with me, my child, and free humanity from the web of dangers it is bound to ensnare itself in," Adam continues his bold speech. Both he and James sit anxious before the portal as they wait for an answer. Each heartbeat stomping through their minds as the seconds go by.

"I humbly accept. As you choose," the voice clamors in uncertainty through the bewildering bridge. A slight pause sits. It seeps through the air sinister and silent, bar the engines. The feeling is overwhelmingly satisfying.

"May you take on the role of whoever you choose through your journey. Regardless of who you become, keep only this in mind. The fate of the world rests in your hands. You may go now, my prodigy," Adam's words deliver. An absence of a reply haunts the tense agreement for a moment before the relative silence is broken. James' thoughts become speech as the two sweaty men work together for a moment to close down the communicative gateway.

"I didn't know it could do that," James stutters for a second to Adam, who turns around rapidly in response. James voices himself once more before Adam can find the breath to retaliate. "How long have you known that it has the ability to allow people to live for so long? Or, no. Never mind that. How did you even find out about such a… powerful ability?" James rants as his face flushes with red color. His feet hit the floor as he straightens the rest of his lanky body, sharpening his tone of voice to produce greater volume. "Why didn't we just fucking use that in the first place? Extract the energy and save everyone that way, boom! Easier, safer, and everyone would be happy." James towers over his chair, with arms flailing in frustration. His voice echoes mildly in the still room as the engines die down.

"Relax! I had an encoded message in an extension of the message I got earlier that I showed you. About the divinity sphere being 'all too powerful' and whatnot," Adam explains almost frivolously, using demeaning air quotes.

"Well, that would've been nice to know, man. I don't get heated about a lot of stuff, but you threw me for a loop there!" James bounces back, walking back to his chair. An awkward silence procured a stealthy grasp on the choking air.

"You sack of shit, you could have at least told us. Kept us in the loop or somethin'?" Simon chirped from the active communications device. James decides to continue for him.

"Hang on. Wait a second. If you knew this entire time that the sphere could do that, why didn't you tell me? Why didn't you tell any of us? Did you… keep it from us on purpose?" he pauses.

The radio communications go silent. Halted, with bated breath, Simon and John listen intensely. It takes a few moments before anyone dares to intrude.

"Surely, we need all four of us to be in the know if we want this to work out. Why do I have to tell you that teamwork is so critical?" John asks, several hundred meters below, still holding the demulcent engines in place. Again, there is another pause. A smirk sneaks into Adam's mouth. He reaches into his pant pocket.

"Yes. Well, I'm afraid that it will no longer be necessary," he says softly, just enough for James to hear, into the eerie tension.

"Wait, wha–" James attempts to speak.

There is an utter end to the conversation. With a spark, a bang, Adam goes deaf.

James' speech is cut off by the earsplitting slice of Adam's finger squeezing the trigger. The horrible noise cuts all tongues silent. Time dwindles to milliseconds at a time, passing painfully slowly. His body is motionless other than the tremors that course through his sweat clogged hand. An electric surge of energy wriggles and frolics throughout his twisted mind. Its power strikes him at intermittent moments throughout floods of ecstasy and sorrow. In the dead of the night, James kneels. His knees imprison the moment with a thud against an immaculate floor. It rings for several seconds, painting the sound black.

His blood spatters across the side wall. A lifeless corpse falls on the spot, his brain flying in chunks and mouth wide open.

Time speeds up again to embrace reality as Adam monopolizes the conversation, seizing true tyranny.

"Ah, that's better," Adam states. "And as for you two eavesdropping bastards, this'll be a bit easier without a bombardment of questions.?' I'll summarize very quickly. You followed me into something you had faith in. Rather blindly, I might add. Not only does that sound very, very familiar, but you know what?" Adam dangles the freedom to speak their own ideas in front of them like a piece of perfectly tender meat, just waiting to be bitten down on.

"What?" they both reply in unison, their faces lit up with artificial lighting in their visors against the brisk night.

"Sometimes, god doesn't care about everyone," Adam finalizes as he slams down a lever down against the control panel. The idling vibrations cease from the engines as their components are left to wither without power. The lights vanish from the entirety of the Dawne one floor at a time, very rapidly, with the exception of the floor lighting around Adam's feet. In the dreaded nighttime hours, the once-fascinating structure becomes nothing more than a cocoon, a cocoon swamped with an abundance of selfishness for the last insect with an immense desire for control.

"Faintly, I wish I was sorry," he mutters to himself as he smiles broadly.

XXIII

The more I confess, the more I remember. I won't give all the details because we'd be here for years, so back on topic.

I was there and the deed was done. I had successfully convinced a vast majority of people that this was the way forward. I felt for a moment as though I had been floating effortlessly on a cloud as the communication with God ended rather abruptly.

Now, I was falling. I was falling fast, and alone, coming out of the sky like a winged beast clipped of its flying limbs through rays of lost sunshine. I was alone and without guidance, barreling toward the ground. I was soul-bound to a single mission that would consume more of me than I ever could have imagined – eternal life. I thought that couldn't be too bad. It is. And it will turn me into the most selfish being in existence.

The light faded from the crack and I looked up to see the last specs of dust emit from the wall only to die.

"You've got your work cut out for you, then," Jesus chuckled. I joined him in doing so in an attempt to make light of things.

"You're not wrong, my friend," I responded heartily. "Now I suppose it's time to find my lover and share the news," I told him. I did just that. I left my place and began walking back to the center of attention with the most impressive grin on my face. I jogged steadily. Jesus joined me in haste, but I think he was just a bit clueless as to what to do next. We made well with time, but I didn't have to jog for long. She'd already started to make her way back to our home. I ran right up and wrapped my arms around her like it was the first time. I couldn't see her face over my shoulder, but I could tell she had lit up. She never failed to make me smile with her own. We returned to a more publicly acceptable posture and locked eyes.

"You're happy, aren't you? What's happened, my dear? Did you finally figure out how to wink with one eye?" she fired a few questions at me. The three of us laughed a little before Jesus patted my back, I patted his, and he walked off.

"No, haha. It's something a little more impressive, I'd say," I said feverishly.

It took me a few short minutes to give her the full gist of it. She seemed delighted at first, but as I elaborated further, I noticed her smile drop slowly. As we walked back to our house, I had almost finished explaining the situation. The only problem was I couldn't bear the thought of her having to go through even a brush of sadness. I couldn't hold back!

"What's wrong, darling?" I blurted out, mid-sentence. She held my hands ever so tightly. That perfect gaze she always gave me flowed into me and we stood in a silent pause just staring at each other. As this quiet period grew thin, she burst out into a hurricane of tears.

"Hey, hey, now what's going on? I know when you sad-cry. Those aren't tears of joy," I reminded her lovingly. I used the back of my index finger to tip her chin toward the blazing sun and she spoke through the fountain of teary-eyed mist.

"It's just," she sniffled, "if you're gonna live forever with this eternal life deal." She continued to bawl. I pulled her closer by the hips and wrapped around her, squeezing her with a musky strength. "We won't be each other's 'the one'…" A slight paused rang through the space around us as she spoke into my ear. "I won't be around for your entire life. You'll see me die, and then what?" Her cheeks were warm with the human attribute of emotion. I pulled her back straight up again and lifted one of my hands to hold her face beside her chin.

"You are the only one for me, my love. I can promise you that," I reassured her. "And come to think of it, I might just have a solution for us, darling," I told her. We began discussing something that had barely brewed in my mind for a minute, a fresh idea that might just work, a contingency plan. We sat together inside and I revealed to her the second cube that I had been sent. I explained generally how it was supposed to work.

I didn't dare tell her that there were two in the first place and that the only reason our savior Jesus Christ was resurrected was actually a scientific miracle, a make-believe.

No one would have wanted to hear that.

I simply explained that it had been given to me for the purpose of self-reanimation in that case that I was to sustain fatal or near-fatal injuries.

"I'm hoping, now I don't know for certain, that when you pass, I can somehow use this to restore you. I'm going to try to bring you back as you were, much further in the future when I deem fit," I explained.

"What do you mean by 'when you deem fit?'" she quickly asked, and rightfully so, if I'm honest.

"I don't know exactly. Perhaps a time when medicine has evolved to the point where you can also live eternally with me," I explained in a melancholic but hopeful tone.

"It seems like a long shot, but if you think it'll work, then I'll trust you to the moon and back," she said quietly with a little more optimism than what I had shown. We went to bed that night with a void filled, an emptiness between us attached, the creation of an undying unison. Then, we set out together for a journey through time and widespread peace.

Time passed seamlessly as we led a truly commendable life together. There was little to be done in the years that she was alive, and I put my gospel focuses aside slightly while I focused on enjoying a number of marvelous years. She was everything to me, and dear God, I hope she never stops being exactly that. I was fully prepared for and aware of the fact that she would have to go one day. It hung over me like a never-ending nightmare. If I was to live forever, I knew it wouldn't be perfect without her by my side. Eventually, though, time took its toll. She aged with the world and her days were numbered. Life expectancy back then was nothing to brag about, to be perfectly honest. The images of her are as fresh as yesterday on the day she died. We sat atop a mooring hill overlooking the village as a silky and delicate sun grazed the fields in the evening. The sky was pink with love and the clouds intermittent as they tiptoed along. I couldn't have asked God to share another sliver of His elegance. She decided it would be on that hill that she'd die, the place of our first kiss many years prior. So, she did. She'd been sick for some time and I knew it was up and coming. Her last words to me rang clear.

"Is there ever a place you wish that you went after death?" she asked me calmly as we stared into a horizon of paint. The wrinkles tugged against her young soul.

"Not that it really applies to me, per se, but yes. Heaven. And in Heaven I would travel the ocean! What about you, my dear?" I responded contently. She lay back and started to close her eyes.

"I'm not fussy. You know that. Honestly, anywhere, as long as I'm with you," she said. It was with those words that we fell adrift into a short nap. I woke up not thirty minutes later to her face covered in her own blood. She lay lifeless despite my efforts to reawaken her. The inevitable had finally approached us.

With grief, I returned her body to the house, where I would begin the most labor-intensive resuscitation conceivable. Using boiling water and the strange cube, I would tend to her body every day. Using the same process as I had done for Jesus, I gave her several drips of that strange sphere's material seven times a week. Not once over several thousand years did I miss a day. For just a minute every single time and I bared no reason to complain. I could have used tools to avoid the pain of scalding water on my skin. If I could do it for Jesus, I could do it for her. I always will and always do remember every sunset in which I performed the self-sacrificial ritual.

It was, undoubtedly, worth it in the end.

From then on, everything went by in a flash. There were times in which this ritual would have precedence over my religious life, but of course I always held true to my word to God. As the two most important aspects of my life became hopelessly entangled, I had decided to concoct something truly magnificent in her honor. It was my dream for everyone to experience the power of romance, and even encourage it through my religion, thus the normalization of marriage.

When sustainable building materials and a common workforce emerged, some thousand years later, we had put brilliant minds together to create a sanctum of sorts for people to collectively pray, a place for people to reconvene after busy hours and pay their dues for the world given to us by the one true father, our Lord. It was a place to unite man and woman as one for a lifetime, officially. Nothing could compare to its monstrous grandeur and heavenly attention to the tiniest of details. The first church was built from what felt as meek as sticks and stones, modeled after the very first time I heard God speak with other people, my old room. They were organized, row upon row. The process became methodical and organized.

Human souls were easy to control, just how God would have wanted.

All the while, the population of our planet spun out of control. What had started as a humble village was beginning to mount rapidly into something much more. As time flew by, a multitude of churches almost started erecting themselves. I knew I'd done right toward the human race as they began to independently construct and lead these colossal creations all across the globe.

Time ticked past me, slipping through my fingers, as the wait for my one and only to return to life diminished day by day. Things really took off in the seventeen and eighteen hundreds when rules and laws were becoming strictly enforced. The result of such a change in our species was nothing short of spectacular. Churches were being thrown up like nobody's business, and a vast majority of people chose to abide by the divine text of the Lord... in the more successful countries, at least.

It was odd how people continued to focus on similar aspects in the modern age as they did so long ago. I was fascinated as homosexual marriage and adultery were banned by law! Yet people could eat pig and shellfish, and even break many other rules without consequence. 'Humans,' I thought, 'we make an impressive species.'

As the planet evolved into something I never could have comprehended in my early years, peace worldwide had been established. For the most part, any sort of pre-empt to major conflict was reduced in stature by the united front of those with Jesus and God.

The mission I had been given all those weary years ago was turning out to be a massive success. The world ran itself in a way. All the countries were connected, and everyone had their bit to do. Nobody had any reason to disrupt the perfection, at least, until the early nineteen hundreds.

XXIV

If the past were to change, for any reason, so would the present. The universe depends on consistency and balance. So, naturally, as previous years are altered, everything changes entirely.

Things that did not exist before do now. Thoughts and memories are changed as the human race remembers a different world than what had previously existed. Most vitally, though, the physical space of the modern world alters and bends to conform to the crucial changes of the past. A different reality is shaped. Inevitably, not only does one's perception shift noticeably, but the world evolves to fit the very force of nature that created it. Reality becomes unpredictable.

Adam stares out of the window at the lightening blackness of a crumbling night. The very edges of the empty horizon are spotted with the tiniest specks of a growing shade of azure. The world before him begins to spiral into something he had only dreamed of. He towers over the stagnant corpse with his hands behind his back and a gentle grin across his lips.

"This," he mutters under steady breathing. "This is perfect," he continues slowly as his hands appear from behind him. "Evelyn. I do this for you and us." His hands rise gradually in a semicircle motion, stopping halfway up. His words radiate a passion that is just a day too old, lost in the surge of power at his fingertips. His silhouette is cast against the mountain of computers behind him. The blue shade that lies so far away ignites the horizon.

As he speaks, the world begins to transform from its desolate and corrupted state. In the distance among the brightening calamity, a vague shadow appears, an extended line of pointed tips beneath a blooming sky. The grin across Adam's soulless face widens as he basks in the glory. The stalky line slowly changes in the faraway boundary of the desert. His smirk slows down for a second in a moment of pause and questionability. He squints rather marginally.

"Those *are* trees, aren't they?" his lips almost silently produce.

As his lips seal after the letter *Y*, a radiant blast consumes everything in white. Instantly, a powerful wave of energy emerges from the air. A visually blinding flash floods his eyes. He feels senseless in a crack of confusion. He does not move in the presence of such power. His skin begins to sear, white-hot, as he's pushed back a few inches with the shock. An earsplitting shriek, like a sonic wave, stuns him in a moment. Paralyzed, he's lost in the light. There is nothing but a blank everything. The world before him seems erased, empty, gone, a clean slate.

With the placidity of a trickling waterfall, he opens his eyes to the grandest sight he's ever seen, transformed by the light.

Fingers extended in a generous posture, he gazes at the freshly formed phenomenon before him. He takes in the ranges of luscious trees that extend far beyond the field of view. The morning sun cascades across a beautiful landscape, expanding further than the eye can see. Colors explode in the brightness of day, writhing within the newborn environment. Amidst the prodigious architecture, he finds himself no longer isolated as he witnesses an ocean of high-rise buildings. To the left and right, the ground is carefully covered with layers and layers of comfortable, safe housing. Adam's breath is suspended as he takes in the order of it all. Everything is connected with paved roads. Lights that actually work are dropped precisely over consistent intervals. Cars litter the streets playfully rather than sitting still as broken husks.

A brightened perspective illuminates a formerly darkened world. Without a speck of dust to be found, he releases the held breath in amazement. Now, the world is anew for real.

He grasps at a few seconds to examine the more clearly defined wrinkles on his aged face. They come from the cold blood.

'The light has brought a new universe to existence,' Adam thinks to himself. There is nothing better than the satisfaction of complete fruition. As his eyes unlock from the stare he holds preciously with the outside world, he steps backward.

"Oops!" he exclaims, bumping into something he didn't expect to. His torso twists and his lower body obliges to face the same direction. A few moments are required to process the impressive congregation of changes. The heap of technology in the center of the room has transformed. In fact, the entire room is completely different, an alteration so powerful that Adam barely recognizes the space. Though, rather than one large room, the floor has been split into several smaller rooms. He places his hand on the plain desk and rubs it smoothly and then pats it twice in a caring fashion. He steps out of the office-looking room to investigate further. A few seconds rush by as he walks by another couple of smaller rooms, a bathroom, and a kitchen-style area with a lowered table in the middle. In the same room he notices three tall figures that look briefly familiar. He pauses for a moment to peer through the checkered window in the door. They look happy, so happy as to say they hadn't been killed and abandoned in an effort to reinvent a timeline. The three men joke around and laugh with one another in adorable synchronization. He looks into the room for a few moments more and then drops his gaze. He places one hand against the gray door gently before backing away into the corridor without causing a commotion. The colorful investigation through an otherwise bland floor leads him to a black door at the end of the hallway. This door, however, does not have a window. Instead, it is sealed on all sides with some sort of rubber fabric. His feet slow him to a halt before grabbing the handle as he reads the sign beside the doorframe. In elegant but fairly simple text, it reads:

Space-Time Continuum Portal
AUTHORIZED ACCESS ONLY

"Space-Time Continuum Portal," he mutters to himself, pondering how naming it would have made it seem more official. 'No, how ridiculous,' he thinks. After creating this world, he's done enough, almost. Without any further thought, an impulse surge through him and his hand forks out from his body as he swings open the door. Some machining hisses spit out at him from the edges of the seal around the door as the entrance opens to a larger room. The moment it cracks open, he hears a muffled deep sound emanating throughout the room.

He peeks his head through the slit between the door and the wall before entering. 'No one there, perfect.' He shivers. In a pandering mess of fear and anticipation his eyes glaze over the fairly recognizable controls. Carefully, he investigates the outer edge of the room. Everything is so neatly compartmentalized. Adrenaline pumps viciously through his bloodstream as he walks around steadily to examine the product of his work in this world. After a minute or so, he takes a few eager steps toward the center of the room and comes to face a questionable arrangement of technology. An oval-shaped hollow disc, about the same size as him, is erected about six inches from the wall. Beside it is a set of controls he identifies immediately. This is it – the portal. He is shocked in awe at how beautifully crafted everything is. Before, it was oddly sketchy and rough. This, however, is a charming summation of everything he has ever worked toward, compact and safe with the support of a presumably functioning economy and an operational world. His ears pick up the voice he has longed to hear since reclamation day.

"Adam, dear?" it echoes through the vacant corridor from outside. He twists to face the door. Sweat begins to form slightly on his forehead as his hands vibrate harmlessly. He stands completely still, staring wistfully at the edge of the doorframe. In a moment that could have lasted years he watched four slender fingers grip the doorframe with determination. An exemplary hand shows itself and then extends into an arm and a shoulder. 'So flawless.' Adam's eyes focus and explode, swelling as a thunderous shiver runs up his spine. The figure comes out of the darkness and into the light. Her face is blessed by the flooding and energy efficient fixtures from above. Evelyn.

"Oh, there you are, babe," she says without any indication of abnormality as she peels away from the door. "We just need you to sign this so we can move ahead with the…" she speaks as she walks forward to him, clipboard and paper in hand. He stands in utter awe. Her face morphs rapidly from a normal expression to a concerned contortion. Her eyebrows dip in the center and lean forward as if to get a closer look at him, retracting her clipboard to her body. "Baby, are you okay? You look a bit pale. What's wrong?" she asks.

"Nothing," he responds, trying to seem as calm as possible while his back grows wet. "Nothing at all." Their bodies enclose upon each other and she wraps both arms tightly around him, keeping a close grip on the clipboard behind his back. The stir of emotion within him unsettles the controlling autonomy he has relied on. He can feel it and swallows. He hopes that it is enough.

"You seem quite stressed, my love. Is everything alright?" she asks him. He plays along, knowing that everyone that exists now has known this life for as long as they have lived. It is difficult to keep down, but he knows that his history never really existed. The smile, that he wishes was not false, on his face fails to falter in any way.

"Of course, honey. Just wait in here with me," he says to her slowly. He walks over to the door to close it, creating a secure barrier between the room and the outside world.

"Wait, what are you doing?" she fires off. "It can't be run without four people. You know this, babe," she warns him.

"I made that rule," he says, assuming it was of his creation in this world. "Do you know why?"

"Not really. I'm assuming that it needs four operators to be handled well enough to work properly?" she responds and rotates her head an inch while raising an eyebrow.

"No. It's so nobody can do what I'm about to do," Adam tells her in anguished confidence. He darts over to the control panel beside the portal and starts to flick organized, labeled switches and turn tiny dials with numbers on them. Ease of use is certainly something they incorporated here, especially in comparison to the risky prototype from before. He hops back and forth between a few smaller stations around the room with lost joy.

"Portal parameters set. Engines are a go," a voice calls out. This covers his mind in a blanket of relief.

"Yes. Silver! It's good to have you back by my side!" he shouts back boisterously. Evelyn raises both eyebrows in astonishment. Adam waits anxiously for the terrifying rumble of engines to shake the building. There is no movement, a stable performance for once. The thick aura of control fills him with delight. A large red button exposes itself on the control panel with the words *'OPEN PORTAL'* inscribed on it. Without a flicker of hesitation, Adam pounds it. The oval-shaped object illuminates and begins swirling with a familiar purple and blue dust. Adam gorges himself on the spectacle. "This is all for us, babe, you and me. Just wait and see," he pauses. "We will be Gods."

As the words slip from his mouth, regret tears through his throat. He can feel the concoction of power mixing in his stomach. His mind is consumed with the rush. With an arrogant face of storm crossed brows, he swallows the sentiment.

XXV

Two thousand and twenty years. Two thousand twenty years and eighty-nine days. Two thousand twenty years, eighty-nine days, and sixteen hours I waited for God to respond to my first call. I had constructed a world worth living in for every reason but one. I'd refused to call him, though. I was best off to leave it for the right moment. I don't really know what I was expecting after all this time, but something would have been better than nothing. However, as time passed and we bounded into the modern era, the mere idea of Him was enough to sustain my burning passion for peace on Earth.

I was happy with where I was, as I drew nearer an awakening. She consumed my life almost as much as my devotion to God.

The year was 2020, a year I would consider to be the end of an era. Oh what an era it was. I'd seen a heck of a lot more than I anticipated in that time. However, that is a story for another time.

We'd recovered from several worldwide conflicts that had been resolved by 'doing the right thing,' which really just means heeding to the Bible a little more tightly. World War three was a bit of a riot to say the least. People became wary of their actions as technology blew up to make life easier. Everything was just right. The world was a better place with everyone confined morally within the boundaries that my religion had defined. Whether they believed it or not, at this point, everyone had some sort of connection to the belief that some greater power would always be watching and that their actions would have them sent them to heaven or to suffer in the unending pits of hell.

Wherever I went, I took the body of my second half with me, rejuvenating the cells daily with the mystical substance. An incomprehensible number of hours of scalding water and burns on my hands were a small price to pay to see her smile once again. The very final specks of life dripped slowly from the object on the night before and I awoke to a scintillating surprise. Two warm hands quietly caressed my abdomen and my chest as my eyes opened on the comfortable bed I'd been resting on for several years.

"Hey, baby. You did it," her words echoed into my ear in a harmony that filled my heart with joyous content. We cuddled and snuggled and made every other cute living thing jealous of our adorable interactions with each other as she recovered.

I'd been planning, though. I was lonely in the time the world had changed. I wished for our bodies to become one just like the old times before God denied our access to such a thing, without marriage at least. And I had had a couple thousand years to think about how I wanted to do this.

My proposal. A big lead-up to a seemingly minor event, I know, but I'd grown desperate through a haunting wait. We went out that evening and I drove us to the peak of a hill where we sat down to enjoy a lighthearted picnic. The sunset was just beginning to ignite over a swarming city. The yellows of the sky were barely greeting hints of orange underneath a sea of welcoming blue. There we were – two tiny beads in a massive universe that changed the entire course of history. I believed that God had shaped this world through me, but who really did all the work?

Of course, I didn't know at the time what had happened. How I had molded an existence from a combination of what I know now to be rumor and science. I believed it and I forced that belief onto others through seniority and practice. I was proud of the fact that I followed the Word of the Lord so strictly. That I created anti-abortion campaigns and held such an aggressive stance towards gay people. I affected more lives than I could count in a negative way and I promise that I never would have done that if I knew what I know now. The faith did me well, yes. I achieved my dreams and made the world a better place perhaps, but I also caused a great deal of pain for many people, too.

Religion is a story cumulated in a set of words or ideas that have been created by someone stringing along a fable into the modern day. Perhaps humans believe it because they don't have faith in themselves and they need something to believe in. I'm not saying having faith is bad; I mean it saved the world, but you can't be so uptight about it. Maybe it's because they need to be given a reason to act appropriately because they are so inherently evil. It's almost as if a majority of people could never have functioned without being told what to do…

We sat at our picnic eating white-bread cucumber sandwiches atop a crested plot of land. We were happy, even though others may not be. And that was right because we followed the belief system. It was okay that others had had a hard time with a variety of aspects of their lives so long as those who went to church were happy. We chatted harmlessly, harmlessly for us. The two of us could never stop laughing at each other's jokes, but that day, I got her to stop laughing. I got her to stop laughing as my silhouette against the blazing orange sky formed the image of a man on one knee. My arms were folded, showing something of importance to a shadow of similar size, with long hair beside me. Our contoured figures seemed like an art form against the glowing background. I asked her a question I had been waiting for two millennia to ask. The words, after her name, 'Will you marry me?' echoed softly. In a spur of raw happiness, she accepted without hesitation. Her smile was the only thing I could see despite the fascinating landscape and horizon covering the vast world around us.

"How do you feel?" I asked her. She had a little difficulty speaking through her intermittent squeals. The diamond ring slid perfectly on to her finger. I may have tried it on her hand before she came back to life. When in Rome, right?

"I'm speechless," she replied. "I love you," her lips mouthed as she blinked slowly. I stared into her beautiful pair of eyes as they reflected a graceful shade of orange crimson from a ribbon-baring sky.

"I think…" I hesitated as I got lost in her eyes, "we should share this moment with God." I nearly stuttered, releasing a heavy breath. She agreed, surprisingly. She loved me enough to understand everything I had done for her and was willing to cater to my needs, despite any adversity.

Now, I hadn't touched the divinity sphere for some time, and I thought my craving for communicating with the Lord had been reduced to nothing more than a long-lost idea. In honor of the completion of the longest endeavor known to man, I reached for the bag beside our red-checkered blanket. I slipped my hand inside and as soon as my fingers connected with the object, my body shuddered. I felt a power come over me.

The skin around my eyes spread wide open to allow the deepest and most absorbed stare to ooze from my face. I squeezed it securely, digging my fingertips into the button I hadn't felt in eons. The power to open such a doorway was nestled in my clutch. Snatched from freedom, I opened the portal with the touch of a button.

The sweet smell of divine presence corrupted the air around us rapidly as the blue smoke swirled carelessly around a circular black opening beside our adorable little setup. Like one's imagination of a miniature black hole, an oval of blackness consumed the air. It was dotted seamlessly with the smallest of white specks. The nothingness from within it spoke aloud.

"Finally, I see you have done your fair share of work," God read to me. I trembled moderately, shaking before the being that started it all.

"Yes. The world is at peace, Father," I spoke gently. I looked at the fair lady beside me, reading the message that bled from her face. "What's more? We have news." I informed him.

"And what might that be?" the commanding voice careened through time.

"We're getting married. Me and Evelyn," I spoke her name. There was a pause. A hefty moment of silence crept through the space between us and the portal. I was unsure what to make of it, so I waited even longer for a response.

"This…" the voice came through, "is perfect." Another swift pause grasped the conversation. "I would like to congratulate you for your work," I heard it say. Adrenaline began shooting into my veins left, right, and center. My vision narrowed and my lungs started inflating much faster. I snapped my left hand out to grab hers beside me in anticipation. God was exciting, but she was and still is worth more to me than He ever could.

"I will gladly thank you and accept." I said, quivering wildly. She looked at me and smiled, leaning forward slightly to kiss me. This day was supposed to be about us, and I wanted it to stay that way. However, one last communication was owed.

"Join me in perfection. I will welcome you to heaven. Take a step into the perplexing colors before you and your dreams will come true. We will welcome you to heaven." The words exonerated everything I had done to reach that point. I found myself a little confused when he said 'we.' I thought He was alone.

"Well?" my raspy voice asked her.

"As long as it's with you, I don't care," she said back slowly with tantalizing lips.

As one, we became ensnared by the mystical properties of the unknown. My hand locked shut around hers. Then, together, we stepped forward. Our feet carried us away before I could even comprehend what was happening to our bodies. I smiled at her and she smiled back with equal joy. Half of my right leg was already well-seated within the conjecture of odd imagery. I caught one final flash of the world I once knew as we were sucked instantaneously inside, still attached to my newly appointed fiancé. The sphere was constricted tightly in my other hand.

Everything was truly black. I don't mean dark like the night where you can still make out distant figures or see your fingers without an issue. I mean seriously, dead black for just the tiniest fraction of time. Then it changed suddenly. The blackness exploded fruitfully into a billion different particles of silver and purple. The sense of sound was entirely removed as I tried to communicate with my lover. We zoomed astonishingly through what looked to be a tube of dazzling lights coming from every direction. We floated through nothing at a breathtaking speed and it was the easiest thing we'd ever done. I wish it had lasted longer, but it was over before I knew what had hit me. All I remember after that was a blur of a clashing white blinding me.

The first thing I noticed was that my feet were touching a sophisticated floor.

Never had I been so shocked. I literally couldn't breathe for a moment, let alone speak, as I took in what I was faced with.

XXVI

Adam stares in unmitigated awe as a skinny, lengthy character bursts from the opening in front of him. Beside it, another one appears simultaneously to emerge from the stirring mess of purples, silver, and blues.

His jaw drops. Adrenaline catapults into his veins through every inch of his ecstatic body. A lifetime of work comes together in a moment of faith and beauty. Out of the corner of his distracted eyes he notices Evelyn's stunned expression. Yes, the world has been fixed. Peace is at hand. Everyone is safe and happy, everyone including Adam, until now.

"But," the figure speaks mere seconds after stabilizing in space. "You're me," it says with a shattered, plummeting voice.

The four people in the room look around in bizarre consternation as the realization sinks in that there aren't four people, but two – two pairs of two different people, four bodies and two identities.

Adam and Evelyn stand tall in their futuristic-looking outfits. Their wrinkles and stray grays become slightly more apparent when compared to the youthfulness of their counterparts. Directly opposing them stand two people that look almost identical to them. It seems almost as though they're looking in a mirror through a sheath-like filter of youth. Evelyn mouths to herself a couple of profane words in a moment of puzzlement. As the unwillingness to speak is replaced with a looming curiosity, the younger version of Adam speaks to the unusual company.

"But I..." he stammers, trying to pick up his words as though he'd just barfed them all over the floor. "Where's God?" he asks aggressively. "I was promised heaven. What is this? Where is He!?" his voice explodes over the simmering hum of the machine behind him. Adam leans over to deactivate the portal, breaking eye contact with his younger self for only a second.

"That would be me." Adam speaks to the youthful character.

"I am the God you have loved for so long. I am the fairytale. Adam. I am you. Only, I'm from the future. God... does not exist."

He explains, "And you have done so well. Dancing around like a perfect puppet petite, doing everything I asked you at the cost of what? A few lives and buckets of blood?" He laughs hysterically. "You and I are about to create the biggest paradox in the universe," Adam continues. "And all of this, everything you see, will be nothing more than a fragment of the past." He smirks beyond what looks comfortable.

"What exactly do you mean? Where's the salvation I was promised? You better explain yourself," his younger self commands, shaking violently in his stance, lifting a finger. Evelyn backs away from Adam now, hesitantly.

"I'm confused too, babe. What do you mean?" she asks him.

"Before I delve any further, why don't you take a seat, Adam? I'll tell you everything you want to know, but you have to do one thing for me in return," he says to his younger prodigy. He motions with his finger, and something about the size and shape of a large dining table unfolds from the floor with two seats on either side. As he awaits a response, he pats the table, placing down a blank book the size of a large block of gold when opened, nearly four inches thick, and an ordinary pen.

"Hmph. Why? What do you want?" he said in response.

"I want you to write down everything from start to finish. Everything you remember about your journey until the moment you came through that portal," Adam requests.

"What? Are you crazy? Do you know how long that would take?" the youthful figure retorts.

"Yes. Yes, I do," he lowers his voice and leans in a little. "But I also know you used the second cube I gave you to bring her back to life," he nods sideways toward the younger female, "so, at the very least, you owe me for that." His younger self stares intently for a few moments of consideration.

"And you'll tell me everything?" he asks, falling deeper.

"Everything." Adam confirms.

"You've got a deal," he sighs back at Adam with discontent, taking a seat. Disgruntled, he plops the sphere on the table into a cup holder. With grit and a million questions, he picks up the pen and begins writing. The older Adam then walks over to one of the glass-paned walls, overlooking the sea of success.

"When you're done, I'll explain things slowly so you can understand," he informs them. He stands straight and still, basking in the completion of turning his dreams to reality.

The women sit at the other end of the table to discuss and whisper as the young Adam scribbles away. Some time goes by as Adam stands motionless before his grand creation. Under the cover of the female voices, he makes his way back to the table. With swift and sly movements, he snatches up the divinity sphere from the table while the younger Adam writes, distracted. Several hours slip by of little chatter on the verge of silence aside from the scratching of a pen. In explicit and vulgar detail, he records everything from the beginning, his side of the story, and his side only is printed rapidly into the eternal markings of a book labeled with a number on the front cover. With attention to detail and an impressive memory for several thousands of years' worth of knowledge, he completes the inscription of his tale.

"Done," the frustrated man says as he puts the pen flat on the book, observing his permanently burned hand and wrist. "Now tell me. Where is God!?"

"Patience, young one. Watch yourself," Adam patronizes, facing the impatient ambassador. As his words silence the women by means of shock, his fingers wrap around the paperbound object. Then, with the sphere in one hand and the book in the other, he pushes a button. Previously used to open a rift in time, now it opens the sphere. Its stony surface smoothly peels back to reveal a half hollow cross section of a semi-sphere with a square hole in the center. He promptly places the scripture inside, that fits perfectly, and closes the sphere using the same means. It seals off with a gentle hiss.

"Now. Are you sitting comfortably?" Adam asks his audience. "The world, our world, was in a desperate time. Humans tore it to pieces like rabid animals. In fact, I'd go so far as to say many of us were. And by our own wrongdoings, we needed an answer before we were faced with extinction." The couple and his own significant other face him as he turns away from them to pace back over to the flawless glass wall. Standing inches from the transparent surface, his breath fogs up a little on the glass with every word. "In desperate times, people rush and make mistakes. They do whatever they can to fix things and make them right," he tells them.

"At first, I was genuinely interested in saving our planet. My life's work had gone into creating a technology that would allow us to one day save mankind and become this. Maybe, even now, it's not perfectly perfect. It is, however, far better than a desolate population of a starving race," his voice renders smoothly as it bounces from the glass to their attentive ears. "But then, I thought about the one thing that I missed more than the survivability of humanity. Evelyn. In this alternate past you were taken from me when our half of the world was split into its two social classes. They dragged you from the house and my last memory of you was a shrill scream, begging to be released." A silent pause sinks through the soft cushion of space. The beginning of a tear begins to form at the edge of Adam's overlooking eye. "I could never forgive myself for taking that job when I could have been with you." His fists clench with a mighty snap. "I had to take matters into my own hands." His gaze falls for a moment. "So, I began communicating with the one person I knew would be strong enough. Myself. I knew it was you, or me I should say, from the beginning because I programmed the portal to track DNA under the noses of my colleagues. Once I had total control over you, I just needed to make sure things were smooth enough so that it was believable for the men I was working with," he said, pacing his monolog. Evelyn looked to face the door longingly. She knew who he meant. "Over time, I lost trust in others, recalling what had happened to me before. I decided secretly to abandon the original mission in exchange for being with you again, Evelyn. Betrayal was at the edge of my fingertips. I just had to hold it in long enough to succeed!" he says proudly, almost shouting now. "From then, it took a few back-and-forths with you, Adam. Getting you truly convinced was the key. And I grew to realize that this power was," he says, looking at his curling fingers, "unimaginable. The fascination inside me was nothing like I had experienced before." He pauses again as they all gawk impatiently at the window. As Adam starts talking once more, they mutter amongst themselves quietly, leaving him to ramble. "My goal was to have Evelyn by my side, but I wanted more," he elaborates, lost in his own world of hearing his own voice. His eyes scan the world frivolously through a faint and barely recognizable reflection. "That sphere you're holding is said to contain the power to transform someone into an all-powerful being. Sounds familiar?" He turns, now walking quickly back to the three of them who have started their own covert conversation. "All I had to do was make sure that when you finally called me, and your task was completed, you'd have the object in hand, so I carefully orchestrated your love and necessity for it. And now, here we are," he finishes, closing his eyes momentarily.

"Right, yes," young Adam perks up. "Hang on. You're not telling me that everything I did… was for nothing?" he ignites. Evelyn looks at him and her reflection. She scoots beside him to cordially connect their hands despite the revelations. He tightens the grip. "That I stayed up late every single FUCKING night for two thousand years!? Just so you could say hi?!" his voice roars deeply with a blistering fire. His knees launch him up from the sitting position as he gets out of his chair as one with his woman. "We will not be some pawn in your stupid fucking game!" he screams at his older, sinister self.

"I'm afraid it's a little too late," the response comes back.

"Now, let me explain. If one of us is holding it, all that we have to do is touch. Two living beings of the same identity co-existing, touching, is more than enough paradoxical energy to set it off," Adam explains to his defensive correspondent, who immediately backs up against the wall.

"You're sick and twisted. Did you really do all this so you could have some rumored godlike powers?" the younger man's fiancé asks Adam. Her eyes sting with an affection that the older Evelyn longs for. "Pass me your phone," she says to her older female counterpart. In compliance, Evelyn pulls a phone from a loose back pocket and hands it over. Her fingers fire off in a flurry of methodical button-pushing.

"No. I did this so I can be eternal with the love of my life. I did this for her. I am here to avenge the wrongdoings of a corrupt government! Adam and Eve will conquer the universe!" Adam rages furiously, blind to the events in front of him. He's the only one in the room who fails to see the falseness of his own words.

"Adam. God. Whoever you are. You're abandoning your wife as quickly as you did those men. How true is what you just said, really? Did you do this for her? Or for yourself?" the younger man asks him, distracting him from his fiancé's finesse. The older Evelyn sighs under her breath, unheard by the others.

"What... what do you mean?" Adam questions.

"There! Sent!" the badass Evelyn shouts as she holds up the modern maiden's phone. Three of the four members look around, waiting for something to happen. Her phone reads in reasonably large letters the exact message that Adam received on his graft recently, just hours before, an unlucky attempt to prevent the end of the world.

"Oh, I suppose that makes sense now," Adam mutters quietly, quickly dismissing the betrayal.

"Adam, you can't do this. Look at them," Evelyn interrupts him. Her head nods in the direction of the love-imbued couple. "They don't deserve this. They've worked so hard to be here. Don't do this. Please." She stands and steps toward him, holding his hands in hers. "I need you to trust me on this," she says with a pounding heart. "Most of all, I need you." Her eyes lock with his in a fiery moment among what was once a wild force of love. They connect with their lips, like animals, before he breaks free of the taming reigns. "Now, give me the sphere," she says in a delicate but sensual manner. Knowing that this may be the last chance to win back her trust, he places the sphere in her hand in a lost attempt to discover what is nothing more than a shadow of who he has become.

"I missed you. So fucking much," he says to her. A tear bubbles from his eye and slides gracefully across a vengeance-ridden cheek. The sparks of emotion stir within his machinated corpse.

"Adam, even though I have believed in a higher power for two millennia, I learned something that maybe you could benefit from," the junior hero speaks up. "No God or religion can steer you to success. You have to find it within yourself. That doesn't mean that religion is bad. It just helps," he clears up. Nearly a minute passes with each couple holding each other as they wait for him to make a decision. In this time, the younger Adam leans over to place his mouth beside his partner's ear, covering it, as his jaw moves up and down. The pressure in the air could not be more emotionally charged with love and stress. Breaking the deadly silence, Adam speaks through a teary-eyed face.

"Fine. I'll keep things the way they are. On one condition," he demands with irritation teeming through his voice.

"Sure, baby. Anything. We can make it through anything," she says, rubbing his shoulders. Her slender fingers slide down his arms as they hold hands in a delicate, deceitful manner.

"We give these honest people a decent goodbye," he says as the old idea-box tinkers, one final attempt to realize the dream. In the performance, he trudges over to the controls where his fingers dance across them one last time.

He returns by her side and squeezes her hand tightly for a moment but soon releases the grip almost entirely. The connection between their fingers remains just as frail as the bond they share beneath her convincing act.

"Of course," she replies in concealed obedience. "I, well. I don't know what to say. You two are clearly the perfect couple," she says, looking away with evident disappointment. "This has been, well... a good story if nothing else," she explains. "Come here." Her soft side emerges through the cover. With arms outstretched, she walks over to the younger couple.

Adam tries to clench a grip on her fingers but his hand slips. The brittle connection between them breaks. His smirk is eradicated. Hers lights up as she pulls away. The separation between them is clear. 'How could I hold on after this?' she thinks to herself.

"Wait, no!" the younger man wails out. His face is wide open.

As the two ladies enclose in adieu, their skins touch.

They are two beings of the same consciousness,

existing together, touching each other in the same timeline.

At lightning speed, the orb erupts into a kaleidoscope of colors.

Everything freezes in place for the most precise instant.

Beside them, Adam's dying sneer is the final perceivable image. His cheeky grin finds finality as it fades into the blaring fog. All things implode simultaneously as the spherical device is the only stable structure. A vociferous, reckoning blast dominates every sense as reality is bent to conform to the weak will of one man and the minds of two women. The fabric of space and time becomes warped and destructed as every living thing, every inanimate object, and every molecule of the unmentioned is torn apart. Like a deafening clarion, the blast expands to consume not only their planet but their galaxy. It spreads faster and faster, gaining momentum. It goes off, devouring everything like a grenade being watched at quickening slow-motion speed. The unhallowed clang of white energy eats star after star, expanding to the very edges of the known universe and beyond.

In the millisecond it took from Evelyn embracing her younger self in a goodbye hug to the downfall of their dimension, nothing was created. And nothing was all that was left.

The end

And the Beginning

How often have you put together a sandwich?

You paid perfect attention to the thickness of the mayonnaise, the juiciness of the sweet, sweet tomato, and the crustiness of the browned bread as it bounces out of that searing hot toaster. You adore it and nurture it to maturity while you tend to its specifications. You slice diagonally and enjoy the crunch that fills your ears with a great wet appetite.

Every element seems just right. It looks, smells, and even sounds impeccable. You raise the production of your time to your mouth and bite down deeply through the layers of ingredients. And you eat that damn sandwich with pride.

Now every single piece of that sandwich is thoroughly orchestrated. Each fragment is splendidly melded together. It's perfect until it comes out the other side. It seemed so fantastic in the beginning, but as time goes on, push will always come to shove.

However, no one will never have the ability to predict this.

It is important to note that patience yields a Panacea, eventually. It's funny how things work out.

A moaning and groaning stir in the blackness. Mumbling occurs through the starless space.

"My head *really* hurts," a voice complains. As the eyes are pried open through a stumbling series of attempts, the blackness fades away gradually.

"I'm... alive?" the female voice resonates through the lack of matter. She grudgingly pulls her hands from her eyes to observe what is left of the universe. Soft hands look like an exoskeleton made of jelly in comparison to the looming emptiness. A second set of groaning sounds mixes with the settled chaos. She turns to notice a silhouette floating steadily beside her.

"Where am I?" the second voice questions immediately.

"Evelyn?" the response unfolds.

"Call me Eve. I may be younger than you, but I was dead for two thousand years, and my Adam worked damn hard to keep me in stasis. Don't you fucking try and give me your toxic name," she barks back. "On the other hand, would you like to tell me where we are?" she demands.

"I'd like to think I know how to answer that," Evelyn informs.

She raises her hand swiftly to wipe her nose but is caught off guard as a white streak of light appears with a rapid motion. It unveils a shooting star.

"Wait," the second voice says abruptly, wiping her eyes for one last time before opening up to the vast expanse, "you don't think it actually worked… do you?" Eve poses inquisitively. As her hands manipulate the very construction of reality, little beads and strokes of light appear and dissipate back into the void with each motion of her fingers.

"Oh, maybe you're right." Evelyn adds little to the conversation. "So, what? *We're* Gods?" she pauses for a moment. "But I thought it was supposed to be me and Adam…" her voice drags on longingly.

"No," Eve corrects her, pondering., "we were the ones who connected." Another deadly pause seizes the emotional boundary and snaps it in half. "Your husband, Adam from the future, solved many puzzles, my dear." Eve informs her. "But it's too bad he couldn't figure out how to love anyone but himself." She floats upward a few feet and casts down a staring gaze to Evelyn.

"We could have had it all in the end, more than we needed, though. We wouldn't have had to lift a finger." Evelyn sobs a little in the reality of the failure. Her voice emerges again, broken. "His sexy mind was his own downfall…"

"Exactly." Eve confirms without sympathy. "I thought you disapproved of his plan. That's why you helped me send that letter." They discuss the matter, floating in a steady circular rotation among the emptiness.

"I did, mostly. I think deep down, however, I was proud of him. I looked forward to living with the power," Evelyn explains. "Either way, I ended up here with a lot more abilities than I could have ever asked for."

"You know, there *are* two figures with Godlike powers in the Bible. Only, one of them is more of an angel. The right hand of God, to begin with," Eve coaxes her into an illusion of reassurance.

"Oh, really?" the doe-eyed Evelyn wishes for an answer to her self-righteous issue.

"One of them is God, of course. The other, the devil. I'd say judging on how your precious heartbreak easily encompassed all seven of the deadly sins that you fit the bill," her glowing figure speaks across the dead space.

"So, you're just appointing yourself as God… Do you even know how to use the powers we've been given?" Evelyn inquires.

"Not yet." Eve lets out a cosmic sigh. "But I do know that you abided by the rules of a man that would watch endless suffering of an entire dimension with a grin. So long as the two of you were happy, nothing else mattered. Really, did it?" Eve explains as her celestial silhouette swoops back and forth. "You're as selfish as him and I have no reason to believe otherwise. The sooner we get rid of the evil that lives within you, the better. Goodbye, Evelyn. Or shall I say, Lucifer," Eve's voice rises in a controlled and authoritative manner. Her final words to Evelyn are followed by a swift swing down with her arm which then emits a blinding pulse.

Evelyn's body drops like a sack of potatoes. Her skin sizzles against the light. The ray of divine punishment shatters the outer layer of her ethereal form and ignites it into a hellish magma-red. She descends at a horrifying rate, losing track of all perception for several seconds before her rear end slams to a halt. She awakens in a smoldering, barren pit empty of everything except an endless roasting heat accompanied by the distant screams of everlasting torture.

Miles above, Eve begins caressing the void with her hands in a mesmerizing fashion as she practices her transcendent endowment. The ability to fabricate anything from nothing flourishes between her fingertips. Sparks between the ends of her fingers create rocks and planets as she experiments with this and that. Much to early dismay, they fail rather quickly and diminish to nothing. With an eternal focus and limitless resource pool, she trains constantly without hesitation. For what would be considered nearly two thousand years, she practices and practices the divine arts before she finally gets it right. She snaps her fingers. An entire solar system is generated. With the close of a fist, it is resolved to nothingness. Her mystical gifts are honed to a fine point. Then, with an astronomically colossal clap, there is the beginning.

A white light erupts from the epicenter she would call her hands.

Similarly, to the world-ending blast that created the emptiness, an explosion crosses the universe in an instant. Matter is created. Planets are conceived. Star systems formulate across an endless sea of speckles. She smiles and sits back to enjoy the spectacle of the interminable power. In an instant, though, she's reminded by her own existence that the presence of life is crucial in the enthralling expanse. Humans. She contemplates for some time. Should they be reintroduced to the universe for their inexcusable behavior in previous lifetimes? She ponders many directions to take them to slow down their advancement.

"What if we say men came first? Let's make men 'in charge.'" Her fingers mimic air quotes and then snap. She chuckles to herself. 'I won't make the same mistakes' she thinks to herself. She was right, she was making all new ones.

The universe as we know it is born.

In the beginning, God created the Earth.